Pretty little DREAMS

ALSO BY JENNIFER MILLER

Pretty Little Lies

A PRETTY LITTLE LIES NOVEL

Pretty little DREAMS

JENNIFER MILLER

Copyright © 2013 Jennifer Miller
Cover Design by BookFabulous Designs
Edited by CDK & Associates
Formatting & typography by Inkstain Interior Book Designing
Proofing by Second Gaze Editing
Photography by Stephanie Williams, This Modern Romance

ISBN 978-0-9894074-9-6

PRAISE FOR . . .

Pretty little LIES

"Pretty Little Lies has it all: humor, great fashion tips, and a witty heroine. Add in a hot guy and sizzling romance, and this is the perfect book for a day at the beach."

- Destiny Ford, author of *The Devil Drinks Coffee*

"Jennifer Miller does a great job of exploring the nuances of dating for a newly single woman. Olivia's outlook on each date adds the perfect balance. Readers will hang on each page to see what happens next."

- InD'tale Magazine

"If the super cute Fashion Tips that start each chapter don't immediately capture your attention then the second-chance romance will definitely have your toes curling and heart palpating for more."

-Yara; Once Upon A Twilight.com

"Pretty Little Lies is a love story that gives second chances to those who could never let go, even with the passing of time."

"There is nothing better than reading a story that takes you back to a special time in your life and that's exactly what Jennifer did for me, butterflies and all."

"Pretty Little Lies made me laugh out loud, shout, cry and gasp in shock - all things I like in a good read."

"Jennifer Miller is now on my "Authors to look for" list. She is amazing and her writing talent goes above and beyond in Pretty Little Lies. This chick gives it 5 outta 5 stars!"

PRAISE FOR . . .

Pretty little DREAMS

"Pretty Little Dreams is an on the edge of your seat page turner with the right combination of drama, humor, heart wrenching emotion, and sexiness. Jennifer Miller nailed this second installment of Olivia and Luke's story!" - Jennifer Domenico, author of Beautifully Twisted and the Sunflower Trilogy

"Pretty Little Lies is heart pounding and gripping. I couldn't put it down! Get ready to fall in love with Luke, all over again." - Mary Ting, Amazon Best Selling Author of Something Great, From Gods and the Crossroads Series

"Jennifer Miller once again brings her words to life in Pretty Little Dreams. It's an experience that takes your breath away. Jennifer manages to make you laugh, cry and hold onto the edge of your seat until the very end!" - Lustful Literature.com

To my mom.
Thank you for being my biggest cheerleader. Your support and unwavering faith in me means more than you could ever know.

1.

FALLING TO FREEDOM

Olivia

I'M LYING IN bed with the man I hate. I wake up, and for a brief moment I am at peace. Then, as fast as fashion lovers rush to a sale at Bloomingdales, I remember. I'm painfully and vividly aware that the peace I momentarily feel is not real and that the man I'm lying next to is not the one my heart longs for.

Another day in hell. I have no idea how many days it has now been. I don't know how long I was out before I woke up and found myself bound and gagged lying on a bed. Deacon injected something in my body to knock me out initially, but I don't know what. When I would arouse during our journey here, he would force me to drink a liquid – water, I think, laced with some kind of sedating drug. The drug would immediately impose a haze and then a deep fog would engulf me, until once again, I was oblivious to everything. Just as today, there was no rest or peace during that sleep, but rather a repeated, tormented struggle: at times a longing to find consciousness and formulate a plan for securing my freedom and, at other times, as fear suffocates me, a desire to sleep into eternity.

I feel myself start to panic again, recalling those moments of pure hysteria when I finally woke up. I can't go there. I can't let myself feel what I really want to feel right now. Instead, I lock the fear in a box. If I don't, it will consume me. I can't let myself think of the unknown, of the what-ifs. When the fear starts to drag me into its dark abyss, I defy its grip and force my thoughts to focus on the people I love. Pyper. My parents. And then, with my heart twisting painfully in my chest, Luke. I roll onto my side in a slow, deliberate and cautious manner, as close to the bed's edge as possible, careful not to wake the living, breathing, nightmare lying beside me. Putting my back to him provides me the illusion of placing even more distance between us than I actually can. I hate being in bed with him.

My pulse starts racing as I give that too much thought, so I quickly lock my feelings and thoughts up in that box again, putting them away to pursue later. Effortlessly, Pyper again comes to my mind, and I could swear it's like she's standing before me waving her arms to get my attention. I smile at her image. I hope she's okay. The last thing I remember before Deacon took me is my best friend tied up, helpless, echoing the wide-eyed fear I also felt. As our eyes met, I tried to convey to her how much I loved her. We both knew what was going to happen. I begged Deacon to leave her, to not hurt her. Whether he listened to me or not, I have no idea. I only know from asking him over and over again about Pyper that he left her tied up on the couch, but in what condition, I do not know, and he refuses to say. He only states that his major objective was to take me. And he was willing to do so at any cost. I can only hope he did not hurt her, that he merely left her as he said. But honesty is not one of his strengths. Regardless, I pray to God that someone found her quickly. I hope she's alive and well and not worrying too much. I hope she was able to tell Luke what happened.

Luke. During my darkest times when I'm most afraid, thoughts of him are constant. He's my happy place. I daydream frequently about him holding me, whispering to me, kissing me. Sometimes, I even let my thoughts venture to the life I wish to have with him some day. My favorite is when I picture us in a home. Our home. Not an apartment or townhouse, but a house. I know without a doubt that it will have to be a house, because Luke will want something that is ours. In my daydream, our house looks like one of those old plantation estates in Georgia. It has a wraparound porch, with his and hers rocking chairs in front; our favorite spot. Luke and I sit in the chairs, sipping iced tea on a warm summer day. Our chairs face each other and my feet are in his lap. I smile, listening to him tell me about the new night club he is excited about opening, while he rubs my feet, his enthusiasm evident. His voice, combined with the breeze blowing through the trees brings me contentment. A dog, a golden retriever named Dakota, is lying next to our chairs. While we talk, I drop my hand down to scratch the top of his head. I think even the dog smiles with contentment. I don't know if dogs actually smile or why we have one, I just know there is one in my perfect day dream; the daydream and the life I hope and wish to have with Luke. I miss him so much that the ache in my heart nearly crushes me, takes my breath away and I find myself gasping for air. The pain is incredible. It's worse than a punch in the gut, the unfairness of it all. After seven long years, we have finally reconciled, and then Deacon comes and ruins our plans. Ruins our dreams.

I still thank God that we found each other again. After hearing him tell his mom I meant nothing, when I took off and married Deacon, I really never thought I would see him again. Thoughts of Luke would venture into my mind often, but I always stubbornly pushed them away. While painful, the best thing that could have happened for me and Luke was the time I caught Deacon cheating and finally took a stand against him and his abusive ways by divorcing him. Moving back to Chicago was the right choice because eventually, surprisingly, and unexpectedly, it brought me back to Luke. And I was finally happy again.

I confess that at some level, I am still in denial. I had no idea that Deacon would do something like this. I knew he was angry and has been obsessive and borderline crazy over my leaving him, but I never thought he would go this far. I never thought he would take me - kidnap me - from my own home. I've tried to reason with him, to ask him what he's thinking, to make him feel guilty, and to try to scare him. I've begged him to just let me go. I've promised him that I won't tell anyone, that it will be our secret. I've told him to just leave me here and save himself before it's too late. He refuses. He shakes his head, laughs. Instead, he makes me do things I don't want to do, and makes it clear that I am far from being in charge here.

My thoughts are suddenly interrupted as I feel Deacon moving next to me, his fingers touch my back, and I stiffen, acutely aware that he's awake. He asks me the same thing each morning, "Have you come to your senses yet? I'm tired of your refusal, no more games."

Jaw clenched so tight my teeth grind together, I roll over and bravely stare into his eyes, "Let me go, Deacon. Each day you keep me here, you're only digging yourself deeper and deeper. There's still time for you to do the right thing." I respond the same each time too.

"I have plans for us tonight." Ignoring my comment, Deacon rises from the bed, completely naked. I avert my eyes from his body.

"Plans? What kind of plans?"

"We are going to have a nice dinner together, for starters."

I scoff, "I don't want to have dinner with you."

"Too bad, you don't have a choice."

The room I'm being kept in isn't bad. We are in some house in the middle of nowhere, as far as I can tell. I'm in a room that has the bare necessities. A large bed and a dresser, there is also an attached bathroom, but it too has the bare minimum. There isn't even a mirror. I can, however, see where the wall paint changes color, indicating that at one time, a large one had hung above the sink. I wonder if Deacon removed it, and if so, when that was. How long had he been planning this? Each time Deacon leaves me alone, which isn't often, he locks me inside the bedroom. Sometimes I hear him talking to someone through the door. There was a time when I wasn't sure if he had someone helping him or if he was talking on the phone. I think back to the time when I found out the answer to that question.

Rolling out of bed, Deacon pulls on a pair of pants. "I will be back. Don't do anything stupid while I'm gone."

"Be back? What do you mean? Where are you going?"

"Aw, isn't that sweet? Are you concerned about me? Are you going to miss me, princess?" he asks, walking over to my side of the bed.

"No. I don't care where you go. I'm just surprised you would leave me alone."

An angry look flashes across his face and he leans over me, grasping my wrists hard, holding them up near my shoulders. I turn my face to the side trying to avoid him. "You better start caring, princess, or you aren't going to like what happens." Then he moves his hands to the side of my face, forcing me to face him again. He kisses me hard on the lips.

As soon as he lets go of me, I wipe my face with the back of my hand. He laughs as he walks out of the room, slamming the door behind him.

Throwing the covers back, I run to the door and press my ear against it – all I hear is murmuring on the other side. He must be on the phone again. It isn't long before I hear a hard slam which I assume is a door closing. I think I'm alone; this could be my only chance for a while.

I run to the sliding balcony doors and creep out onto the balcony. This is the first chance I've had to come out and take in my surroundings. Deacon told me when he locked me in this room that we are in the middle of nowhere and I could yell and scream as much as I want – no one will hear.

Looking around, I see he was telling the truth. There doesn't appear to be anything for miles. I'm too high up to jump down and tying my sheets together would be useless; I couldn't even reasonably reach the ground.

Frantically, I start running around the room, looking for something, anything, to use as a weapon. I search the dresser, the top of the closet, under the bed, the bathroom cabinets. "Dammit." I can't find anything.

Running back to the bed, I rip the sheet from it and wrap it around my hand. Heading to the balcony doors, I brace myself. If I can manage to shatter the door, I can use the glass as a weapon. Please let this work. I take my fist and slam it against the door as hard as I can. I scream. Not even a scratch and all I managed to do was hurt my hand. In anger, I beat against the door over and over until I'm a heap on the floor. I pull my hand out of the sheet and glance at it. It's beginning to swell, but I hardly feel it.

There's nothing here. Nothing. Feeling defeated, I walk back out onto the balcony and decide it's worth a try, no matter what Deacon said.

"HELP! PLEASE SOMEONE! HELP ME!" What do I have to lose? Maybe I will luck out and someone is around.

I wait a moment and then try again.

"HELP! I'VE BEEN KIDNAPPED. SOMEONE HEL..."

Suddenly, I am grabbed from behind and dragged into the bedroom and thrown on the bed like a rag doll. I try to roll onto my back but instead a weight settles on my back, and my face gets shoved into the mattress.

"Shut the fuck up, bitch."

The voice is not Deacon's. I freeze as shock runs through my body from head to toe, paralyzing me in fear.

"Lover boy isn't here to save you. It might be worth facing his anger to shut you up permanently."

I don't speak. I'm afraid to move. Who is this man? He moves off me so he can roughly flip me over. I stare up into his hard eyes. He's not an attractive man. Light hair, pointy nose, and lips so thin they're hardly there at all. He has a scar that runs from the tip of his eyebrow to the middle of his cheek. "Leave me alone."

"I don't think I will... what does he call you? Princess? I don't think I will, princess." He says mockingly. Then, to my horror he runs his hand down the front of my body, squeezing my breasts painfully and then gripping my hip. His breathing starts quickening.

"No, please don't touch me."

"That's right, beg, you bitch. Next time you will think twice about breaking the rules and trying to yell for help."

Oh God. He's going to hurt me, or worse. I do the only thing I can. I start struggling. I kick my legs like a three-year-old having a tantrum. I throw my head back and forth and get one of my hands loose and scrape my nails down the front of his face. "Let go of me!" I scream.

He roars in pain and touches the side of his face where I scratched him. The next thing I know I feel a hard smack on the top of my head. I see stars and I panic, afraid of what he will do to me when I can't defend myself. Just as I start to lose consciousness,

I hear Deacon yell, "WHAT THE FUCK?!" Against my will, I succumb to the darkness enveloping me.

My eyes well up from that awful memory. I remember when I came to, Deacon was angry. "You don't have to worry about Ronnie, princess, I took care of him. He will think twice about ever touching you again," he said while stroking my face. My head hurt too much for me to react to his touch, until I realized I'm completely naked. I ran to the bathroom heaving into the toilet, not sure if I was sick due to the ache in my head – did I have a concussion? - or the fear coursing through me as I had no clue how I had ended up naked or what, if anything, had happened in addition to what I could recall.

Deacon distracts me from my thoughts when he yanks open the closet door and grabs a box I've never seen before from the top of the closet. He turns towards me, and throws the box on the bed. "You will wear this to dinner tonight."

Opening the box, I pull out a slinky black dress that I can already tell will barely cover my body. "I'm not wearing that."

"Oh, yes you are, princess. We are going to have a nice, romantic meal, and you are going to wear that dress."

"I'm not dressing up for you, Deacon."

Faster than I can blink, Deacon is on me. I shrink back as much as I can, trying to avoid his nakedness from touching mine. Grasping me by the top of my arms, Deacon's face is mere inches from mine, "You will wear the fucking dress, Olivia. This is not up for discussion." As he speaks each word, he shakes me and squeezes me tighter, making me cry out in pain.

"Deacon! You're hurting me."

"Stop making me hurt you. Do you think I like this? Do you think I want to hurt you? Why do you keep making me hurt you? Just do what I tell you to do and we will be fine. I've told you over and over again that this is our future. You and me, princess. Once you accept that, the happier you'll be."

"Okay. Okay, Deacon." I force the words out of my mouth because it is the exact opposite of what I want. I've learned the hard way what happens when I don't keep my mouth shut or if I don't say or do what he wants.

"Good. I will be back later. Make sure you are dressed and ready." And with that, he grabs some clothes off the floor and leaves the room.

WHAT MUST BE a few hours later, I'm running a brush through my hair. It's one of the few personal items Deacon allows me. I have no idea what I look like. I have the hideous dress on and I keep pulling it down. The scrap of fabric barely covers my ass and my boobs are barely contained. I look like one of the very girls I tell all my readers on *Pink Sugar Couture* not to emulate. My inner fashion diva has officially curled up and died.

Entering the room, Deacon whistles low, "You look hot, princess."

I feel revulsion internally and just stare at him. He's dressed for dinner in what I can't help but notice is a well-cut, charcoal-colored, European suit and tie. Where he gets the clothes, I have no idea. Not for the first time I wonder where we are exactly, and how this house is associated with him. The things that I don't know about this man continue to shock me. How I was ever married to him, I don't know.

He walks toward me and places his mouth on mine. I refuse to open for him and I know it will only make him mad, but dammit, I hate feeling helpless in all of this.

9

Pulling away from me Deacon looks into my eyes, "I'll let that one slide, for now. Come with me."

Grabbing hold of my arm, already covered in bruises, I slightly wince at the discomfort, as he hauls me out of the room and down the hall. Bringing me into a large sitting room that includes a dining table, I see that he has set up a candlelight dinner. Dread fills me. What is he up to?

Steering me towards a chair, I take a seat - or more accurately, am seated. The table is set and there are even silver domes over what I presume are our meals. Deacon takes a lighter from his trouser pocket and lights the tall candles set perfectly in a silver candelabra at the center of the table. As he leans over, his suit jacket opens slightly and I see a gun tucked into the front of his pants. It certainly isn't the first time I've seen it while I've been here, but it is just as disconcerting this time as the first. I secretly hope when he sits, the gun will go off and shoot his dick off. He certainly deserves far worse. I smile at the thought.

Deacon, seeing the smile on my face, returns it with one of his own. "I knew you would like this, princess. I wanted you to see that we can have wonderful, romantic dinners like this. You don't have to spend so much time locked up in your room. Once you finally realize this is where you should be, we can have dinner like this every night."

"I don't want to have dinner with you every night. When are you going to get a clue, you fucking douche?"

The smile that was just present on his lips quickly vanishes and anger seizes his entire countenance. I know I should just shut up and play along with what he says, but I can't; I will never stop fighting. Not ever. I will not let him strip away who I am.

After taking a few deep breaths, Deacon's eyes once again meet mine, "Tonight, things are going to change. The time for you to start accepting that we are together again is right now. I've apologized to you over and over for sleeping with Tracey. I'm so sorry you walked in on that, but I'm done apologizing for it. I've forgiven the fact that you betrayed me with that man, so you will forgive me about Tracey. I know once you forgive me, we will be fine. Everything will be fine, princess, and we will be happy."

"Not for the first time, you are out of your fucking mind. Tracey was merely the straw that broke the camel's back. I quit loving you long before that."

"ENOUGH! I am done being easy on you."

I laugh at that comment. Easy? He calls this easy? My laughter only angers him.

He rips me out of my chair and yanks me against the front of his body. "You are my WIFE and you will do what I say. You *will* provide your wifely duties. You are no longer allowed to talk back to me."

"Fuck you, Deacon. I am no longer married to you. I don't love you. I love Luke. I will ALWAYS love Luke."

He pulls me just far enough away from him to give him room to backhand me across the face. I feel pain, blinding pain, and taste blood in my mouth.

"DO NOT SPEAK HIS NAME TO ME!" He screams. Then, while seething with fury, he continues, "I will not allow you to talk about the man you whored yourself out to. Do you hear me?"

Before I can respond, his mouth is on mine. I want to throw up. He pulls me tight to him and I can feel that he is obviously turned on from the violence. His erection presses against my hip and his hands are all over my body. I'm stiff and don't move, refusing to participate in his complete violation.

Then suddenly, an idea enters my mind. It's crazy, but it may just work.

Hesitantly, I reach my hands out and run them up Deacon's arms. He stiffens, surprised at my touch. I never return his touch.

Leaving one hand on his arm, I cup the side of his neck with the other hand and start returning his kiss. When his tongue enters my mouth, I shudder and Deacon mistakes it for pleasure, pulling me closer and moaning deep in his throat. I grab the hair at his neck, and squeeze it into a fist, deepening the kiss while my other hand starts unbuttoning his shirt, one button at a time.

Deacon pulls away from me and looks into my eyes questioningly. It kills me to do it, but I whisper, "I want you, Deacon. You're right, we belong together. Kiss me."

He wastes no time pulling me back to him and kisses me hard once again. His tongue is brutal in its exploration of my mouth. He starts sliding my dress off of one shoulder and just as I reach the bottom button of his shirt, I quickly pull the gun from his pants and back up, pointing it at him.

"Back the hell up right the FUCK NOW." I feel like a bad ass. Finally, I have the upper hand and I feel euphoric.

Shock is displayed all over his face. He's breathing hard and his eyes are glassy. I can tell it's taking him a minute to completely comprehend what has just happened. He takes a step towards me.

"I SAID TO BACK UP, DEACON."

"You aren't going to shoot me. You don't even know how to use a gun."

Calling his bluff I click the safety off the gun and see his eyes widen.

"That's right, motherfucker. I guess you don't know everything about me, do you?"

"You won't shoot me, Olivia. You don't have it in you."

Deacon starts walking towards me again and I take a step back for every step he takes forward. Before I know it, my back is at the doors leading out onto a balcony. I'm trapped, but I refuse to give up. I reach behind me and open the doors, happy they aren't sliding glass like the bedroom. The cold air takes my breath away.

"Just give me the gun, Olivia. You don't want to do this. Give it to me, and we will go back to dinner. I made your favorite, cheese ravioli. Come on, I will show you." He takes another step towards me.

I keep backing up, "I said stay away from me, Deacon. I am not afraid to use this. I *will* shoot you."

I feel the railing at my back. I don't know what to do. I can shoot him and then try to find a phone and call 9-1-1. That's what I will do. It's all I can do.

I grasp the gun with both hands, and before I can get off a shot, I see the intent in Deacon's eyes right before he lunges for me.

I overcompensate for his lunge and throw myself backwards, right over the side of the balcony. I see his eyes widen in horror as the gun goes off and he reaches for me, but it's too late. I'm falling.

The fall feels like an eternity, and my life flashes before my eyes as expected, but another thought occurs to me as well... *where are parachute pants when a girl needs them?*

2.

I DON'T WANT TO WEAR THIS FUCKING SUIT

Luke

ER SPIRIT LINGERS here. Initially, I was afraid that being in her room, surrounded by the very essence of her would be too painful; that I would just be hurting myself more by staying here. Instead, I've found that it gives me peace, at least on some level I don't quite understand, and I also feel closer to her here. Since that dreadful day, I've pretty much moved in. I can't find it in myself to go.

At first, when I couldn't leave, I told myself it was in case she came home or if the police had news, perhaps they would come here or call here first. I think in part, that's true, but the truth is, it comforts me to be here. I can bury my face in her pillow. Look at her pictures. Touch her clothes and the knick-knacks she keeps on her dresser. I've spent a lot of time doing that - trailing my fingers over her possessions – because I know her fingers and hands touched them before mine. Does that make me pathetic? Maybe. Probably.

I'm embarrassed to admit that I sit in her closet at my lowest moments. The intoxicating scent that is uniquely hers – while everywhere - is strongest there. The simple act of smelling her perfume brings back so many memories. Seeing her for the first time again after seven years; wanting to kiss her so bad, but being afraid I would scare her away while I was still trying to win her back. Her kisses. Her touches. Each act is a memory that haunts me. And still stirs me.

With a sigh, I stand up from my corner in her closet and unzip my garment bag, taking in my dark suit, crisp white shirt and tie. I don't want to do this today. At all. Carrying my clothes, I grudgingly walk to the bathroom so I can change. Once I'm dressed, I take in my reflection in the mirror before me. My eyes look sad. I have dark circles that have become a permanent fixture, given that a good night's sleep hasn't been easy to come by lately. My shoulders appear to be drooping slightly. I sigh. Not much I can do about it.

I want to rip this fucking monkey suit off my body. Every part of me is begging me to do it. I just want to head back to her bed and shove my face in her pillow again. I want to pull the covers over my head, drown myself in her essence, and escape from reality for a little while longer. Wanting her here has turned into a physical ache; a pain deep in my gut and chest that can't be calmed or relieved.

I catch myself rubbing at my chest like I can smooth the pain away. It doesn't work.

"Luke? Are you almost ready?"

The sound of Pyper's voice snaps me out of my thoughts. Walking out of the bathroom, I look at Pyper, taking in her appearance. She looks nice. She's wearing a black dress and smiling a little at me, but it quickly falls, as if smiling on a day like today is sacrilege. She's sporting dark circles under her eyes as well, and there is sadness in her eyes too.

"I don't want to do this today, Pyper." I confess.

Closing the distance between us, she starts straightening my tie. "I know this is something neither of us wants to do right now, but it will be okay. You can lean on me for support, and I will lean on you. It's all we can do, okay?"

I give her a slight nod, my thoughts drifting elsewhere. I can't look at Pyper anymore without my mind automatically going back to that awful day. It's the day that my life took a brutal nose dive into the fucking abyss.

"Olivia! Pyper! It's Luke! Open the door!" I become more and more frantic as my hard pounding on the apartment door goes unanswered. Why aren't they answering?

Nothing.

BAM! BAM! BAM! The echoes of my fist pounding on the door resonate through the hallway. An old lady down the hall peeks out of her condo and gives me a look of death, but I couldn't care less. She should just mind her own damn business. "OLIVIA! PYPER!"

When I was at the office and received Olivia's message, I just knew something was wrong – Olivia's text didn't make any sense. Thanking me for flowers I didn't send. Telling me she would see me in a moment. "Please God, let me just be worried for nothing." Grabbing my car keys, I ran out of my office and out of the club as fast as I could, ignoring the questioning calls from a few staff members as I flew by. I immediately try calling her cell phone and she doesn't answer. I try again, and again. When my calls go unanswered, I can't think about anything else aside from getting to the condo, and making sure everything is okay.

Something's wrong. I can feel it in my bones. It's a monsoon of fear that starts at the top of my head and runs all the way to my toes, like a bucket of cold water over my head. I'm not going to wait anymore. I start trying to beat down the door by ramming my shoulder into it again, and again, like I'm some fucking linebacker. It isn't working. I frantically search the hallway looking for something – anything- I can use to help me break down the door. I exhale sharply when I see a mini fire extinguisher enclosed in a glass case, in case of emergency. Fuck it. If this isn't an emergency, I don't know what is, and I don't have anything else. I open the case, yank out the extinguisher and just start beating the shit out of the door knob until it is so beaten to hell it's just hanging there so I can get inside. If Pyper is pissed, she'll have to get over it - and maybe she'll even laugh at my trying to be the hero.

What I see when I'm finally through the door makes me freeze. The back of Pyper's head, she's just sitting stiffly, not moving, on the couch. She makes no attempt to look at me. I immediately know something is wrong; I know she would have answered me if she could have. Running to the couch and rounding to the front, I see Pyper tied up from head to toe, her mouth taped closed, and tears leaving trails down her cheeks.

"Oh God. Oh God. It's okay. It's going to be okay." I try to reassure her as I place my shaking pointer and thumb fingers at the corner of the tape across her mouth and whisper a hurried, "I'm sorry," before I rip it off her mouth so fast that the skin around her mouth tears in a few places.

Pyper screams in pain, "Oh God. Luke. Olivia. He has her. She's gone. She's gone!"

My world freezes. For a moment things feel like they are moving in slow motion. My heart; my heart feels like it has stopped. My breathing becomes difficult, I feel like fear is suffocating me, paralyzing me, and it takes effort to force that fear to the side. I can't help myself from reaching out and grabbing

Pyper's upper arms, shaking her. "What? What do you mean? Who has her? Where is she?"

And then she utters words that set my whole world ablaze, "Deacon. Deacon has her."

I squeeze my eyes shut and try to shove the image of that day out of my mind. Pyper and I have spent exhaustive hours going over everything that happened. She told me how Deacon knocked on the door, shoved his way inside, tied her up, took Olivia, and...well, the rest is history. I didn't want to leave any stone unturned, in hopes of absorbing any hint about where he took her. I know it all – I know Deacon was nervous, but excited about what he was about to do. I know everything he said to Pyper and Olivia, I know how he looked at Olivia with what Pyper called a 'menacing hunger' in his eyes. I even had Pyper tell me every excruciating moment from the time Olivia showed up until he took her. Pyper's account was complete, precise and likely very accurate, even if only from her perspective. I can still close my eyes and see it vividly, even though I wasn't there. I even dream about it. The worst is when I dream that I show up and rescue her, only to open my eyes and realize I was too late and I wasn't there and didn't save her.

I wasn't there. It echoes over and over in my mind like an accusation. Sometimes I hear it in my own voice, which is painful enough. But when the accusation takes Olivia's voice, it's crippling.

I will never forgive myself for going into the office that day. I was going to just wait at her condo for her to get back from lunch, but instead, I figured I would get some work done while she was out doing her thing. Maybe if I had stayed there and waited for her, things would be different. Why didn't I just do that? All I had to do was stay there.

I follow Pyper out into the kitchen and she automatically walks to the refrigerator and grabs me a bottle of water, as well as one for herself, and hands it to me wordlessly. I glance at my watch, "The limo should be here by now. We should head down."

"Okay, let me grab my sweater. It's always freezing in funeral homes."

I wait for Pyper at the door, holding it open for her and when she walks through, I follow her to the elevator, but spin back quickly and catch the door before it closes, realizing I forgot something. "Just a minute." I walk back into the kitchen and take the vase full of pink roses off the island counter. "I almost forgot them." Pyper gives me a sad smile as we close the door behind us, heading to the last place on earth I want to be.

"I'M SO SORRY for your loss."

I take in the woman currently grasping my hand, and see the sincerity of her words in her eyes. I nod at her, "Thank you for coming."

I make my way through the sea of black, with Pyper at my side, her hand on my arm silently lending support. I'm happy she's here. She and I have gotten a lot closer lately, leaning on one another, just taking it one day at a time. I feel like it's a moment-to-moment battle, trying to prevent the madness that so desperately seeks to claim my mind and my soul. There are moments when I know I'm toeing the line between sanity and complete and utter devastation.

Reaching the front, I take a seat and take in the room around me, purposely avoiding looking at the casket in front of me. I'm not ready for that. I head to the table next to the casket and place the pink roses there.

The viewing room is large. Chairs and couches are placed sporadically around the room, I suppose so people can sit and share memories or just be still with their thoughts. The sickly sweet smell of flowers is everywhere. You can smell them as soon as you walk into the room. Boxes of tissues are conveniently located in every nook and cranny and on every table top in the room. I can hear several whispers and sniffles around me, but I try not to make eye contact with anyone. While I appreciate them being here, I already know I'm only going to be able to handle so many sad looks, before I want to scream.

"Are you doing okay?" Pyper looks up at me from her seat beside me.

I smile in what I hope is a reassuring way, "I'm fine, I was just thinking that there is going to be a limit to how many sad looks and condolences I can handle before I want to lose it and scream my freaking head off."

Pyper smiles just a little, humor glimmering in her eyes for just a moment, "Scream?"

I shrug, "A manly scream, of course."

She full on smiles now, "Well, of course."

"Excuse me, Luke?"

I look away from Pyper and see a woman who looks vaguely familiar. "Yes? Hi."

"I just wanted to tell you that I'm so sorry for your loss. If there is anything you need or anything I can do, please don't hesitate to give me a call."

"Okay...thanks...umm..."

Thank goodness my father chooses that moment to save me, "Thank you so much Mrs. Donovan, that's very nice of you. Thank you for coming."

Mrs. Donovan smiles, nods her head, looks at me another moment, and then walks away. My father squeezes my shoulder in support and I give him a reassuring smile as I stand to face him. Pyper looks from me to my father, "Luke, I'm going to the ladies room, I'll be back."

"Okay."

"How are you doing, son?" My father's brows are furrowed in concern.

"I'm doing fine, dad, please don't worry about me."

"As a parent, that's an impossible request. You'll understand one day when you have children of your own," he says as he pats my shoulder.

Again, there's that stabbing pain in my heart. Something must register on my face because my father gives me a whispered, "I'm sorry."

Clearing my throat, I change the subject, "There are a lot of people here. That's good."

"Yes there are, but I'm not surprised. It's going to be a long couple of hours."

"Yeah, I'm not surprised either."

At a loss for words, I just stand there like an idiot. I force myself to take in the details around me because I'm not ready to confront the reason I'm here yet. My eyes travel to the front of the room and I take in the dark cherry casket, still refusing to look towards the top. It's pretty, and shines in the light. The front has roses carved into it as well as a bible and cross. There are so many flowers draped over the casket as well as surrounding it, I know she would love them. My eyes keep traveling up and I stop at her hands. They look so delicate; clasped together as if patiently waiting for something. Those hands represent so many things to me, comfort, love, nurturing, kindness...to see them lying there dormant, is painful.

I feel a hand on my shoulder and look back to see Pyper has returned. Tears are running down her face, and the sadness there makes tears fill my own eyes. I look away, back towards the casket, and move my eyes from her hands, and take in her red dress, it makes my throat close. I don't know shit about fashion, but I do know that the color red, today of all days, is fitting. Everyone knows black is the typical color of mourning, but that wouldn't suit her. The red, it's her, and it makes me proud.

I find myself walking away from Pyper, and stepping towards her. I know she would not have wanted everyone to be carrying on and wallowing over her death, but it's hard. I finally make myself look at her face, and the tears in my eyes double, making my vision blurry. I'm not ashamed. She's deserving of these tears and many more.

She looks beautiful and peaceful, even in death, like she's sleeping. I want to rant and rage over the fact that she was taken so soon. I want to scream at God and demand to know why life is so unfair. Why do bad things happen to good people? She should still have years of her life to look forward to. There are so many things she didn't get to do, things I know she looked forward to, wanted, and craved.

The hardest part for me in all of this is going to be to let go of the anger and guilt. I know she's in a better place and all that stuff everyone tells you at times like these, but it doesn't keep the selfish thoughts from surfacing anyway. The fact is that while it may have been God's time, it sure as hell isn't mine. *I* want more time with her. Another chance to tell her how I feel; how much she matters. The complete lack of control we have in life and death is frustrating. I walk to where I placed the pink roses, take one from the vase, and bring it back to lay next to her.

"Luke!"

I snap my head towards Pyper, the tone in her voice setting me on edge. She looks as if she was talking to someone, and is now rushing towards me with a phone in her hand, waving it in the air. At the same time, I begin to feel a buzzing from my phone in my jacket pocket. My brows furrow in confusion, and I pull the phone from my pocket glancing at a number I don't recognize.

"Luke, oh my God!" Tears are pouring down Pyper's face and I run to her, meeting her half way. I feel my father at my back.

"What happened? What's wrong?"

"There's news," Pyper almost wails, "About Olivia."

My heart stops and fear runs through me as I can't decipher anything from the look on Pyper's face. I grab her shoulders trying not to squeeze them too hard in my fear. "Tell me."

She manages to choke out, "She's alive."

My breath catches in my throat and I feel elation. I immediately start making my way to the door and then stop in my tracks as I remember where I am and what today is. I look back at my father, an apology ready on my lips. He doesn't hesitate, "Go, son. Go. Don't even think twice about it. She would understand - she would want you to go."

With one last look towards my mother lying in her red dress, I squeeze my dad in a tight hug, "Thank you for understanding. I'll be back as soon as I can."

Then, without another word, I run to my car with Pyper trying to keep up.

3.

IT ONLY HURTS WHEN I BREATHE

Olivia

*E*VERYTHING HURTS. MY body feels stiff and sore, and there is an insistent slapping on the side of my face. I proceed to roll over and feel a sharp pain in my leg that is so intense; it makes me see nothing but white and feels so excruciating, I'm afraid I'll vomit. "No! Don't move goddammit! Don't fucking move." I realize the slapping is Deacon smacking me. Why do I have a feeling he's enjoying it, the prick. "Your leg is broken. I can't believe you fucking did this! Ronnie! Pull the goddamn car around, there's a bone sticking out of her fucking leg!"

I hurt too much to even care about the fact that Deacon's voice is the one I hear, or that he is being a complete dick. I just want to close my eyes again and escape the pain resonating through my entire body. I'm burning. My whole body feels like it's on fire. It's debilitating, and the hair on my whole body is standing on end. I'm clenching my muscles and gritting my teeth, my breath coming out in pants between them, just trying to stay conscious, and not throw up. I'm ignoring the black dots at the edge of my vision. I know

24

what will happen if I give into them. When Deacon scoops me into his arms, I scream.

"Shit, you have a huge gash in your arm too. I said stop moving! I have no choice but to take you to the hospital. Your injuries are too much – I can't fix them myself. You are so fucking lucky these bushes broke your fall, or that you didn't fall on your head. What the fuck am I going to do with you?"

My whole body is jostled as he runs to the car, causing me to scream out in pain again. I mentally try and take an inventory of my injuries. My left side is hurting, my arm, my leg. My leg hurts so much, that when Deacon accidentally knocks it against the side of the car, I scream yet again. I almost black out from the pain, and can feel something hot and wet dripping down my leg. I taste blood in my mouth; suddenly I realize I'm having difficulty seeing out of one of my eyes.

"Screw... you... Deacon." Every word is painful and takes effort to say, but it's worth every single syllable.

"I hope you are hurting! You deserve it, you ungrateful bitch. All I wanted was for us to be happy. I wanted us to get away, and start over – to have a fresh start. Instead, you go and pull a dumbass stunt like this. Is the thought of being with me so bad you had to do something like this? FUCK!" He shakes me with each of his words, but I refuse to acknowledge the pain his acts are causing me. I'm biting my lips so damn hard, it's bleeding. Does he really think I wanted to do this? Asshole. He keeps talking as he places me down in the backseat of the car, but I just tune him out. I hear the doors close, and the engine start, making the seat underneath me vibrate.

I open my good eye to a slit, and see Deacon sitting next to me with my legs in his lap. Looking down I see his hands are covered in blood and he's holding something against my leg that is also covered in blood. I refuse to investigate further, as just that sight makes me even more woosy – if that's possible. He sees me looking at him, "Hear me right now, Olivia, I have no fucking choice but to leave you at the hospital because of your injuries, but listen to me closely, THIS IS NOT OVER! I will find a way, and I will be back for you. I promise you that."

Before I can form the question on the tip of my tongue, or even find it within myself to care, the black spots surrounding the edge of my vision take over. My whole world turns completely dark.

"Ma'am? Ma'am?"

There's a persistent pest screaming in my ear.

"Ma'am can you hear me?" I can hear him. Why is he shouting? "Ma'am if you can hear me, please, open your eyes."

I can tell I'm batting my eyelashes in an effort to get my eyes open. How is it that just that tiny motion requires so much effort? Finally, I succeed and I take in the man trying to rouse me. His face is very close to mine, he has blonde hair, green eyes and glasses sitting on a rather large nose that is currently so close I'm afraid it will poke me. His brow is furrowed and he's patting my shoulder. "There you are, hi there. Can you tell me your name?" I just stare at him. "What is your name?" he repeats again, but much slower this time.

"Olivia."

"Great, that's great, Olivia. You're going to be fine. My name is Daniel. Can you tell me your last name? What's your last name, Olivia?"

He's talking so loud; I really want to punch him in the throat. My head is aching. Why the hell is he asking what my name is? "Olivia? Olivia? What is your last name?" he repeats.

"Brooks."

"Okay, Olivia Brooks. Good job. Olivia, you are at Trinity Memorial Hospital, can you tell me what happened to you?"

I swallow. My throat feels so dry.

"Olivia? Can you please look at me?"

I do as he requests and he shines a light in my eyes. I flinch. That light is bright, asshole. It makes my head hurt more.

"It appears she has a concussion, her eyes are fully dilated. We need to get her into trauma room B and assess the extent of the damage."

I'm so cold. I feel cold air on my body and I realize I'm lying down and am being moved. My body breaks out into goosebumps all over and I shiver.

"Olivia? Do you understand where you are?"

I don't respond. I feel confused, everything is a blur. The darkness around my vision is calling me again, luring me with the promise of peace. I don't fight it.

Pain. I'm being jostled and it brings me from darkness to white hot light in a blink. I open my eyes, tears instantly blurring my vision.

"Well, hello there. My name is Dr. Arnez. Do you know where you are, Olivia?"

My eyes widen and I frantically look around the room. I hear a constant beeping and note the tubes already connected to my body. I have oxygen around my nose and an IV catheter already lodged into my hand.

"The hospital?"

"Yes, that's right. You are at Trinity Memorial Hospital. You have been hurt, but you're going to be okay. Do you remember that?"

"I think so." My mind does feel a little fuzzy.

"You have quite a bit of damage to your leg and a large cut on your arm. We have to take an x-ray to see the extent of the damage to your leg. You will likely need surgery on your leg, and while you are under anesthesia, we will stitch up your arm. We already took a picture of your head – and it does appear that you have suffered a concussion, but there doesn't appear to be any other injuries. Do you remember what happened to you? Can you please tell me?"

Slowly, like a sun breaking through the clouds on a gloomy day, the reality of my situation dawns on me. I remember tricking Deacon. I remember falling. Most importantly, I remember I'm away from Deacon. I can get help! "Kidnapped. Please...help me," every word is a struggle and to my own ears, it sounds like I'm slurring each word.

His eyes widen in surprise, but he doesn't question me further. He calmly turns to the nurse next to him and says, "Carrie, call the police. Tell them we have an Olivia Brooks here, and she was left at the emergency room. Please tell them she told us she's a victim of kidnapping. If she isn't here in this room when they arrive, she will likely be getting an x-ray or we will be in surgery. I don't want to delay fixing her leg longer than necessary. Thank you, Carrie." he says dismissing her.

Carrie nods, "I will call them now."

"You're going to be okay, Olivia. Did you understand when I told you where you are?"

"Yes... hospital."

"Yes. You are at Trinity Memorial. Hospital," he repeats. "We're already giving you some morphine for the pain, but I want to make sure it is working well for you. On a scale from one to ten, can you tell me how much pain you're in?"

I mentally take in my condition. I can't feel a thing, except that my head is aching. "Three or four or five? My head just really hurts."

"Okay. Very good. Your head likely aches from the concussion." He turns to another nurse that I just now realize is on the other side of me, holding something against my leg.

Dr. Arnez continues his questioning, but all I want to do is just close my eyes again. "Do you have any allergies?"

"No – except...de..on.." I smile at myself. Or I think I do. Good answer I try to tell myself.

"Can you tell me what happened to you?"

"Fell. Off a balcony."

"Okay, Olivia, try your best to relax. We are going to take great care of you." Dr. Arnez turns, as yet another person walks into my room. "Olivia, this is the x-ray technician, Andy. He's going to take you to get scanned now. We are going to have to move your leg around, and I'm going to be honest with you, it will not be comfortable for you."

I try to show my understanding by nodding my head, but it hurts to move and I realize my head is trapped in some kind of neck brace and movement is restricted.

Before I know it, I'm being pushed down the hallway again. When we enter a room, the temperature is freezing, and the thin sheet covering me isn't enough. I break out in goose bumps all over when they lower the sheet, and start cutting the dress from my body. Good riddance, slutty dress.

"Okay Olivia. We have to move you onto this surface over here for the scan, okay? Just try to relax." He lowers the bars of my bed, and then turns to the others in the room, "On the count of three... one... two... three."

The pain is so intense that I don't hang onto consciousness any longer.

BEEP. BEEP. BEEP.

"Her leg was severely broken with a protruding bone. We reset it with pins during surgery. She also had a large and very deep cut on her arm, that nearly severed an artery but we were able to repair it and stitched it closed. There are contusions covering her entire body. She has a scratch over the top of her eyelid, which is causing some swelling around her eye, as well as some other minor abrasions. There are other bruises that look older; but do not appear to have occurred at the same time."

"Did she say what happened? Where she was? Who dropped her off here?" I don't recognize the voice asking the questions.

"No, officers, we didn't manage to get much from her other than her name, the fact she fell, and that she was kidnapped. All we know is that someone came in with her in his arms, and started screaming for doctors and nurses to help her. As soon as she was placed on the gurney, a nurse turned around to ask some questions, and he had disappeared."

"How long was it from the time she was taken on the gurney, that they realized he was gone?" Another voice asks.

"The nurse said it couldn't have been more than a minute or two, tops."

I crack my eyes and see the blurry figures of Dr. Arnez and two policemen standing there.

"How long will she be asleep?" one of the officers asks.

"Likely, a few more hours, or so. Her body needs to rest in order to heal itself."

"Okay, well we need to be notified as soon as she wakes up. Time is of the essence and we have several questions we need to ask her."

"I understand. I will let the nurses know, as well."

"Does she have any family or any friends here yet?"

"Not that we've seen, no."

"Okay, well we contacted her parents. As soon as we saw there was an APB out on her and for the man that is suspected of kidnapping her, we called her local police department for information. They let us do the honors of notifying her parents. They should be on their way here now, from what I understand."

"Great. Having family surrounding her will definitely be beneficial to her recovery."

"We would like to keep an officer posted outside of her room. That way we can be sure to be notified as soon as she wakes up. Is that a problem?"

"No, not at all, officers. Again, I will be sure my staff is aware of the situation."

"Thank you."

I close my eyes again. While I can hear them, I am not sure who they are talking about, but somehow have the understanding that they are discussing me. They aren't coming completely into focus and I can't move at all. My body won't listen to me, so I just give up, and surrender myself to the dark once again.

4.

PINCH ME SO I KNOW IT'S REAL

Luke

*I*T FEELS LIKE it has taken me days to get here, instead of mere hours. As soon as Pyper got the call from Olivia's parents, I've felt a rollercoaster of emotions. The private investigator I hired called me with the news at the same time Olivia's parents tried to reach me. The relief I felt at hearing, "She's alive," was staggering. I can't even begin to put it into words. I didn't want to admit that in the deepest part of my mind, I was afraid of the worst. She's been gone from me for four weeks, three days, five hours, nine minutes. Every moment has been mind-numbing and terror-filled, and in many ways felt like a lifetime. I couldn't concentrate or think of anything else; barely a moment passed without wondering where she was, if she was okay, what was happening to her, if she was alive. That question was the most painful. That and wondering what was he doing to her.

I have no idea what state I'm going to find her in. I know the extent of her injuries, my private investigator told me on the phone. But emotionally, how is she going to be after four weeks with that monster? Can she heal from this? How will it have changed her? Is she going to be the same Olivia after such a traumatic experience? Will l be able to help her through this? Moreover, will she let me? Or will she blame me? Will she want to be with me? Can we move forward from this? Can I? l want to find him and kill him – to obtain my revenge for all he has done to Olivia, to us. For what he has taken. l don't care how irrational that is. The legal system will never be able to exact the penalty needed. So many questions, so much anger and pain, and each question, each issue is driving me crazy. And truthfully, I'm terrified of the answers. Terrified of what l might do. Or who we will have become. Will that stop me from rushing into her room to see her? Keep me from holding her, and telling her l love her? Hell no. Even if it's the last time, because she can't bear to be around me, I will take every moment, every second l can with her. l would walk through a pit of hypodermic needles if it meant she was on the other side. l will fight like hell to keep her in my life. Nothing will ever take her from me again.

After l got the call and found out Olivia was in St. Louis, l went to my condo in order to pack and make travel arrangements. l stood there for just a moment, feeling completely overwhelmed from all the emotions running through me. l had so much to do, yet felt paralyzed, unable to process even where to begin. l stood like a school girl on her first day of school, staring at my closet, trying to decide what to pack before l even realized what l was doing and that it didn't matter - she wouldn't care and l certainly didn't care. l then merely threw the first things l saw into my suitcase while calling the airline to arrange for a flight and rental car for both Pyper, and me. All tasks that had to be completed, but l was furious with the time it took to accomplish it all. What l really wanted was to take action, to get in the damn car and take off and drive, but that would ultimately have meant an even longer time before I could see her. So, I did my best to put emotions aside, and just do what needed to be done.

The flight seemed to take forever, but upon arrival at the Saint Louis International Airport, while hard for her, Pyper chose to wait behind for Olivia's parents, while I went on ahead. They shouldn't be far behind us, scheduled to have arrived within a half hour of our flight, but I couldn't wait another minute. I have to get to Olivia. To see her. My heart won't beat right again until I do.

"In one mile, turn right on Hospital Plaza. Your destination will be on the left."

Finally. Thank God for GPS since I have no clue where the hell I'm going. The twenty two miles seemed so far and seemed to take so long. I couldn't drive fast enough, yet, knew that getting a ticket would only make things worse; require time that I do not have to spare. And I can only imagine how an interaction with a cop would have gone down – not very pretty. So, why St. Louis? Why did Deacon bring her here, of all places? I finally reach my destination and quickly swing into the first parking space I see. I don't give a fuck that it's a handicapped spot, my life has been one big handicap without my girl. Anyone that has a problem can call the cops, I couldn't care less.

As I fly through the hospital entrance, aware that this is a fucking big place, I abruptly ask the volunteer Olivia's room number and the directions to the elevator. They really do wear pink at these places. Could one elevator take so long? Arriving on the 12th floor, flying through the doors, I am confronted by a large nurse's station and a young nurse who seems oblivious to my arrival. There are no signs that I can see indicating where I should go, so getting help is necessary. She's twirling her hair, snapping gum, and talking on the phone - awesome. I swear she turns her chair slightly away from me. "Yeah, I know right?! Thank goodness it's kind of a slow night tonight. If I'm lucky, I'll get off early."

"Excuse me, Miss? I need directions to Olivia Brooks' room, please."

She sighs and rolls her eyes, "I gotta go, Joey. I will see you during break. Uh huh...yeah. Oh really? They're serving fish again? Ugh, gross, who wants to eat fish from a –"

I reach over the counter and disconnect little Miss bubblegum's call, "HEY!"

I take a deep breath, and try again, "I said, where is Olivia Brooks' room, please?"

With another sigh, she taps on her keyboard before finally telling me, "She's going to be in room 1236, but right now she's in recovery room three, down on the second floor. The elevators are through that entryway over there," she says pointing to the right. "Oh, yeah, you know that right? I mean you just came up them. But maybe you came up on the other ones..."

"Thank you."

"Yeah, whatever," I hear her mumble under her breath.

I take off in a near run and find myself again stabbing the elevator button with impatience. I barely acknowledge the individuals on the elevator with me, and begin the second longest elevator ride of my life. Once I'm on the floor, I confront yet another reception desk. I again ask for Olivia and after providing my name, rank and serial number, am allowed through the doors that lead to her current room. There are no doors, only curtains, and the numbers are posted outside each cubicle looking space. I'm so close to her, my stomach is in knots, my heart is aching, and my mind is full of so many questions. I'm just steps away from seeing her, holding her.

When I see the policeman standing outside the curtain of room number five I abruptly stop. Looking at me, eyebrow raised, the officer says, "Can I help you?"

"Uh, yes. Is this Olivia Brooks' room?"

"Who are you?"

"I'm Luke Easton."

"Okay, I was told you were on your way here, but I need to see some identification first."

"Oh, yes, of course." I hurriedly take my wallet out of my back pocket and pull my driver's license out, showing it to the officer. He holds it up and inspects it carefully, looking from my ID, to me, and back again.

He hands it back to me, "Okay, thanks. The last time I checked, she was still unconscious from surgery. We are still waiting to get a statement from her about what happened. As soon as she wakes, I need you to let me know. Time is of the essence, if we are going to find the man that did this to her, okay?"

Just the reference to that bastard makes my fists clench as anger rushes through my body. I tap it down because now isn't the time. Instead, I nod and reply, "I understand."

He nods, "You can go on in."

I don't waste another moment maneuvering the curtain back, anxious to see her. I stop in my tracks at the sight. She looks so small; the bed almost swallows her whole. She has an oxygen tube around her nose, an IV running in her arm, some type of device attached to her index finger, and is connected to various monitors that are producing both a rhythmical beat and hum. Her right leg is suspended slightly over the bed, being held in place by some sling contraption, and her left arm is wrapped in a large bandage. She has visible bruises and scratches in nearly every place where her skin is exposed. She's still resting, but her eyelids move rapidly and her brow is furrowed in sleep, as if she's trying to solve a problem.

I have to keep myself from falling to my knees at the sight of her. My legs buckle, tears flood my eyes, and I feel a ball in my throat. Her beautiful ivory skin is so pale; it wrenches my stomach.

I can't help but miss the beautiful flush her skin has when she's laughing or excited by my touch.

I don't want to wake her, but the desire to touch her is a physical ache I feel all the way to my toes, making them curl in my shoes. Walking to the foot of her bed, I simply stand there and take her in. Tears I had been trying so hard to contain fall freely from my eyes. It has been one hell of a day – between my mother's funeral and now this – it's all too much. Wow, I've hardly thought about that in all of the urgency and rush to get here. Leaving my mother's funeral, while difficult because I know my dad could use my support, was the right thing to do. I have no doubt about that. Once upon a time, I chose my mom over Olivia, trying to make everyone happy, and the consequences of those actions took me years to make right. Choosing Olivia, prioritizing her, even at this time wasn't even a question, and I know she would understand. Wiping my face, I find myself at the side of her bed reaching my hands out to touch her. I hesitate because with all her scrapes, bruises and cuts I don't want to hurt her. There isn't a spot on her that appears to be a safe choice.

Finally, I settle for her cheek. I can't stop myself from trailing the back of my fingers down her profile, and as I do more tears escape, and I don't even care. I will gladly hand in my man card. I was so afraid I would never see her again. I love this woman with every part of me. She is my past, my present, and I hope she's my future. If she can forgive me, I will spend my life trying to make it up to her. I don't want anyone but her. I've spent seven long years of my life living without her, always wondering where she was, if she was happy, if she ever thought about me or remembered us at all. I can't imagine going back to that. It would kill me. I need her like the earth needs the sun.

Cupping the side of her face, I whisper, "Oh, my angel. I'm so sorry. So, so, sorry. Please forgive me. I should have been there. I wish I had been there."

Without warning, Olivia turns her face into my hand, nuzzling it. Her eyes open to slits and she murmurs, "Luke?"

"I'm here, love."

"Am I dreaming?"

Those words make my heart wrench hard in my chest, "No angel, you're not dreaming. I'm here."

"Luke, please don't leave me. Please God, I know this is a dream, but please, let him stay a little longer." Her eyes close and it takes her a while to reopen them. I can tell she's struggling to stay awake.

Her words gut me. "I'm here. You're safe now. I'm not going anywhere."

Her lips turn up at the corners making my breath catch in my throat. Her smile is beauty amongst so many touches of pain. "This is the best dream so far. I love you, Luke."

My breath leaves my body in a harsh exhale. I don't think I will ever tire of hearing those words pass her lips. "I love you too." I bend down and place a soft kiss upon her lips. I can't resist. She doesn't respond, and I know she's slipped back into sleep once again.

I'VE PLANTED MYSELF in a chair at her side, with no intention of leaving. They have moved her to the room on the twelfth floor. She hardly aroused when the nurses told her what was happening, choosing instead to sleep through the entire process, commotion and elevator ride and all. I'm guessing it's part medication and part exhaustion. I'm holding one of her hands, and can't stop myself from repeatedly tracing circles over her knuckles. Since we arrived in her room, three more times she's regained consciousness, each time, her eyes find mine, she asks me if she's dreaming, and falls back to sleep. It splits my heart open every time.

I just want her to open her beautiful green eyes and know without question that I'm here. I want her to know she's safe, and that I will do everything I can to make sure this never happens again.

Pyper is here, as well as Olivia's parents. She's not yet been able to be aware of their presence or even take in the room. She seems unaware of anyone, except me, and that is just fine. Olivia continues to ask me if she's dreaming each time she wakes, and it has made them emotional as well. All of us are wondering the same thing... what happened to her during her kidnapping?

I know I should probably move from my vigil at her bedside and let Pyper and Olivia's parents be closer to her, but I can't find it within myself to move. They haven't asked, so I think they understand. And so, we all just sit here, watching her sleep, thanking God she's alive, and waiting for her to open her eyes again.

"Luke, we are going to go to the cafeteria and get some coffee and something to eat. Can we bring you something?" Joy, Olivia's mom, asks.

"I don't know if I can eat anything right now. Maybe just some coffee, please."

She gets a scolding look on her face that I remember well. It may have been years since I've seen Joy and Nelson, but I still remember that look from the days Olivia would get home late and her parents didn't approve. "You need to eat something. You won't be good to anyone if you're tired and hungry. It will only run you down."

Pyper is smirking at me, likely because Joy just stated exactly what she was thinking. It's written all over her face. "Okay, you're right. Maybe just a muffin or something would be fine."

"I'm going to go with them. Will you let us know if she wakes up? I have my cell phone." Pyper asks.

"Of course."

They head out of the room and I resume rubbing circles into Olivia's soft hands.

Fifteen minutes or so have passed since they all left the room, when I notice Olivia's eyes flutter. I squeeze her hand automatically in response, and am overjoyed when her hand squeezes mine in return.

"Olivia?"

Her eyes open, and she stares at the ceiling above her. For a moment, her face is peaceful, and then I can tell the instant clarity arrives, because her face registers panic before she realizes where she is. Her body jerks, and for a minute, she looks like she's trying to sit up, but then she whimpers in what I assume is pain.

Immediately, I tighten my grip on her hand and stand next to her running my hand down the side of her face, trying to soothe away the hurt. Her eyes focus on me. "Hi, angel."

"Luke?"

"I'm here. You're safe now. It's okay. Do you know where you are? Do you remember being brought in here?"

She doesn't respond, she just stares into my eyes, and I'm bracing myself for when she assumes I'm a dream once again. Then, without warning, she clutches my shirt with her right arm and pulls me to her. She tries to wrap her damaged arm behind my neck to pull herself up. "Luke! Oh my God, Luke!"

I place my arms around her the best I can, given the contraptions and restrictions her body has right now. "I'm here. I'm here. Please don't hurt yourself. You need to take it easy right now."

I hold her against my chest carefully, and run my fingers through her hair. "I love you so much, Livvie. So, so much." I can't quit telling her, reminding her. I thought I'd never get the chance to again – I don't know if I'll be able to any time soon.

In response, Olivia's body starts shaking, and when she makes a choked sound, I pull back and look at her face, afraid. She's trying to hold it in, but the dam breaks and she starts sobbing. Tears fall like a waterfall down her cheeks and her whole body trembles, breaking me into pieces. I don't know the right words to say, or how I can make this better. I want to make it all go away for her, but I know I can't. At least not yet.

"I never want to let go," she cries, "please don't let me go."

"Never... I will never let go. I missed you so much," I wipe the tears from her face the best I can, but they continue to fall, despite my efforts. "I died a little inside every day that you were away from me. I'm so sorry, angel. I'm so, so sorry." I stop talking because now I'm afraid I'm going to lose it too, and that's the absolute last thing she needs to see.

Pulling away from me, Olivia looks up at me and loosens her grip on my shirt so she can swipe at her teary eyes. Her green eyes are shining brightly from her tears and I move her hand aside and wipe them from her cheeks with my thumbs again. I lean in and place a gentle kiss on her lips, feeling her lips respond to mine immediately. My whole body responds and I can feel myself tingle in places that are highly inappropriate, given the situation. I can't help it though; I always have this reaction around her. My body has a mind of its own. I want so much more. I need so much more. I want to crawl inside of her, take care of her, and protect her. I need it so badly, but of course, now is not the time to lose control.

"Sorry? Why are you telling me you're sorry? You didn't do anything, Luke."

"Because I wasn't there. I wasn't there to keep you safe. I wasn't there to keep this from happening to you." My voice breaks, the pain in my chest becoming too much to hide.

"Luke, no. I cannot handle you trying to blame yourself for this. There is only one person who's to blame. Please, don't say that again."

"But..."

"No! I mean it. Don't."

I brush her hair away from her face and lower my lips to hers. I have to. It's a need I have no control over. I kiss her, and in that kiss, I try to convey to her every emotion I'm feeling. My despair at losing her, my desperation and determination to bring her home, and my pure joy to finally have her back again. Pulling away, I look into her eyes, hoping that mine somehow tell her everything I'm too choked up to say. I open my mouth to try and form the words, but before I can do so, we are interrupted by the door opening.

"I just came back up real quick to bring you-" Pyper stops mid-whisper when she realizes Olivia is awake. The coffee and muffin she's holding are forgotten and crash to the floor, and then there is nothing but a red blur as the tornado that is Pyper rushes to her best friend's side.

"Olivia! Oh my God, Olivia!" Pyper is sobbing and Olivia is crying in response to Pyper. I should probably back the hell up and give them their moment, but again, just thinking about moving away from Olivia's side gives me a physical ache. I can't make myself do it.

"Pyper! I am so happy you are okay. I asked... him... I asked... and he told me... he told me you were, but I didn't know if he was telling me the truth." Olivia can barely speak in between her sobs.

Pyper embraces Olivia and they hold onto one another and cry.

5.

THE INTERROGATION

Olivia

M Y ROOM IS crowded. Luke is here, plus Pyper, my mom and dad, two police officers, a doctor and a nurse. I appreciate their concern, I really do. I get that they were scared for me and need to see me, but I feel like I'm suffocating. My chest feels tight, my breath keeps catching, and already I'm picking at my new cast on my leg. It's too much. I think it's due in part to the fact that I know what's coming – the dreaded questions. Just thinking about them makes my stomach twist and churn.

The reunion with my parents was an emotional one. My mom kept running her fingers through my hair, and stroking the side of my face like I'm a little girl. Silent tears fell down her face as she told me over and over again how much she loves me. Even my dad, whom I don't know if I've ever seen cry, was emotional. His eyes became glassy and he kept clearing his throat while asking me repeatedly if I'm feeling any pain. Before we could do or say much else, the police officers came into my room. Once they heard I had awakened, they were ready to begin questioning. They keep telling me the timing is so important if they are going to catch Deacon. I don't tell any of them that I don't think he will be found.

"Hi Olivia, my name is Detective Kline." Nodding to the other man with him, he says, "With me is Officer Timpleton, and we're here to ask you some questions about your kidnapping."

I take in Detective Kline's dark hair and dark eyes. He has a five o'clock shadow, hinting at a long night, and full lips. I decide he could totally be on one of those cop shows. I store that information to discuss with Pyper later. She'll appreciate it. And it could be great conversation to use as a distraction from me and how I'm feeling. I know she will agree that he's easy on the eyes, and speaking of eyes - his reveal compassion and kindness. They immediately put me at ease.

His partner, Officer Timpleton, looks younger. He has blonde hair, blue eyes, and a young, boyish face. He continuously sways from side to side, with his hands clenching and unclenching. I get the impression he would much rather be running someone down on the street, as opposed to questioning me. I can't really blame him. I would give back my favorite Jimmy Choo's if it meant I could get out of this. Well okay, maybe not, but close enough.

"Okay, I'm ready."

Before the officers speak again, the doctor and nurse excuse themselves, likely not wanting to interfere. I give them a smile as they head out and then return my attention to the officers.

"First, I want to say I'm sorry. I know you just had surgery, and that you were just reunited with your family. I promise, we will try to keep the questioning short, so you can get back to your time with them. As we mentioned, time is of the essence if we are going to have any luck tracking Deacon down before he gets too far."

I flinch. It's an automatic response to Deacon's name. I can't help it. Trying not to show my fear, I nod in response, and brace myself for a round of questioning that I know will be difficult.

"Are you okay with your family being present during this round of questioning?"

I look around at all of their faces. This is not only going to be hard for me, but it will be for them as well. "Yes, it's okay."

"Okay." The officer clears his throat and then begins, "Olivia, let's start with the day that you were taken. Can you tell us what happened?"

Taking a deep breath, I give them a nod and dive right in. That day has played over and over in my mind more times than I can count. I couldn't forget it, even if I tried. I begin with the roses I received at the restaurant. They ask me specific details about everything, from where I was in the restaurant when I received them; who gave them to me; how many there were; and what color they were. "I assumed the roses were from Luke," tears fill my eyes and I glance at Luke and see a tick in his jaw, "that's why I texted him to tell him thank you. When I got to the condo, the door was closed –"

"Did you notice any signs of forced entry?"

Shouldn't they know this already? This seems pointless. Then I remember that I'm not in my home state where the incident occurred. I should be more patient. "No, I didn't. If I had, I wouldn't have gone in. I would have called the police, assuming there was a break in."

"What happened when you went inside? Walk us through it, please."

"I saw the back of Pyper's head," my eyes well up again, making me sniff in an effort to hold them in, "I remember thinking it was strange that when I called her name, she just sat there. She didn't turn around, didn't acknowledge me at all. I walked toward the couch, instinctively knowing something was wrong." I swallow hard, and take a deep breath, "When I saw she was tied up and gagged," I pause a moment as the memory of Pyper sitting there floods my memory.   Tape over her mouth, tear tracks down her cheeks, fear and pleading in her eyes. "I didn't even think twice about removing the tape from her mouth to help her, and find out what happened. Before I could, Deacon appeared with a gun in his hand."

"What then?"

"He said, 'hello, princess', and pointed a gun at me."

"Did he say anything else to you?"

"He said lots of things. I don't see how any of that is helpful." I want to cry. Remembering how I was forced to leave my best friend on the couch bound and gagged makes me want to lose it. I've spent hours and hours running that day through my mind. I've asked myself what I could have done differently, time and time again. Could I have helped her? Freed her? Or prevented his taking me somehow? I was so afraid for Pyper, so afraid for myself. I'm getting that tight feeling in my chest again, and I find myself gasping for air.

"I'm sorry, I'm sure this is difficult for you, but we need to know everything – no detail is insignificant. Everything you tell us will only help our investigation."

I take another deep breath and count to ten. Luke walks to my side and takes my hand. "Do you need some water, angel?"

I give him a small smile, "That would be great, thanks."

After taking a sip, I continue. "Deacon made me leave Pyper on the couch. I pleaded with him to let her go immediately. I told him that it was me he wanted, and that Pyper had done nothing wrong. I told him..." I hesitate and take another sip of water before continuing. "I told him I would do anything he wanted." Tears instantly blur my vision as I recall my desperate pleas to Deacon. They went unanswered. "He ignored me and brought me to my room. I-", I need another minute. I'm so weak and angry with myself. This wasn't even the worst of my experience, and already I need a moment. "I opened my mouth to scream and he shoved his gun down my throat." I choke on my words. Luke's hand tightens around mine and my mother gasps in horror. Tears start streaming down Pyper's face, and I clench my teeth tight in an effort to stop the tears from falling.

I lose focus for a moment as I remember exactly what he said to me, *"Don't even think about it bitch – if you make a fucking sound, I won't hesitate to walk into that living room and blow your precious friend's brains out while you watch. Do you fucking understand me?"*

"Olivia?"

I blink several times trying to clear the image from my mind. "He told me if I wasn't quiet that he would hurt Pyper. So, I remained silent while he used rope to bind my arms and legs. After that, he put duct tape over my mouth. He said he couldn't trust me to keep quiet. When he was finished, he threw me on my bed, pulled out his phone and made a call."

Understanding my distress, the Detective's voice is soft, "Who did he call?"

"I didn't know then. Now, I'm guessing it was probably Ronnie."

"Ronnie?" Officer Timpleton takes over questioning, "Who's that?"

"Ronnie is the man who helped Deacon kidnap me."

Detective Kline and Officer Timpleton exchange a look before Timpleton asks, "Helped how?"

"He was always there. When Deacon would leave, he... he would be with me. He is also the one that drove the vehicle here."

Detective Kline takes back control, "Okay, we will get to that. What happened after he made a call?"

"Deacon came back to the bed where I was lying and pulled a syringe out of his pocket. Before I could even comprehend what he was about to do, he stabbed me in the neck with a needle, and I lost consciousness."

Luke cursed. Pyper choked on a sob. My mom used a tissue to catch her tears. My dad looked away. I'm regretting my choice to let them stay. They don't need to hear this.

"Did he ever mention what was in the syringe?"

"No."

"Did he use it again?"

I hesitate. "Yes," I whisper.

"Please explain."

"I was drugged consistently. Sometimes, as soon as it would seem like it was wearing off, I would get stabbed with a needle again and put under. Sometimes I would go out completely. Other times, I was in and out. I lost all sense of time. I have no idea how long I was under its influence each time. I lost total awareness of time."

"Where have you been the last four weeks, Olivia? Where did Deacon keep you?"

It was my turn to gasp. The days just seemed to all melt into one another. They seemed long and endless. I thought I would never get away. Somewhere inside of me, I started to resign myself to the fact that I was doomed to a life with Deacon. I hated myself because the truth is, there were times when I just gave up. I welcomed the darkness the drugs would bring. It wasn't until I woke up naked the first time that I started to be terrified instead. I was afraid of what was happening during the moments I wasn't aware, but they didn't need to know that.

Before I can stop it, a grainy memory assaults me, *"You like that baby? Being touched there feels good doesn't it?"* Deacon's rough hands on my breasts, pinching, pulling, hurting... I shake my head, wishing the action would shake the memory right out of my mind.

"Four weeks? I've been gone for four weeks?" Oh my God. What my family must have felt. I squeeze Luke's hand and look into his eyes. I see the pure agony he's trying his best to keep hidden. I know that every moment I was gone must have felt like a lifetime for him. I know if it were him who had been missing, I would have felt the same way. I want to soothe the hurt away, but I don't know how.

"Yes," Luke says, "four very long weeks," his voice is raspy and full of emotion.

Detective Kline asks again, "Can you tell us where you've been?"

"I've been in a house somewhere. Locked in a bedroom."

"What can you tell us about the house? About the bedroom?"

"There was no way out."

Luke's hand is squeezing me so tight, it's beginning to hurt. I know he's doing it subconsciously. I hate that he has to hear this, because I know him. He's blaming himself for all of this.

"You tried to escape?"

"Yes."

"And what happened?"

I hesitate. I look at Luke, Pyper, my mom and dad. A squeeze to my hand makes my eyes meet Luke's. He runs the back of his fingers over my cheek, lending silent support.

I open my mouth and start telling them about the time I tried to look for an escape from the bedroom where I was being kept. I told them how I searched the room, and desperately looked to find a weapon of some kind to use. How I tried to scream for help, when that got me nowhere, how I swung at the glass doors trying to break them so I could use the glass as a weapon. I told him how I found out Ronnie was in the house.

"What did Ronnie do when he came into the room?"

"He threw me to the bed and told me it didn't matter how loud I screamed or cried, that no one would hear me."

49

"Olivia, how did you get these injuries? How did you end up being brought here to the hospital?"

Again I hesitate, knowing the answer will be hurtful to those that love me. "I... well I umm... fell."

His brows lowering in confusion, Officer Timpleton asks, "You fell? How?"

"I fell off a balcony after I managed to take Deacon's gun from him and threatened to shoot him. He called my bluff, went for the gun, and I overcompensated by throwing myself off a balcony."

"Good God," my dad exclaims, "you are lucky you didn't die!"

Pyper and my mom hold onto one another. It looks like if they let go, one of them will fall over. My eyes meet Luke's, and his are full of pure fear and agony. I squeeze his hand, knowing where his mind is, and at the same time wanting to reassure him that the worst didn't happen. I'm here. His eyes soften, but a lone tear falls down his cheek. I wish I could move toward him to wipe it away.

"Do you remember what happened after you fell, Olivia?"

"I came to and Deacon was over me. Some bushes had broken my fall and Deacon was cursing at me and telling me that I was stupid. He told me..." I stop. Pure fear runs through my body in a rush when I repeat his words, "He told me that he had no choice but to bring me to the hospital because of my injuries but he said," I stop again, then whisper, "he said he would be back for me."

"I dare him to try." Luke says with pure heat behind his words, "I will kill the bastard."

Officer Timpleton and Detective Kline look at Luke, but say nothing. I see understanding in their eyes when they look at Luke.

"Olivia, we have a few private questions to ask you. I don't know if you would prefer for us to conduct them one on one."

"Privately? Why?"

"They are personal in nature."

At first, I don't realize what he is trying to say to me, but then it clicks. And my whole body stiffens. Luke looks at me curiously. "We are her family, I'm sure whatever you have to ask, we can be here. Right, love?"

I feel like I'm going to suffocate again. He can't know. I don't want Luke to know that Deacon had his filthy hands on me. What will he do? What will he say? Will he still want me? Am I tainted? I am. I'm tainted by Deacon. I'm not pure. I know that while it wasn't in my control, my body was violated while my heart, my very soul belonged to Luke. Is that cheating? When it isn't in your control? What will Luke think? I can't... I just can't...

I look at Detective Kline and I know he sees the pleading in my eyes.

"I'm going to need to ask that everyone leave the room, please."

"What, why?" Luke asks, his eyes going from me and the detective like he's watching a tennis match.

"We have a few questions that we must ask her privately."

Luke looks at me, and I don't say a word. I know he wants me to say that it's okay, that he can stay. That there is nothing that they could ask that he, Pyper, or my parents couldn't hear, but that isn't true. I close my eyes, avoiding having to see the worry and confusion in his.

"Come on, son," my dad says to Luke and under any other circumstances I would have smiled at the 'son' reference.

"I will be right outside that door okay, Olivia?" Luke asks.

I open my eyes, look in his, and give a nod.

They all leave the room and Luke looks back at me once more. I try to give him a reassuring smile, but I know it looks like a grimace instead. I'm sure he can see the residual fear in my eyes.

Once they are gone, Detective Kline hesitates, "I'm sorry Olivia, but we have to ask..."

I nod my head, waiting for him to say the words.

When the Detective takes a deep breath, I almost believe for a moment this is as hard for him as it is for me. "Olivia, other than being drugged, were you abused in any other way - meaning, physically or sexually?"

My breath catches, tears fill my eyes as they lose focus, *"Oh God, you feel amazing princess. It has been too long since I've been with you. You belong to me. Do you hear me? You belong to me."*

"Olivia?"

A whisper, "Yes."

6.

PUNCHING A STEERING WHEEL
HURTS LIKE A BITCH

Luke

I DON'T WANT to leave her. I feel hurt and confused that she didn't tell me I can stay with her. What could they possibly have to ask her that I couldn't, or shouldn't, be here for? Each step towards the door is a challenge; I feel like I'm trying to walk through cement. I look back at her and when our eyes meet, I hope she will tell me that I can stay. Instead, her eyes lower, and she look sad, scared and...ashamed? Why would she feel ashamed?

I've just gotten to touch her, hold her and see her again after fearing the worst - I don't want to leave her. I swear I'm not a pussy, and I know that I'm being irrational and unrealistic, but I don't want her out of my sight. Even in a room with police officers. I just need to be able to keep an eye on her right now. To know that she's safe – and okay, maybe also so I can keep reminding myself that she really is here.

Pulling the door behind me, I start to latch it closed, but then stop. I know I shouldn't do this. I should respect her privacy, but I can't help it. I just need to be within listening distance. If something distresses her, I want to know about it. I want to be there in a second if she needs me, and I just feel better knowing she's basically within my reach. This stupid door feels like a huge barrier, and the fact that it is all that is keeping me from her is putting unease in my stomach. I want to rip it off its hinges so that the obstacle is no more.

So, I make a decision. I don't close the door all the way behind me.

I'm not standing here long before a voice trails out to me. I can barely make out what's being said. I want to try not to listen, I really do, but I abandon all my best intentions at the words I hear.

"Olivia, other than being drugged, were you abused in any other way, meaning physically or sexually?"

I stiffen.

I can't breathe.

I don't fucking move.

My stomach has dropped to my ass.

I can't hear the response from Olivia, but what I hear next confirms my worst fears.

"Okay, we are going to let our forensic nurse know. She's the nurse who will help us gather evidence. She will do a medical exam, gathering samples required for the rape kit protocol, perform a vaginal inspection, draw blood for testing, and take some pictures."

"Pictures?" I hear her voice now and the sound of it, makes my knees shake. She sounds scared.

"Yes. We need pictures for evidence purposes."

Suddenly, it feels as if the walls are closing in. I can feel my heart pounding in my chest, and even though I'm standing still, my body rocks forward a little with each beat. No, it's more of a thud. My heart may be exploding from my chest. My breathing becomes rapid and shallow and my face must register excruciating pain and shock, because pure alarm flashes across Pyper's face. She steps toward me and takes my hand, "What is it? What's wrong?"

I open my mouth to reply, and find that nothing comes out. My mouth and lips suddenly feel dry and I'm pretty sure if I don't walk away right now, someone will be summoning a nurse for me. And some poor custodian is going to have to clean up the goddamn puke I'm about to project all over the damn place.

I'm rescued as Joy suddenly approaches us, "I know it's awful here, but we are going to go get some more coffee. Can we bring you anything?" She's looking at me, and it takes extreme effort to make my lips move and give her a reply.

"No, thank you," my voice sounds unsteady, raspy, "I'm fine." Part of me wants to break out in hysterical laughter at the word 'fine'. I'm anything but fine.

"How about you, Pyper? Can we bring you back anything?"

Pyper, with her eyes red from crying and looking extremely tired and disheveled, doesn't look away from me when she answers. "Some coffee would be great, thank you."

"Would you like cream and sugar?"

"Yes, please."

"Okay honey, we will be right back."

Pyper nods at Joy, but I don't acknowledge her leaving at all. I don't think she noticed though. Pyper continues to stare at me, though now appearing to be in a state of confusion. I'm sure Pyper thinks I'm nuts. I'm not budging from Olivia's door, and I know I have a look of horror frozen on my face. I can't help it.

"Olivia, other than being drugged, were you abused in any other way, meaning physically or sexually?"

Those words are an echo...continually reverberating in my brain. *"Were you abused... were you abused.... were you abused..."*

"Luke, are you okay? Something is wrong. I can see it on your face. What am I missing?"

The last thing I want to do is tell her. I don't want to worry her, and as much as I want to talk to someone about it, I couldn't ever betray Olivia that way. So I lie. "I'm not feeling so hot all of a sudden, uh...stomach upset" I mumble. "Gonna go to the bathroom." I gesture down the hallway.

"Do you need anything?"

"No, thanks."

I can't look at her as I walk away. I'm trying to appear casual when all I really want to do is take off in a sprint at the fastest pace I've ever run. The overheard conversation is getting louder in my head. And won't stop. I want to scream. But that wouldn't help anyone. I just want to get the hell out of here. For a moment, I contemplate going to the bathroom, and shutting myself in a stall, but the lure of the outdoors and fresh air is far too strong.

Once I know I'm out of eye sight, I do take off in a run. People look at me curiously as I pass - and I almost take out the nutritionist pushing her food cart - but I can't bring myself to care. I mumble an apology, but I don't stop. I can't get out of the hospital fast enough.

Once I'm outside, I take big gulps of air like a fish out of water.

I brace my hands on my knees and stay that way deeply breathing in and out for several minutes.

"Were you abused...."

I hear someone exit the hospital behind me, which brings me to awareness of where I am. Standing here is probably not the smartest move. Nor is it far enough away. I race through the parking lot, making my way to my car. Once there, I unlock it, and practically lunge inside, still trying to catch my breath. I'm breathing so hard it sounds like I ran a 5K at a dead sprint. I clutch handfuls of my hair, as if doing so will get the words I keep hearing over and over out of my brain and the noise to stop.

"Were you abused..."

It echoes like a drum in my mind, beating against me until I scream out and start pounding on the steering wheel over and over and over.

"AHHHHHHHHHHHHH FUCK!" I can't hold it in. It feels good to scream. To rant and rave and punch. I keep punching the wheel until I feel my skin crack and bleed. The blood catches me by surprise because I just feel numb – the only pain is from my bleeding heart.

"Goddamn it. God fucking damn it. Not my beautiful girl, not my Olivia. This is all my fault. All my fucking fault."

I can feel beads of sweat on my brow. My shirt feels hot, itchy and suddenly constricting and uncomfortable. And I am suddenly sweaty. I still can't catch my breath, so I start my car and blast the air conditioner, looking for relief that I know damn well I'm not going to find in here. The kind of relief I need comes from just one look by a dark haired, green-eyed angel that has my heart in the palm of her hand.

Each slam of my heart in my chest feels like an accusation screaming, "Failure, failure, failure."

Oh god, he touched her. He put his hands on her; hurt her. Closing my eyes, I picture her face. Her beautiful face. I wonder if she has any idea that her green eyes twinkle with love and a hint of mischief when she looks at me. Such expressive eyes. I can tell what she's thinking by just one look. Those eyes are the window to her soul. I thought I would never see them again. The thought makes me groan in pain.

I picture her skin, her hair. I hear her laugh. I can see the curves of her body. In my mind, she's smiling at me. Then, like a flash of lightning I see her eyes alight with fear and I picture her lying on a bed somewhere, drugged up, with a monster. I see him touch her, look at her, want her. I imagine him kissing her. Squeezing her too tight and hurting her.

"Were you abused..."

Suddenly, the devil invades my mind like a thief in the night and my thoughts take an unanticipated flight, bringing me agony and pain. I'm consumed and tormented by thoughts I don't want to have. Did she, oh god, did his touching her arouse old feelings; make her remember how she felt about him at one time? Did she like it on some level? I wrack my brain trying to remember what it's called when you fall for your kidnapper. Did that happen to her? Does she miss him? Want to be back with him?

I whimper like the pansy-ass bitch I am - a hiding pansy-ass bitch. What the fuck is wrong with me? Why would these thoughts even occur to me? I know better than this, how dare I even think such things; yet the thoughts invade my mind anyway, and all I can think is oh god, he touched her.

When I touch her, will she think of him? Will she be able to stand being touched by anyone now?

He touched her.

What can I say to her to make everything better? How can I even begin to apologize for this? I don't even know how. Can she ever forgive me? How could she? Can I even forgive myself? I should have been there. How could she possibly get over that when I don't even think that I can?

He touched her.

What am I going to say to her? She doesn't know I heard. Will she tell me?

I put my head in my hands. And I cry. I just fucking cry, gut wrenching, soul screaming sobs. I cry for the woman she was before this. I cry for the woman I know that is forever changed because of what she endured. I cry because I didn't prevent this. I cry for the fact that she has to go through this. I cry because I'm afraid things will never be the same. I cry because I wish my mom were here, and that she could offer me advice on how to help Olivia get through this. I cry because I love my girl so fucking much and I don't know how, or if, I can make this better.

In the dark recesses of my mind I wonder... can I touch her again? Will I be able to kiss her, touch her, look at her and love her without thinking about the fact that his hands were there too? Are Olivia and I strong enough to get through something like this?

I use my shirt to wipe my eyes and I put the car in reverse.

I've made my decision.

I need to get out of here.

7.

NUMB

Olivia

"Hi, OLIVIA. My name is Katie. I'm the forensic nurse that is going to perform an evidence collection exam that you agreed to have. This can be a difficult and intrusive process, so I won't pretend that I can make you comfortable, but I will proceed at whatever pace works for you and want you to make sure to tell me if you need a break or have a question during this process, okay?"

I nod, feeling numb, not able to do much else. I want this over now.

"I'm going to do a few things, including a vaginal inspection, collection of some hair and nail samples, and blood draws. I will explain what I'm doing as we go. Do you have any questions before I begin?"

"Since I'm not positive that... he... " I take a deep breath, but she doesn't make me continue.

"It's best to be precautionary. While findings and evidence is most reliable when this process is conducted within 72 hours of an assault, that doesn't mean that any evidence we obtain here won't be helpful down the line. It will also help to determine if you acquired any ailment or disorder. If that occurred, we will provide the appropriate care for you promptly."

"Okay."

Katie gives me a small smile while she eases on a pair of exam globes. "I've already gathered the clothes you were wearing when you were brought in, so we are going to start with hair and nail samples."

"When was the last time you showered?" Katie asks unemotionally. Her calm, steady speech and effortless, easy motions are simultaneously reassuring and unsettling. She has obviously done this many times.

"I...I'm not sure. I don't even know what day it is. It's likely been a couple days at least, I guess." I respond, trying to be equally impassive.

"Okay. Don't worry that you don't remember exactly. That's fine." Katie proceeds to cut my nails, capturing each one in a plastic bag. "Next, I need to gather hair samples from your scalp. This is going to sting just a little. I need to pull one hair out of your scalp in five places. One on each side of your head, the center, and then from the front and back."

I remain silent as I feel her selectively comb and then the sting and snap as she pulls a hair from each place on my scalp, and then places them in their own plastic bags labeling each one.

Next, she approaches me with cotton swabs.

"I need to take swabs of your saliva, please. Just open your mouth for me."

I open my mouth and wrinkle my nose at the feel of cotton in my mouth as she swabs my gum line, and the inside of my cheek. When she's done, she smears the samples on glass slides. The process is repeated with two more cotton swabs, but these are not placed on slides.

"Normally I would collect samples of the blood from each of the scratches on your body, however each of your punctures and scratches were cleaned and medicated when you were brought in. Next I need to retrieve pubic hair samples, as well as do a pelvic exam. Do you have any questions about that?"

"No." Is she crazy? I don't want to ask her questions. I want to pretend none of this is happening and drift off to la la land.

"Okay. I know this is going to be difficult with your leg cast, but we will make it work."

"Okay." What else am I supposed to say? Should I say 'great' or 'thanks', because I don't feel either of those things.

Katie comes to the side of my bed and presses a button that makes the bed rise into a sitting position. She can't lift it too much because the cast on my leg does make it difficult, as predicted.

"Are you ready?"

I can only nod – or at least I think I did, because she efficiently pulls the cover and sheet back as she deftly adjusts my gown to assist in providing needed access without undue difficulty.

"I now need to help you disrobe down to your waist."

I start to try and awkwardly pull the hospital gown off my shoulders, but the bandage on my arm makes me clumsy, and I only manage to get one side – and not fully off. I can tell getting dressed each day is going to be an interesting experience. Joy.

Grabbing her camera from a nearby table, she matter-of-factly states that she needs to take a few pictures and begins taking photos. I look down at myself and gasp when I see all the scratches and bruises covering my torso. There are even a few bandages on places where fluid has leaked through enough to show on the other side.

"Can you tell me how you got these marks, Olivia?"

"I'm assuming most of the injuries were sustained during my fall."

"Yes, I would assume that too, however, what about the marks on your arms that look like fingerprints?"

I just stare at her. Is that a rhetorical question? I think the obvious hand prints speak for themselves.

"Did Deacon Brooks do this to you, Olivia?"

"Yes."

I don't realize until after she asks, that she's making notes on a notebook.

"What are the notes for?"

"I have to make sure I have notes that correspond with each photo I'm taking."

"I see."

The flash is on the camera and it is blinding. I don't realize how much I'm batting my eyes, until they start to water. I close my eyes, just trying to shut this out and more tears fall down my cheeks in silent succession. I want to blame it on the flash, but I know better.

"We belong together, Olivia. Do you hear me? You are going to stay in this fucking room until you get that through your head."

"Deacon, you're hurting me."

I open my eyes, hoping that doing so will make the images of him shaking me go away.

"Okay, let's put this back up on your shoulders," the sound of her voice startles me and I realize she had pulled the covers up in an attempt to provide modesty while she was taking pictures and writing, "then I am going to pull the bottom up to your waist and pull the covers down one more time. We need to do a pelvic exam now, and I can take pictures of your leg and hips, if needed, at the same time."

"Okay."

Katie is gentle. There is kindness in her eyes, and I know she's trying to make this as easy as possible. But, is there an easy way? Is that even possible?

Katie lowers the bed back down so I'm lying down once again, "Olivia, please bend your knee on this leg," she says tapping my knee, "and relax it to the side."

Oh God. I hate these things. Once a year is enough. I force myself to relax and open my leg to make her job easier. It's not easy. I feel vulnerable and completely violated.

"This may pinch a bit. I have to collect ten hairs the same way I collected the samples from your head."

I squeeze my eyes closed. This is humiliating. The first thing I'm doing when I'm better is getting back to the spa for a wax and a full-on pampering session. I try to remove myself from the situation. Luke's face comes to the forefront of my mind. I saw the confusion and hurt on his face when he looked back at me as he left the room. He wanted to stay, he wanted me to tell him to stay, but I couldn't. I don't want him to know about this.

I feel alone, and on one hand I wish he were in here with me holding my hand, telling me it will be okay. I want his lips in my hair and his sweet words in my ear. But, I know Luke, and I could see it on his face, in his eyes; he already blames himself for what happened to me. The last thing I want is for him to blame himself for this too. It's bad enough already, and selfishly, part of me doesn't want to deal with his emotions too. I can hardly handle my own.

I just want to move on and pretend this never happened. Do I think that will be easy? No. Do I even think that is healthy? No. But I refuse to let Deacon dictate my life. I refuse to let him and his sick obsession ruin everything I want in my life.

"Okay, Olivia, I'm finished with the exam. You can relax now." She tucks my gown back down and covers me up again. "The last thing I need to do is scrape your fingernails in case you have any of his DNA trapped under your nails, that didn't come off with the clippings."

"Alright." I am patient and quiet as Katie goes about her task.

I could have lied to the police when they asked me if I had been physically or sexually abused. I thought about it, for a moment, but I'm not stupid. I have no doubt the doctors already saw some of the marks on me during surgery, so if I lie, they will know it. Plus, I know that eventually, this is all going to come to a head and the more evidence I have on my side, the better. Documenting this is important. So I keep telling myself that, because knowing doesn't make this any less demeaning.

"Oh, one more thing. I'm going to leave this cup. The next time you get up to use the restroom, I need a sample."

"A sample?"

"Yes, a urine sample, please."

"Okay. Why?"

"We have to run a pregnancy test."

I feel faint at her words, "A... a pregnancy test?"

"Yes, that's standard in a situation like this. We have to do that as well."

I can't even let my mind go there. Oh God, no. Absolutely not, I can't be.

The nurse smiles at me with sympathy, obviously seeing my distress. "Okay, Olivia, that's everything. I'm going to ask one more time if you have any questions?"

"No. I understand everything that occurred."

"Olivia, what you have been through is very traumatic. There is a counselor on staff with the hospital; I would encourage you to talk to someone. Can I have them come in and speak with you for a bit?"

"No."

She looks at me questioningly, and I see her open her mouth in order to argue with me. Before she can, I tell her, "I will remember that, and call a counselor when and if I'm ready."

"Fair enough." Katie squeezes my shoulder, "you take care. We will get the evidence tested and will let you know when we have some results."

"Results?"

"Yes, of course. The pelvic exam..."

I just stare at her blankly.

"Well they will check for STDs and HIV. We will let you know the results."

I blink away tears. How could that not even have occurred to me? "Yes, yes of course. Thank you."

Katie nods and walks out of my room. I breathe deeply trying to calm my fears and choke on a sob. I force it back when the door to my room opens immediately and Pyper walks in.

"Is it okay if I come in?"

I smile to myself because of course she asks this while she is already standing on the side of my bed. "Of course."

"How are you feeling?"

"I'm doing okay." I wish I could tell her the truth. How I feel ashamed, dirty, destroyed...but I can't. I won't.

"Who was that lady that was just in here? What did they want?"

Shaking my head, I change the subject, "Can you believe these hospital gowns Pyper? What the hell? In all this time they haven't updated them?"

Pyper does exactly what I hope she will – she allows the change of subject but not before she gives me a meaningful look, letting me know she is completely aware of what I'm doing. "What's the problem, Livvie? You don't like your ass hanging out the back end?"

"Ha. Very funny. But just for the record, no I don't."

"You may be able to catch the attention of a hot doctor in that gown. Hmm, come to think of it, maybe I should put one on too."

I laugh and I hope it sounds genuine, "I think you should. I dare you to put one on and walk around the hospital halls with your ass hanging out. Tell me if it works. It can be a test."

"I like this idea. It can be like the movie, *How To Lose A Guy in Ten Days*, but instead, it's how to snag a doctor in – hmm – how many walks down the hallway do you think it would take?"

"For what? How many walks until you get a date with a handsome doctor? Or, how many until you get that sweet ass of yours kicked out of the hospital?"

"Either or," she states matter-of-factly.

I laugh out loud, this time with a lot more feeling. Not only at her response but because at that very moment, she is rummaging through the closet in my room to see if they have any gowns in there.

Before I even think about what I'm saying I blurt, "It feels good to laugh."

Pyper immediately turns towards me and the look on her face is one of sadness, guilt, and anxiety. "Olivia?"

Even with our fun and games I know she needs to get something off her chest. It will kill her inside until I let her. "Tell me."

She walks to my bed and sits. Her mouth opens and she chokes on a sob. She snags some tissues from the side of my bed and I reach my hand over to clasp hers, and wait.

After a few more deep breaths, Pyper says, "I just want to tell you that I'm sorry."

"Sorry for what?"

"I'm so sorry I couldn't keep Deacon out of the house that day. He... he rang the doorbell and avoided the peep hole. I opened the door and he forced his way inside."

"That is not your fault, Pyper."

"Yes it is! Don't you see?! I never should have opened the door if I didn't see who was on the other side."

"That's silly. You had no way of knowing Deacon would possibly be on the other side of the door."

"It's my fault, Olivia! All my fault! If I had never opened the door, this may never have happened."

Tears are chasing one another down Pyper's face and her eyes are so full of remorse and sorrow that my eyes fill just from looking in hers. When she sees this, she bows her head. I brush the hair that is shielding her face and tuck it behind her ear. She looks at me again and I take a good look at my friend. Her eyes are red and swollen. Her nose is shiny, her face is flushed, and I swear she's aged just a little since I've seen her last. She could even use a good hair coloring. Gosh, what a pair we make. It's obvious this has taken a toll on her too, and all I want to do is make her better.

"Pyper, I don't blame you. Not even a little. I would have done the same thing. I understand that you feel bad. If the situation were reversed I would feel the same way, but let's not focus on that, okay? I'm here now. That's all that matters."

"But... are you okay? What did he do to you? I can't even imagine what it must have been like."

I hold back a flinch because I know that would only make her feel worse.

"I can't," I clear my throat and try again, "I am not ready to talk about that yet."

"Well, when you are, I'm here for you. I hope you know that."

"How could I forget?" I attempt a smile.

Pyper smiles enough for both of us, and it is a sight to behold. My friend is beautiful, and her smile makes me finally produce a smile in return. She stands up and opens the closet once again and pulls out a hospital gown, "So, about that dare..."

8

CATCHING UP

Olivia

MY SIDES ACHE from laughter. I feel my eyes widen when Pyper walks into the bathroom to change into a hospital gown. As I am thinking that there is no way that she will really go through with it, she proves me wrong as she walks out of the bathroom fully changed into a gown. As she proudly struts out of my room with her perky ass hanging out, I start laughing so hard, I'm pretty sure my laugh sounds more like wailing because my poor mom comes flying into my room in a panic. "What's going on? Olivia? Are you alright?"

She runs straight past Pyper, not even paying attention initially, until I point to Pyper because I'm too choked up to speak. My mom's head whips around in Pyper's direction, and upon getting a look at her, one eyebrow raises in question. With her face flaming as red as her hair, Pyper does a little twirl for my mom. The look she gives Pyper is hysterical. "I don't even want to know."

Pyper reappears, and with speed that makes me giggle, she goes into the bathroom, apparently to change back into her clothes. My mom looks to me for an explanation, but I just shake my head and shrug my shoulders. Mom comes to the side of my bed, and takes my hand, totally encapsulating it in hers. As she closes both hands around mine, she offers a soft, reassuring smile, overflowing with love and concern – expanding on my response to Pyper's antics. It's then I become aware of her bloodshot eyes, rimmed in dark, nearly black circles, unhidden, despite an attempt to use concealer. She looks so tired and weary, and I know I'm to blame.

"How are you feeling?" She gently inquires while brushing the hair back from my face, her hand lingering at my cheek for a moment before pulling away.

"I'm doing okay. I think the pain meds are helping because I'm not feeling any discomfort."

"Good. What can I do for you? What do you need?"

"All I really want is to go home."

"I know, honey, I'm sure you do. You won't have to be here much longer. They said 48 hours at the most. They don't seem to keep patients long these days."

"Thanks goodness for that, because home is just where I want to be. With Luke. Speaking of Luke," my eyes dart towards the door and back to my mom again, "where is he?"

My mother smiles at my question, "I'm not sure. We went to get coffee, and he was gone when we came back. I'm sure he just went for a breather. He hasn't left your side since we've been here."

I nod at her but I can't help feeling like something is off. It isn't like him to leave and not say a word to anyone about it. But, I'm sure she's right – he probably just needed a break.

Having let go of my hand, I notice my mom is wringing her hands subconsciously and I know she just wants to do something to feel useful, to feel like she's fixing something that we both know is not fixable. "Can you adjust the pillow under my leg, mom? It's a little uncomfortable."

"Sure!" She goes to my other side quickly and starts fluffing and moving the pillow. "Is that better?"

"Yes, thank you. I would love some water, or juice."

"You have some right here," she grabs the cup I already saw from the table next to my bed, and holds the bendy straw to my lips. I'm certainly capable of holding it myself and feel somewhat ridiculous, but I indulge her, and take a sip.

"Better, thank you."

When she turns back to me, I see the sad look in her eyes. I know we need to have this conversation, but I don't want to. She cups the side of my face and I turn my head into her hand just a bit, accepting the comfort and warmth it brings. "You know I'm here for you, right? If you want to talk about what happened, or need a shoulder to cry on," her eyes fill with tears, "or if you just want to rant and rage at the unfairness of it all, just remember I'm here for you. Always."

"I know that mom. Really, I do."

"Olivia, are you... are you okay? I can't imagine what you've been through, and I don't know how to help you."

My eyes fill with tears, "I bet they don't teach this kind of thing in the parenting 101 classes, do they mom?"

She smiles and chuckles just a bit, which was my goal. "No, they certainly don't."

"I'm okay, mom. It will take some time, but I will be better before you know it."

"I know you will. You're my strong girl, you always have been, even when you didn't know it yourself. But honey, you can't do it alone."

I smile at her, "I know. I just can't talk about it right now. I... I've never been so scared mom. I started to lose hope." I choke on a sob. Again. I'm turning into a regular cry baby these days.

My mom just strokes my hair and my face to soothe me and lets me cry, all the while wiping my tears away with a tissue. "It's okay baby, let it out."

Eventually, Pyper joins us and sits close to us, offering silent support. My tears and the emotions held within them, make me tire quickly. I smile gently at my mom, close my eyes, and drift off.

I WAKE UP to the doctor coming in and checking on me. Pyper is sitting next to me reading a fashion magazine. She politely excuses herself.

"How are you feeling, Olivia?"

"Okay right now."

"Good. I see no reason why you can't go home tomorrow or the next day at the latest."

"Oh, that makes me so happy. I just want to go home."

He smiles, "I'm sure you do. I also wanted to let you know that the results came back from your blood tests and exam." My stomach drops. Is that a sympathetic smile I see? Is the news bad? He doesn't leave me long to fear, "The results are all negative. There are no diseases, or other concerns."

"Oh, thank God." I feel like I can breathe a little more now. Like maybe some of the weight that has been on my chest is relieved just a little.

"In these kinds of circumstances the tests get a priority status in the lab. I knew you would want to know the results right away."

"You're right. Thank you so much."

He gives me another smile and this time, I know it's because he's a kind and caring man. "You're very welcome. Now get some more rest. When you get home, lots of rest will be on the agenda there too. You need to let those bones heal, okay?"

"Sounds good."

"Okay then."

The doctor leaves and Pyper quickly walks back in the room. She's looking at me intently like she's expecting me to break down on her watch or something. "Everything okay?"

I smile at her, seeing her visibly relax when I do, "Everything is fine. I get to go home tomorrow or the day after at the latest."

"That's great!"

"I know!" I look around the room even though I already know Luke is still nowhere to be seen. I'm not sure how much time has passed, "What time is it? It feels like I slept the day away."

"You did for the most part, but the doctor said that is normal, your body needs the rest so it can heal."

"Why thank you for the feedback, Dr. Pyper."

"You are most welcome, my smart ass best friend."

"Oh come on, you know you love me."

"Too true." She grins.

"I'm so excited. I want to go home so bad!"

"I know you do! The nurse was in here while you slept and she left you some fancy shmancy crutches." She gestures to the crutches already leaning against the wall in the corner of the room. "She said someone from physical therapy will be here to be sure you know how to use them."

"Yuck. That is not going to be fun." I look at them with a frown. I'm clumsy as hell already, this is not going to be good.

Pyper gives me a wink, "We will make them work! I already have a thought about that." Oh great, that statement could mean so many things.

"Why does that not give me comfort?"

"Oh relax, I promise it won't be painful or anything."

I look around the room again and finally ask the question that's been on my mind since I woke up, "Where is Luke?"

"Why? My company isn't good enough?"

"I'm sorry. I didn't mean it like that."

"I know you didn't, I'm teasing you. I'm not sure where he is. My guess is he is getting some much needed rest. Your parents went back to their hotel to do the same. I bet you he spoke to them."

Hmmmm. I remember that before I fell asleep my mom hadn't spoken to him, but that was hours ago. Is he okay? I push it from my mind, I'm sure I'm being silly. "What are you reading?"

"Oh, just the latest, and greatest in the spa world." She turns her *Spa Me* magazine towards me so I can see what she's reading.

"Must be fascinating."

Suddenly I have a thought hit me out of nowhere and it makes me gasp, "Oh my God!"

Pyper jumps at the sound of my gasp, "What?" I really need to stop doing that to her.

"My blog! Pyper, I haven't blogged in ages. I had articles that were due for magazines that had hired me. Shit! The key to a good blog is consistency. It's going to take me ages to get caught up."

"Olivia, calm down. I blogged for you."

"Um, what?" I really do make an effort to pick my mouth up off the floor.

"Oh, don't look so panicked. It isn't anything special. I can't do what you do, but I posted an announcement online about what happened. We used it, in part, as a way to have people help us find you. Your readers are wide spread so we posted your picture on the blog, and tried to use it as a tool. I would post updates as to the progress, so your readers know what's been going on."

"Wow," I stare at her stunned.

"There was nothing we wouldn't do or try, in order to find you."

I nod my head, and look away, "Well it seems to me there is only one thing to do then."

Pyper's brows scrunch, "What's that?

"I need a paper and pen. We need to start making a list of potential blog posts. I'm not letting a stupid cast get in my way. I've got to get back on the ball! Who knows what trends have already come and gone in four weeks' time!"

Pyper snorts at that comment, but then she gives me a serious look, "Olivia, I'm not sure that's such a good idea. You need to rest, get your strength-"

"You're wrong."

Pyper stops mid-sentence and stares at me. "Getting back to normal, as much as possible is exactly what I need," I insist.

Staring at me for another moment, like she'd like to object more, she sighs and gives me a slight nod. "I have a pad of paper and pen in my purse," she says as she starts rummaging around in her ginormous designer bag. "A-ha!" She holds it up like a trophy and hands them to me.

"Thanks!" Holding them is a little awkward with my cast, but I will get used to it. "Okay, help me make a list!"

By the time we are done, I'm thrilled with my blog topic ideas. Everything from the new fall makeup colors to the gorgeous lace trend in clothing. We even have articles about what to do to help keep your body in shape, since technically that's related to beauty too.

I catch Pyper yawning out of the corner of my eye. She's trying to make herself all comfortable on a couch pull out, and I know that's not going to work. "Hey, why don't you go to your hotel? I'm sure you're just as exhausted as everyone else. You need to get some rest."

"No, I'm not leaving you alone. I'll be fine right here."

I have to admit the thought of being alone terrifies me right now. Part of me wouldn't mind her leaving because when Luke comes back, we can have some one-on-one time. But, while I mean what I say, about Pyper getting rest, I don't want her to go either.

"Are you sure?" I ask quietly, unsure about my wish for her to stay too.

She looks me straight in the eyes, and I can see the sincerity in them, "I don't want to be anywhere else."

"Thank you."

"You're welcome. Besides, I've missed my roommate."

I smile, "Me too."

I use my good arm to place the notepad and pen on the table next to me, and then pull the blanket up to my shoulder. I know I just woke up not long ago, but I'm tired again. My mind once again wanders to Luke, and how it has been hours since I've seen him. I wish I could tell him good night and give him a kiss and hug. I don't want to be clingy girlfriend, but I missed him so much. I thought I would never see him again, and all I want to do is hold him close and never let him go. I also can't help but feel a little angry – where is he?

"What's wrong?" Pyper interrupts my thoughts with her question. I look at her and I realize she was watching my emotions play out over my face while I was thinking of Luke.

"Honestly, I'm feeling a little hurt that Luke isn't here. I mean, I wasn't sure I would ever see him again. I wasn't sure if I would see any of you again," I involuntarily shudder at the thought, "I just want to be close to you all right now, I guess. I'm trying not to be selfish, but it's really hard."

Pyper sighs and looks away. The problem with that is I know her as well as she knows me, "What is it? Why do I get the feeling you aren't telling me something?"

"Because I'm not, but I'm not sure that I'm the one that should tell you."

"Okay, well now you have to tell me. You can't say that much and then just stop."

"Olivia, Luke should be the one to tell you."

"Pyper, you're scaring me."

"I'm sorry, I'm not trying to," Pyper sighs. "Okay, I will tell you because he wouldn't want you to worry, but while you were... gone... Luke's mom took a turn for the worse."

"Her cancer? Is she okay?"

"No, she's not okay."

"Is she in the hospital? Is that why he's not here? Oh no! He should go be with – "

"Olivia, Luke's mother died. Her funeral was the same day we found out you were here in the hospital."

"Oh my God." I cover my mouth with my hands and tears build in my eyes and then fall down my cheeks. My heart feels like it drops into my stomach and I feel like I'm going to be sick. I can't imagine what Luke must be feeling. "Oh my God," I repeat.

Pyper comes and sits beside me, and hands me a tissue. "I just think Luke has a lot on his plate right now. The loss of his mom, his grieving father, your return, his anger towards Deacon...my guess is, he passed out for a bit. The emotions and stress of the last couple days probably took him over. He'll be back. I just wanted you to know what's going on, so you understand he's dealing with a lot."

"I'm so glad that you told me," I take Pyper's hand and squeeze it. "He should be with his dad. He shouldn't be worrying about me."

"Olivia, don't be ridiculous. There is no place he would rather be. When we got the call about you, there was zero hesitation, except to tell his father what was happening. Even his father understood and pushed him out the door. Choosing you wasn't even a question."

I shake my head, trying to wrap my mind around it, "I just can't believe she passed away that fast."

"Well, once she found out that it had spread everywhere, she decided to stop the chemotherapy treatments. It took her very quickly after that."

I wipe the tears off my cheeks as I think about the man I love, and how far we've come. I can't imagine what it had to feel like for him to be faced with a decision like that. Having to choose to stay at your own mother's funeral, or to come be with the woman you love who had been kidnapped. As soon as I'm able, I want to visit his mother's grave and leave her flowers. I know it would mean a lot to Luke too. I can't imagine what he's been through these past weeks. Watching his mother begin a journey he knew he wouldn't be able to follow, all the while waiting to find out if he and I would get to continue ours.

Like a balloon, my heart swells with love in my chest. I didn't think it was possible to love him even more.

9

NOTHING I CAN'T FIX

Luke

WHEN I PULLED out of the hospital, I drove with no destination in mind with the question "*were you abused*" playing over and over in my mind like some sick joke. It was like I thought I could outrun the fears and problems that were chasing me, nipping at my heels, begging me to confront them. They were telling me there was no way in hell I could take the easy way out and simply run from them.

Eventually, I stopped and pulled over to the side of the road, and just sat there. My eyes tried to focus on the miles of pavement before me, but all I could see was Olivia's face staring back at me. I saw the eyes I love, and that mouth of hers that curves up at the corners when she's amused or being sassy. That sexy pout of hers that just begs to be kissed. I saw her body. Curves that I haven't spent nearly enough time rediscovering, and kissing every inch of. I saw her cute nose that wrinkles when she is thinking hard about something. I saw her heart – a heart that I hold inside my own. A heart that didn't ask to be hurt and abused and God knows what else that monster did to her. I love her, and I'm a lucky bastard to have her love in return. My love for her is unconditional. I'm certainly not going to let some asshole ruin what we have. I'm not going to let my stupid insecurities ruin it either.

Sitting on the side of that road, I picked up the phone and called my dad. In no uncertain terms he told me to turn my ass around. He told me the life before us was going to be a bumpy one, but that just means we are no better than anyone else. Love isn't supposed to always be super easy – if it were, how would we grow to truly appreciate its beauty? How would we know how rare and special a love like we have is if we didn't have the tough times to make us appreciate it? He promised we would talk more when I returned to town; and I look forward to it. He always knows the right thing to say.

The truth is, I'm just scared. I'm scared of losing her at the end of all of this chaos. I can't go through that again. I would not be functional when it was all said and done. No way in hell. Her kidnapping proved that much. I mean, damn, what was I expecting to have happened when that fucker took her? I certainly didn't think he was feeding her chocolate in bed and discussing feelings and the weather. I knew he would hurt her. I felt it, like an ache in my bones. I just hoped and prayed that maybe he still had some semblance of a soul and conscience.

I decided right then and there that I am going to fix this. I will get Olivia to talk to me about what happened, and we will deal with it, whatever that takes. I wish like hell that this didn't happen and I will blame myself for an eternity for not being there, but I can't change it. I can wish it away all I want, but it's not going to work.

By the time I was ready to confront reality, it was too late at night to go back to the hospital, and try to explain where I'd been. I knew Pyper or her parents were with her, so the best thing for me was to turn in and get some rest. It's been a very stressful few days.

Now, with a new day before me, thinking back through the last couple nights, I feel a little like a pansy. I acted like a douche and now, I can't wait to get my ass back to the hospital to see my girl.

I throw my clothes on, and before I know it, I'm back at the hospital, walking through the halls once again on my way to Olivia's room. When I get there, I disturb a sleeping Pyper. As soon as she wakes and sees my face, she gives me a small frown and mouths, "Where have you been?"

I whisper, "Later."

She nods, stretches and walks out of the room with a whispered, "Be back later."

I turn towards Olivia's bed and looking at her makes my hands twitch in automatic reaction to the sight of her. I can never keep my hands to myself when it comes to her. Watching her sleep, her face so peaceful, I can't help but brush my thumb across the lips that give me such a thrill with each kiss. She can take me from zero to ready for her in a matter of seconds with those beauties. Unexpectedly, she awakens to my touch with a start.

"Luke?"

I don't use my lips for words. Instead, I place them gently on her forehead. Her head pushes against gently into my lips, as if seeking comfort, and I begin to trail kisses down her nose, then to her cheeks. I even kiss her closed eyelids before placing my lips on hers. I hold her face in my hands and stroke my thumbs over her cheeks, trying to put everything I'm feeling into the simple act of touching her. I don't want to scare her or make her uncomfortable. Maybe she's not ready for contact like this, given what's happened to her, so I start to pull away until her mouth opens under mine, and I realize her small hands are gripping the front of my shirt, pulling me closer to her.

The small noise she makes in the back of her throat is almost my undoing. I explore her mouth with my tongue and can't help but tangle my fingers in her hair. My belly is on fire, and I start to feel some movement below my belt. Before things can get out of control, I pull away from her with a smile on my face, and touch my forehead to hers.

"Hi, angel," she smiles at me, and I feel a heavy feeling in my chest, like my heart just split wide open at the sight. I will never tire of seeing that smile. "How are you feeling?"

"Amazing, now that you're here."

I chuckle because I feel the same way. I missed her. I still can't stop touching her. I may have pulled my lips from hers, but other than that, I can't bring myself to break the connection.

"Where have you been? I mean, not that I'm trying to be an overbearing, nagging, controlling girlfriend or anything. I just... was worried... and I missed you," she says almost shyly.

"I'm sorry, love, I just needed to get out of here for a little while. I got some rest, did some thinking, and now I'm back. I'm really sorry I worried you. I hope you aren't too pissed at me." I give her the smirk I know she loves, hoping to charm her a bit. Shameful, I know, but I can't resist. I know I should feel bad for not telling her the whole truth, but I don't. I figure I deserve to give myself a damn break. Besides, the space and rest was much needed. She just doesn't need to know about my freak out. I had feelings to work through, and I did.

"I understand. I mean, of course you needed rest and a break. I'm sorry; I didn't mean to suggest you need to be here every minute."

"You didn't and besides, there is no place I would rather be. How are your arm and leg feeling?"

"I'm fine. In fact, I'm supposed to be released today, just with some extra equipment." She points to the crutches in the corner of the room.

"Mmmm... that's going to be hot."

She laughs, the sound once again making me feel light and happy, which makes me smile too. "You're crazy. Me hobbling around on crutches will be hot? I don't think so. I'm going to look like a baby giraffe trying to get her balance, or something."

"A baby giraffe?"

"Yep," she says popping the p. It makes me chuckle.

"Oh angel, you could never be anything but hot." I wiggle my eyebrows at her making her laugh. But then, her laugh cuts off.

"Luke?"

"Hmm?" Maybe this is it. Maybe she's going to tell me what happened. I try to smooth my features to hide my anxiety, and hope the only look on my face is open and curious. I notice her hesitation, and squeeze her hand, and give her what I hope is an encouraging smile.

"Last night, Pyper told me about your mom."

Her words rip through me, making my chest feel tight and leaving me breathless. That is not what I expected her to say. "She shouldn't have told you about that." I run a hand through my hair in frustration.

"Yes, she should have! I'm so sorry, Luke. I can't even imagine what you're feeling; what you're going through. You should be with your dad, not having to worry about m– "

"Stop right there, Livvie. I will be honest. It has been really tough. Not only have I spent these last few weeks frozen in fear, worried about you, but I also watched my mom disappear before my eyes. I won't mince words and pretend it hasn't been hell. But, first of all, Pyper shouldn't have told you, because you are dealing with enough. Second, I know you. You are going to feel guilty because you think I should be somewhere other than here, and I am telling you right now, don't even go there. When I got the call..."

83

I take a second and look directly into her eyes, and for a moment, I lower the façade and let her see the pain in mine. She squeezes my hand, and I struggle to give her a small smile, and continue after clearing my throat. "When I got the call, it wasn't even a question as to where I needed to be. Not only does my dad understand, but I know she understood too. She spent the last moments of her time with me telling me not to give up hope. She refused to let me think otherwise. Livvie, she knew how much I love you, and she knew I would have done anything to get you back. Leaving that day, wasn't even a choice, it was a need - plain and simple."

"But still, what timing..."

"I wouldn't have it any other way. I like to think that my mom had a hand in the timing. Her way of making up for her hand in our past."

"That is a nice thought."

"Yes it is. Now, any idea when I can bust you out of this joint?" I squeeze her hand reassuringly.

"I think my discharge papers are supposed to come any time."

"Great. Have you talked to your parents? What are their plans? Are they going to stay with you for a while?"

"They want to. My mom offered to come to the condo and stay with me for a few weeks if I want her to. I think she was really hoping I would take her up on it, but I didn't. I told her what I really need is to get my life back to normal. As much as possible, anyway. I love them for being here, and I understand her need to want to stay with me, but it just isn't necessary. So, I encouraged them to head home after I get back to Chicago. She made me promise that I let her know immediately if I change my mind and need them."

"I will talk to them too and reassure them that I will be helping take care of you until you are back on your feet. Quite honestly, until that asshole is found, I don't intend on letting you out of my sight very often."

"Luke, you have a business to run, you can't be with me every second."

I raise my eyebrows at her in challenge, "Watch me."

"Luke-"

"Olivia," I fire back at her, "Look, I get what you are trying to do, and if you're trying to tell me that you don't want me there, then say it. Otherwise, I need you to understand that right now, and likely for the foreseeable future, letting you out of my sight is not going to be easy for me."

"Well, if you insist..." I'm pretty sure that is a mischievous grin I see on that mouth of hers.

"I do."

"Well, okay then. Please, just promise me that if something comes up – something at the club, or with your dad - you won't put your life on hold for me."

"Angel, you are my life." I enunciate each word, wanting to make it clear. Doesn't she get that? If not, I'm going to make it my mission that she does.

Her eyes fill with tears and she whispers, "And you're mine."

I can't help it. I kiss her again. I hold her head in my hand and run my tongue along the seam of her lips, silently asking for entry. When she gives it to me, it doesn't take long for things to heat up between us – our kiss is raw; demanding. She's once again pulling at my shirt and my body is more on the bed than off of it at this point. I pull away again and place my forehead against hers. Our breathing is fast, and I close my eyes to gain control of my hormones.

"Luke, I have a favor to ask you..."

"Anything," my voice sounds raspy with longing and need.

"It isn't going to be easy, but do you think you can help me wash my hair and my body? I just really want to feel...well, clean. Other than Pyper helping me brush my teeth and my hair, I haven't had a chance to truly freshen up and I think I would feel so much better if I could. I mean, taking that tumble and getting banged up, and then lying here in this bed..."

Oh god, my body is an evil bastard because I'll be damned if just the thought of her naked doesn't do things to me. I swear my cock just twitched, and my breathing that was getting under control, has picked up once again. Somehow, I manage to choke out an "Of course," but I have no idea how I am going to make it through this. It is going to be pure torture.

She eases the covers off the top of her and I very gently help ease her off the bed, being very careful not to bump anything. Her body looks so fragile and small. I feel like one wrong move, and I'll break her. When she stands, she sways on her feet. "Screw that." I sweep her up into my arms.

"Luke! I could have made it on crutches, I need to get used to them anyway."

"I know you could have, but maybe I wanted the chance to hold you in my arms." I give her my best mischievous smile and walk us into the bathroom.

"Thank you for doing this," she whispers.

"Don't thank me. I want to take care of you. I'm going to set you on the toilet while I get the water warm, okay?"

"Okay."

The bathroom contains a large stand up shower. I pull the curtain back and see a bench, which will be helpful, since she can barely stand on her own. Fortunately, the shower is also big enough for five people. I twist the faucet on so the water can start warming up.

"Can you grab those bags and rubber bands off the sink? We have to wrap my cast in them because I can't get it wet."

"Oh sure."

I walk over and grab the bags and a towel while I'm at it. When I turn back towards her, I stop dead in my tracks and stare. She's pulled the gown off her body and she's naked. Usually the sight of her glorious body always takes my breath away, but this time, when I can't breathe, and try not to gasp - it's for an entirely different reason. She's covered in more bruises and scratches than I can count – and they are located everywhere - from head to toe.

10.

KISSING THE PAIN AWAY

Olivia

*L*UKE'S GASP MAKES me look up into his face. His gaze is roaming over my body from head to toe and I feel my skin turn red in embarrassment. A flush starts at my face and runs down my chest. I know I'm a horrid sight. The fall wasn't kind to my body, and the bushes that broke my fall scratched or cut my body everywhere. I'm covered in scratches, bruises and there are quite a few bandages as well. Some of the bruises have started to heal, so my body is a plethora of colors from black, blue, and yellow. Aside from the hurts that mar my body, I'm sitting here in nothing but skin; I'm completely exposed. Not only physically, but emotionally. All of me laid bare for him to see.

I feel tainted on the inside. No matter how much I tell myself that this isn't my fault and that feeling this way only gives Deacon power, I can't brush the thoughts from my mind as easily as I'd like. Can he tell that Deacon touched me? Does he know that I'm sure I was taken advantage of in my drug-induced state? Do I look different to him? Used somehow?

His eyes meet mine and I give him a timid smile, but I don't move. I'm terrified of his gaze. I'm afraid of what I'm unknowingly revealing to him. I feel cold heat in my chest and it bursts from me like a water balloon and runs down to my belly, covering me in fear. What if he doesn't want me anymore? I couldn't bear it. I hate that I need his help with bathing and letting him see me in this vulnerable position, but I trust him more than anyone. Before I can even second guess seeking his help, he pulls me up and presses my naked body against his fully clothed one. He holds me close, kisses the top of my head over and over while swaying us back and forth. Right then I realize he's blaming himself for every single mark on my body, as if he's personally responsible.

I grasp handfuls of his shirt at his back, reveling in the comfort he's offering. My arm hurts a little where my stitches are located, but his embrace and the soothing support it offers my spirit and mind, makes it not only manageable, but nearly imperceptible. I nuzzle my face into his chest and squeeze him to me. His scent – a combination of coffee, mint and a brisk, fall morning - make me feel whole. For a few moments, while swaying back and forth, I take deep gulps, letting the essence of him fill my soul. It nurtures me in so many ways. Eventually, I pull back and look him in the eyes. I want him to see their sincerity and pleading for agreement, when he takes in my words, "I'm fine. None of this is your fault."

"I should have been there," he whispers so softly, as if we are in a room full of people and he doesn't want to be overheard.

"No, you shouldn't have. Being in a relationship doesn't mean we stop living our lives. You have responsibilities, and so do I. You did nothing wrong, Luke. Nothing. It was just a day...up until then...a day like many others, and hopefully many more to come. Listen, if we are going to move on from this, you must stop blaming yourself."

He doesn't argue with me, but I know he doesn't agree. I feel his arms tighten around me a little more, and suddenly I feel a shift in my awareness. Out of nowhere, I'm extremely aware of how erotic it feels to be naked against him, even though he is fully dressed. Each breath he takes presses his chest against my breasts; the sway of our bodies creating a sweet friction. His tendency to shift his weight and leverage his one leg slightly between mine in a gesture of offering me increased support and steadiness, awakens me. A feeling I haven't felt for weeks runs through me like a waterfall, and pools in my lower belly. I want him to help take the memories of Deacon away. My hands start moving like they have a mind of their own, and start running over his chest, feeling the hard muscles underneath his soft shirt. I lift my head and look at Luke's lips. They are full and inviting, and I don't think twice before I move my mouth towards his. I gently take his lower lip between both of my own and nibble.

A soft groan of contentment comes out of Luke's mouth, and now I couldn't stop myself, even if I tried. His encouragement prompts me to capture his mouth with my own. I take control of our kiss by wrapping my arms around his neck, running my fingers from one hand up the back of his head, gripping his head with my good hand, and pressing him closer to me. I let my tongue and lips speak for me in their actions--not words--making sure he knows exactly what I'm thinking. I pour my love and need through each movement, and when he groans again, I capture it against my mouth.

He pulls away from me breathless, and his eyes are overflowing with lust and longing, no doubt mirroring mine. "Let's get you in the shower." His voice is raspy and sounds sexy. It makes me feel complete feminine satisfaction knowing that I affected him that way.

Right now, the last thing I want to do is get in the shower, but my need to feel like me again, and to wipe the last traces of Deacon off of me is overwhelming. As much as I want and need to go further with Luke, I feel tainted; contaminated, impure. Before we can go any further, I need to be unsullied, unblemished. Clean. Will it ever be possible?

I immediately push that thought from my mind and instead watch him place the shower chair under the water. Once he has it secure, he turns back around and starts securing the plastic bags and rubber bands over my cast.

"We should probably put one over my stitches too. I know the bandage is there, but they said not to get them wet for a couple days."

"Good idea."

He puts a bag around the bandage on my arm and then helps me get under the water and settled onto the chair.

I let out a sigh. The warm water is soothing and comforting and feels amazing on my skin, and I feel like it's already washing the last few weeks away. It's healing some part of me with each drop. I close my eyes and enjoy the feeling of warmth that runs over me in continuous waves. I open my eyes to see Luke rolling his sleeves up. When they are above his elbows, he grabs the soap, lathering it up between his hands. As I realize his intentions, my eyes meet his and I smile, encouraging his thoughts. I love that he wants to take care of me, and the truth is I need it too – on more than one level.

Reaching in to trail his hands over my shoulders requires a longer stretch anticipated and I notice that his sleeve and shift begin to get wet. He mumbles, "Forget this," and before I can blink, he's unbuttoning his shirt. "I'm coming in with you, it will make this easier."

My mouth instantly waters and I almost laugh at the feeling. With all the seriousness I can muster, I manage to say, "Yes, that's a good idea. I don't want you to get soaked or for your clothes to be ruined."

I watch him like a starved animal. I swear it's like everything starts moving in slow motion. I see the buttons of his shirt come apart one by one, each accomplishment revealing his flesh, inch by stunning inch. I want to touch and taste him. Feel him beneath my fingers; watch his muscles move. He's barely undressed and already I feel warmth between my legs. When he starts to unzip his pants, my mouth goes dry. I feel like I'm ready to combust, and he's completely oblivious to the effect he's having on me.

I continue to observe with unashamed fascination as he slides his jeans and boxers down his legs, at the same time toeing off his shoes, and lastly lifts his legs one by one to remove his socks. When he's standing before me, I practically dissect him. Beginning at the tips of his toes, my eyes move to his muscled calves and thighs, and stop at the juncture of his thighs. My own body aches in response at the sight of his. I miss him with a physical desperation that shows itself in the tightening of my stomach, the hardening and pronouncement of my nipples, and the quickening of my breath.

I advance my gaze to his hard abs, chiseled chest, strong neck, full lips, and then meet his glorious blue eyes. He's looking right at me and I feel not the slightest hint of embarrassment that he was standing there, silently encouraging my exploration. I wonder when he perceived that task turned to pleasure, and oblivion became interest and desire. Hopefully, the water helped mask any drool that may have escaped my mouth. His eyes reveal longing and lust - the curve of his lips show amusement. I clear my throat and tip my head back in the water, trying to distract myself.

I swear I hear a chuckle, prompting me to open my eyes, and when I do, I'm startled to see him right in front of me. Since I'm sitting and he's standing, it makes for a rather interesting display.

I smile and look up at him, his grin is ear-to-ear and I laugh. "You know exactly what you're doing, don't you?"

"Maybe."

I shake my head and quit talking when his soap covered hands once again start running over my collar bone, shoulders and down my arms, carefully avoiding the wrapped part of my arm. "Raise your arms over your head." I do, and he even gets my armpits with the soap. As his hands go over my chest and stomach, he bends closer and lower, paying special attention to every mark and bruise. My breath catches when his activity abruptly ceases and he lowers himself to his knees. He is no longer looking at me, but appears to be analyzing my body with glassy, glazed over eyes. I start to reach out to touch his face in comfort, but freeze as he leans toward me and places his lips against my skin, gently kissing the worst bruise on my good arm. He leaves his lips there a moment and then I see his eyes move to the next mark and he kisses that too. He takes his time, lovingly touching and kissing every spot. It doesn't matter how small it is, he gives it attention. He even kisses the scratches on my knees and the few bruises and scrapes on my legs.

When a tear falls down his cheek, silent tears of my own immediately match his. He looks up at me when a sob catches in my throat that I can't disguise. If I wasn't already sitting, I would fall over at the look in his eyes. Outrage. Sadness. Desperation. Guilt. Compassion. Love. He cups the side of my face, brushes his fingers over my cheek, and then kisses my tears away too. "I love you, Livvie."

I take his head and cradle it to my chest. I run my fingers through his hair and let my tears continue to fall. "I love you too," I whisper.

"I didn't mean to make you sad."

"You didn't. You make me feel loved."

He gives me a soft smile and then it changes to a smirk as he grabs the soap again. His hands run over and under my breasts, holding them in his hands for a moment, making my breath catch. I know he's trying to change the heaviness in the air around us. The bastard even brushes his thumbs over my nipples and chuckles when they pucker immediately in response. I indulge his efforts.

"You're an ass."

"Hush."

He continues the cleansing of my body, over my hips, down my legs, even washing between my toes. He moves behind me to get my back, and then wraps his arm across my chest, "Hold on to my arm angel." His hand tucks under one of my arms and he pulls me up a little bit and I brace my weight against his arm. It's a good thing too because when his other arm touches the area between my legs I almost fall right then and there. "I'm just being thorough. We want to make sure we get everywhere."

All I can manage is an "Mmm hmm." It isn't only his hand between my legs, it's also the feel of his hardness pressed against my ass. I can feel that this is affecting his body as much as it is mine, making my need for him triple. My breathing starts getting crazy, but once again, my thoughts are stopped in their tracks when he sits me back down. I barely resist a groan in protest.

"I'm going to wash your hair for you."

"You don't have to do that, I can do that much."

"I know you can, I want to."

"Okay, then."

His hands in my hair stop all protests. I don't know what it is about someone else massaging and touching my scalp that feels so amazing, but it does. I practically whimper, "Okay, I'm pretty sure I would be fine with you doing this every day."

Luke chuckles, "Oh yeah? So, you don't want to do it yourself anymore?"

"Nope. No idea what I was thinking. I'm pretty sure we are going to need to take all future showers together for this very reason."

"Mmm, I can get on board with that."

I sigh, happy in the feeling of contentment that washes over me. Luke's mere presence makes me feel safe and secure, but this type of spoiling and generosity engages a keen sense of protection and love. I have so much to work through physically and emotionally, but Luke has no idea how much he's helping. He's the perfect medicine for my mental and physical wounds.

When he finishes, he shuts off the water and reaches for a towel. He removes the plastic coverings he placed over my arm and leg as he dries me off, then dries himself. He tosses the towel over his shoulder, reaches down, and picks me up, holding me close to his body, taking care to avoid contact with the worst of my wounds and bruises. I capture his lips again in another kiss.

I want more. I know he was going to be distant, not wanting to start anything that he doesn't think I want to finish, but he couldn't be more wrong. I want to be with him. I need to feel him against me and know that he is with me in mind and body.

I increase the pressure of my kiss. He swiftly moves across the bathroom floor and sets me down gently on my hospital bed and before he can choose his next move, I caress his face and make my intentions clear by pulling him closer to my body. He comes willingly and I press my breasts into his solid chest. The contact makes me gasp into his mouth. Luke keeps things gentle initially by holding my face still in his hands, like I'm a breakable china doll. But I'm not. I don't want him to treat me like something that's been broken. I don't want to be treated differently, not by him.

I pull my mouth from his, look into his eyes, "Luke. I want you." I want him to help make the memories go away; to cover the pain and fear with love and passion.

He stares into my eyes for a moment and I can see the internal battle going on inside of him, "I don't know, angel. Your leg and your arm – I don't want to hurt you."

"Please, Luke. I need you right now. I don't want you to treat me differently. I know that he... please," I whisper. I swallow and let him see the pain and uncertainty in my eyes, "Don't you... don't you still want me?"

"Oh angel, I couldn't want anything more. It's not even a question of that."

"Prove it. Please. I need you to show me."

He looks at me again for another beat and then, in a flash, his lips are once again on mine. His tongue is begging for entry and I immediately give it to him. I relish the taste of his mouth, his lips, and the heat they create in my belly and between my legs. Just his kiss makes me feel like I'm on fire."

Tearing my mouth from his, I take his hand and place it on my breast, "Touch me."

He wastes no time answering my request by kneading one breast in his palm while he trails kisses down my neck, across my collar bone, then down to one breast. Taking my nipple into his mouth, he teases it into a hard point and releases it with a loud pop. Then he moves across to the next breast, giving it the same attention. I can't help the moan that escapes my throat. All I want is him, all I feel is him. He's removing the memory of the touches and fear from another on me, and all I see is Luke.

"Now, Luke. I need you now."

Luke groans, and positions me like the weight and awkwardness of my cast are nothing, placing his mouth at my neck and bites down gently while he slowly eases into me at the same time.

"You feel so good, Livvie. So wet, so tight. You were made for me."

"Yes, you. Always you, Luke. Only you," I pant in response.

He slowly starts moving in and out and I have an ache deep in my belly that is begging me to meet its demands. I want more. Luke moves his hand between our bodies and starts rubbing the part of me that is aching to be touched.

"Oh god, yes. That feels so good, don't stop. Don't stop."

That ache moves through my body like a song reaching crescendo and before I know it, I'm falling off the edge and losing sense of everything, other than riding out my body's screaming demand. I never want this to end. My release wracks my whole body, and makes tears instantly come to my eyes and fall down my cheeks. I feel amazing, but want to cry at the same time, so many feelings are inside of my body and heart that I can't even make sense of.

Luke is unaware of my tears, with his head buried in my neck, and is moving faster now. I tighten my good leg around his hip as tight as I can encouraging his pace, wanting him harder, wanting him faster, wanting him to show me with every pound how much he wants me. Needs me.

He cries out with his release, the sound muffled by my neck, and we stay with our bodies pressed together, trying to catch our breath without moving. I want to stay like this. Safe, loved, secure in his arms. There's no danger here; no fear.

"You okay, angel?"

I smile, "I'm perfect."

Luke chuckles, the sound making my heart skip a beat. He eases out of me, helps me recline in the bed, removes the towel that somehow has remained in place, and helps me tidy up. His touch is gentle, his eyes full of love, and I want so much to return his smile and pretend that all is right in the world. But I can't, because deep inside of me, scratching at my throat and pushing behind my eyes, is the need to scream and cry.

11.

TRYING TO CONTAIN A VOLCANO

Olivia

I'M PROPPED UP in bed with a fluffy pillow elevating my leg. My Kindle is on my lap, a drink sitting within easy access on an adjacent table, and the remote control snuggled next to me in case I get a yearning to watch TV or listen to my favorite music. Luke has been waiting on my every need, ensuring that I have anything and everything I could possibly want or need. I'm snuggled and wrapped like a cocooned butterfly, all nice and warm in my comforter and I'm finally wearing a pair of my favorite pajamas. They are kitschy pink and patterned all over with shoes, purses and lipsticks. It's a nice change from that stupid, ugly hospital gown.

Speaking of which, I have an idea about those. I look at my laptop and read through my post again about the evilness of hospital gowns. I seriously think I should start a petition about the need for new hospital attire designed with a trendy look. I mean come on, yes people may be sickly, but it's not as though they don't know what they have on and a stylish gown might go a long way towards making them feel better. Add that to the fact that no item of clothing - well, perhaps except those drop seat pajamas for children - should ever be designed that allows ones ass to hang out. I definitely think I'm onto something.

It's nice to feel content for the first time in days. At first, it was tough walking back into the condo. As soon as we came through the door, my mind flashed back to the terrifying moment I realized Pyper was tied up on the couch. I saw Deacon standing in the living room with a gun again and I couldn't move past the doorway. Fear made me completely immobile. It wasn't until I felt Luke's reassuring hand on my back that the visions faded and my pulse started to return to normal.

Pyper and Luke are nervous. It's written all over their faces. And they pace a lot and keep fidgeting and asking over and over again if I needed anything and if I'm okay. Sometimes I feel like they are waiting for me to either break down or lose my mind or stab someone or worse... stab my favorite dress or handbag to pieces. I finally made my way to the bedroom to get away from their weighted stares.

I'm dealing with it. One minute at a time. I figure eventually I'll work myself up to one day at a time, but I'm not there yet. My mind doesn't allow me peace for long. Just as I begin to engross myself into some activity, a memory from my time with Deacon assaults me. I keep hoping if I just keep pushing them back into the box in the back of my mind, eventually they'll just quit trying to take over. I simply want to forget.

Luke rarely leaves my side, not that I mind, but he has a life and job he needs to get back to. He can't put his whole life on hold for me - nor should he. It isn't realistic. Or normal. And I need normal. The problem is I'm not sure that he understands how much I need that. Crave it. But, he shuts down any conversation I venture to have with him about it, saying that none of that matters more than I do. And this is his new normal – at least for now. I'm going to have to make him understand and I'm dreading that conversation.

I love Luke with every part of me, but I find myself getting frustrated, aggravated with him easily. Why doesn't he understand that I just need things to be the way they were before? Why do I have to spell it out for him? I have so much anger inside of me. Fortunately, I keep catching myself before I blow. Rationally, I know Luke isn't the source of my anger, he's just an easy target. And that's not fair to him. So I keep it inside.

Interrupting my thoughts is the very man at the center of them, "Wow, just when I think I know everything there is to know about you, I'm reminded that I still have some things to learn?"

I absently look at him as he walks out of the bathroom, "Huh?"

He nods towards the TV, "What are you watching?"

I glance at the TV and quickly do a double take when it dawns on me what he means. The screen shows a glassy, wide-eyed deer lying on the ground, tongue protruding from its mouth, bleeding, obviously having just been shot by a hunter. It's awful. "OH MY GOD, what AM I watching?"

Luke laughs, "Have you decided to take up hunting? If so, we can go get some gear and start planning a hunting expedition. I mean, it isn't what I would expect from you, but I bet you'd look hot holding a rifle. Oh!" He stops and places a finger on his chin.

"What?"

He stares off for a minute and then looks at me at last, "Oh nothing, I was just imagining how hot you'd look holding a shotgun, wearing nothing but stilettos."

"Ha. Very funny," I tell him as he comes back to bed, making himself comfortable next to me. "I was flipping channels and then got distracted."

"Distracted by what?"

"Oh nothing in particular, just thinking."

His brow furrows and he looks away from the gruesome sight that's still on the television and into my eyes, "Anything you want to talk about?"

"No. It wasn't anything important. Just thinking about how I'm happy to be home."

His face registers disappointment so fast, I'm almost sure I imagined it. He grabs the remote and starts flipping the channels, not commenting on my statement.

Turning back to my computer screen, I put the finishing touches on my blog post. I even included pictures of the horrible hospital gowns and made a list of suggested solutions. I bet I could even find gifs from movies where the old guy walks down the hospital hall with his low-hanging ass exposed, just for effect. My post includes ideas like how the gowns should be a nice light weight cotton, or silk. And perhaps cut a bit more shapely and offered in a selection of short, three quarter or long sleeves – or perhaps dolman sleeves to cover up equipment lines and such. Female gowns should have cute patterns like roses or sunflowers, with calming colored backgrounds. For men, an attractive flannel, or just a plain color, like tan, sand, or a nice green might be appropriate. Anything other than little blue dots. And perhaps matching short jackets or robes with non-skid socks.

"Livvie?"

I look up at Luke, and while I know he said my name in some imploring way, he isn't looking at me. His attention is still focused on the TV. "Yeah?"

"Do you... do you want to talk about what happened? "

I grab my glass of water off the table and take a sip, as my mouth suddenly feels dry. "Talk about what?"

His eyes meet mine for a beat, and then he looks away. "About what happened when you were with Deacon. The doctor, well he said it would be good for you to talk about it."

"No offense, Luke, but how could a medical doctor know anything other than the condition of my bones? I'm fine. Really. I don't have anything to talk about."

"Livvie, how can you not? You were held against your will for four weeks. God only knows-" he stops for a moment, runs his hand through his hair, "I want to be here for you."

"The best thing for me is to get my life back. I want things to go back to normal. I want to get back to blogging, writing, and enjoying life again."

"But..."

I snap, "NO LUKE. NO! I refuse to let that man take away any more time from my life. Can't you get that? I will not allow him to take away what makes me happy, and talk about what he..." my eyes fill with tears and I look away from him. I take deep breaths, trying to slow my heart that's suddenly racing in my chest.

Luke puts the remote down and scoots his body closer to me so he can hold me, but I don't want that. I don't want comfort; I don't want to be held. I don't want to be treated like a sick child. I'm not fucking broken. I'm not. And I don't want to be treated like I am.

As soon as Luke's arm wraps around my waist, I push my computer off my lap, and as quickly as I can, I swing my legs over to the side of the bed. "Babe, what do you need? I can help you."

"I'm just going to go to the bathroom. I can manage." I just need a few moments to myself. Time to calm down before I let my anger boil over and explode. And say something I will likely regret. Must keep control.

I grab my crutches that are leaning against the wall and put them in place. They are stiff and hard and not at all comfortable. I know they said not to put all my weight on my armpits, but I think the guy who wrote those instructions never really had to use the things, as not doing so, is nearly impossible. You would think they would make the pads puffier or something. Trying to calm down,

I give extra attention to my crutches and assuming that rhythmic swinging-like motion with my body to make my way to the bathroom. Touch down, swing, touch down, swing.

Once in the bathroom, I sit on the toilet, aware that I did not have to lift the seat. Thanks, Luke, is it really that hard to put down a lid? I grab a tissue from the box on top of the tank lid, and dab at the tears, sitting in my eyes. I just need a moment to cool off before the emotional bomb ticking inside me detonates and Luke becomes collateral damage. I hate feeling like I may erupt at any time and that I'm communicating like some cold-hearted, angry bitch. I hate it. But when he brings up what happened or looks at me with hurt and sympathy, I can't help it. . I see that he blames himself, it's written all over his face and the pure torture is evident in his eyes. But his overbearing nature right now and his somewhat somber mood are all more than I can handle. I have enough of my own emotions I'm trying to work through, I can't take his on too. And besides, this – these emotions and what I went through - is not about him. It's my story. He needs to get over it, just like I am.

Feeling better, more determined and in control, I leave the bathroom after doing a fake flush of the toilet and washing of my hands. Luke looks at me with those sad puppy eyes – sigh - as soon as the door opens, "Do you need help?"

"No, I got it."

He doesn't listen, and as I get closer to the bed, he comes to my side and just stands there as I lower myself to the bed. He takes my crutches and puts them back in place and tucks me in like I'm a toddler. I want to scream, but I bite my tongue. Hard.

Reaching for my laptop, I place it back on my lap and open Google docs, determined to add a survey to my blog post. All those in favor of new hospital gowns can vote and weigh in with their opinions.

I hear Luke sigh and it immediately puts me on edge. I can see him staring at me out of the corner of my eye. I turn my body slightly, attempt to concentrate even harder, doing my best to ignore him, but he isn't going to take the hint. Dammit. This isn't going to be good, I feel the anger rising in me again like hot lava. The last thing I want is to argue with him.

Easing himself closer to me, and slightly moving the computer from its positioned place, he says, "I'm trying to talk to you about this Livvie, and I don't have your attention."

Something in me snaps. It's intense and sounds like the crack of a bat against a ball. "Tell me something Luke, what the hell do you not understand? Have you forgotten the simplicity of the English language? What will it take for you to understand that I DON'T WANT TO TALK ABOUT THIS?" Oh shit, I'm getting mean and I'm yelling and I can't stop it now. "I REFUSE, absolutely REFUSE to let what happened take over my life. What do you not understand? Please, for the love of GOD, tell me, because I will do any damn thing it takes to make sure you GET IT."

I'm breathing hard and sweat has appeared on my forehead. I can practically feel the production of hormones being secreted keeping pace with my emotions. I want to count to ten or a hundred, but can't. Neither can I control this. Exhaustion and rage engulf me and despite my internal alarms, my entire countenance radiates my feelings. I'm acutely aware of the internal turmoil contributing to this outburst. On one hand, I'm struggling with having not been totally honest with Luke, yet I am holding him culpable for trying to pressure me to talk, to tell him...and simultaneously I am enraged at myself, both for shouting and for my attempt at deceit. Trying to gain a semblance of composure, I again make eye contact and the look on his face is pure shock. His eyes that became widened and fiery during my rant are accompanied by a new speechlessness. He's taking deep breaths and I realize it's likely that he has found the benefit of silently counting to ten before responding to me. Probably smart of him.

"I'm just trying to help."

I take an extremely deep breath and look him right in the eyes, "I do not want your help. I do not need help. I want us to move on with our lives." I say each word slowly and with distinctness and clarity. "And, speaking of which, you cannot sit here and babysit me day after day. You have a business to run and you need to get back to it."

"It's fine. I will just take a brief leave of absence. I'm the boss. I can do this-"

"Oh, hell no you won't. You can't. Absolutely not. I will not be babysat like I'm some invalid. No fucking way. What I need... how you can help... is by listening to what I just said. Go back to work; try understanding that I just need normalcy. Be normal. I don't know how many times I have to say it."

He looks so torn, devastated. And defeated. He is clearly battling what I'm asking – no, telling - him to do versus what he wants to do. I'm not dumb, I get it. I know he blames himself at least in part for what happened, but I cannot continually reassure him. I must move on. Tears fill my eyes and I rapidly work to blink them away, because on the tip of my tongue are words to soothe him, to give him what he needs and wants and to tell him to stop blaming himself, but I can't.

Deacon's fingers trail up my leg and he's saying something about wanting me to wake up, but I can't make out the words. It sounds like he's slurring and I can't keep my eyes open. I begin to go under again just as I feel his fingers at the edge of my panties.

NO. I can't. Taking a deep breath, still trying to calm myself down, I look into his eyes. "Luke, I love you, I do. But if you don't listen to me, I'm telling you right now this is going to be a problem for us. I don't want to talk about this, because if we do, I may not be able to control where my mind goes. And I don't want to think about any of that, okay? I need you to accept that, or I need you to leave."

"Angel, I'm sorry, I just want to fix this. I just want to help."

Looking him straight in the eyes I say words I know he won't like, "You can't."

12.

CAVEMEN WERE ON TO SOMETHING

Luke

*T*HIS SHIT SUCKS. I feel completely helpless. Emasculated. Has Olivia ever yelled at me? Certainly not like that. Sure, I admit, seeing her all worked up is kinda hot. Part of me wants to smile and then shut her up with a searing kiss that ends up in hot, sweaty sex. I mean, I am a hot blooded male after all. However, the reason behind her anger doesn't get my blood pumping at all.

No one – not even Olivia – can treat me like I'm weak and powerless. Doesn't she understand that seeing her like this creates a natural instinct in me to defend and protect? The unreasonable caveman part of me wants to throw her over my shoulder while screaming, "ooga ooga" and take her to my cave. I could watch her and keep her safe there. If only it were that easy. The loving part of me wants to soothe the hurt away I see in her eyes. I want desperately to fix this and make it all go away. It kills me to see her this way, and even though she says I can't fix it, I damn well want to try. I want to give her back the peace and security she deserves. I mean fuck, she finds the strength and determination to stick up for herself, leave him and their so-called marriage, to end up in something even worse? What the hell? That isn't fair at all, even if I know and have learned that life often seems unjust. Hell, if it was, I never would have lost her all those years ago, and she never would have met that bastard to begin with.

I can't change that though. She did meet him, and as much as I want all of this to be some kind of bad dream or horrible acid trip, it isn't. All I can do is hope she feels my love, and recognizes that my attempt to help her is to meet her need for security and safety. I want her to find peace in the knowledge that it will be okay. Aside from tracking him down myself and ending this, I don't know how else to make this better.

I knew from the moment Olivia and I met that she was meant to be mine. Not in a twisted, sick way like Deacon. She truly belonged with me – we belonged together - and all I've ever wanted is to make that reality. There is nothing I wouldn't do for her to make her feel safe, secure, and loved. Her inability to lean on me, to help her, causes actual physical distress, real pain in my chest. I absentmindedly rub at my heart through my shirt, as if I can soothe the hurt there. Rejection tries to adhere itself to me like an octopus, and I keep pushing it away, refusing to let it get its tentacles on me.

I know I can make her happy. I know we will be happy. We just need to get through this. Question is, how do I make that happen when she won't even talk to me? She won't admit what happened, won't deal with it all, and until she does, how can we move forward? It's simple - we can't.

"Okay, I hear you. You don't want to talk about it. You don't want to deal with it. I'll try to accept that temporarily, but love, I think we are going to have to at some point. You think the only thing we need is to move forward and get back to normal, or we'll have problems. Okay, I get that...for now. But you listen to me, too. This is our new normal. This is not just a part of our – or your

- past. Not dealing with this, or our failure to deal with it, will create a wall that may get impenetrable and be sure to come between us."

I look her straight in the face as I'm telling her this. It's like gouging my own heart out with a spoon; this candor, this brute honesty. I'd like to forget about it all too, to forget what I didn't do, what I know, what I heard. To erase how I feel. Wouldn't that be easy? To pretend the nightmare never happened and the two of us go skipping off into the sunset like some cheesy *Lifetime* movie? Not that I skip, or anything. Or watch *Lifetime*. Fact is, it did happen. And while she doesn't realize exactly how much I know, she does know I'm not dumb, and I know something went down. I mean, Deacon is a twisted fuck. Of course something happened.

Olivia looks down at her hands twisting in her lap. She won't meet my eyes. "I understand, Luke. Please, just not yet, okay?"

I swallow hard at the pain I hear in her voice. "Okay. And as far as going back to work, you're right, I do have a business to run, but none of it is as important as you. Can *you* understand *that?*"

Her gorgeous green eyes finally meet my own and she gives me a soft smile, since I threw her words back at her. "I'm not trying to say that it should be. Just that I know it's important to you too; it's part of what makes you happy, part of who you are. And I don't want to be the reason you get behind on anything. Maintaining that business is important for our futures. Plus, I need to get back to my work as well. It only makes sense that while I'm working, you should be working too. Baby, I will be fine."

I can't help but sigh in frustration at her statement and one of the thoughts I've had repeatedly spills out, "We don't know that Olivia. Deacon is still out there." Panic rises in my chest, making it difficult to breathe. I do my best to push it away because that won't help either of us. "Until he's caught and put away, leaving you is something that seems to risky – and is going to be very difficult for me to do."

"I get that, I really do. But we've taken necessary precautions as much as we can. The locks on the door have been changed, the security working the building has his picture, and there's an alarm on the door and windows. The police are working on it. On top of that, I won't take stupid risks with my safety and neither will Pyper."

I nod my head absently and look at her when she grabs my hand, "We can't let fear rule our lives. That would be the worst thing for us to do. He would win, at least in part, and we can't let that happen."

I stare into her eyes and feel myself start to give in. She does make a point and I can read between the lines. I think she needs a little bit of space, and I respect that. It isn't going to be easy at all, but I quickly resign myself to a plan I have been formulating. And best of all, she doesn't need to be aware of it. I will talk to Pyper and I'm sure that we can work out a schedule that just happens to ensure that one of us will always be here, just in case.

I say nothing to Olivia and instead look at her in her cute pajamas. Hair on top of her head, her nose is crinkled as her attention has been deflected back to the computer in front of her. God, she's beautiful. I need her so much. Every part of me wants to reach over and touch her. I know she wants time to herself, but I can't stop thinking about how damn good it would feel to kiss and taste her right now.

As if she senses my thoughts, her eyes return to mine and her lips curve up at the corners. Her eyes dart from my own, to my lips, and back again. That's all the invitation I need. I squeeze her hand in mine a bit tighter and give it a gentle tug, pulling her towards me a little as I lean in and kiss my girl. I keep it gentle, hand moving to the side of her cheek, our mouths barely touching. Images from our hospital shower make it tough to pull away, but I do. I can't resist placing a brief kiss on her adorable nose, which crinkles in response, making me smile. Damn, my girl is sexy when she isn't even trying. Things will get out of hand quickly if I don't distance myself.

"Well, I suppose now is as good a time as any to go check in at the club. Pyper is here, so I will let her know where I'm going on my way out. Your cell is within reach in case you need to call me, right?"

She fishes it out of the blankets at her side, and holds it up to me, "I'm good."

"Okay. Please angel, call me if you need anything okay?"

"I will, but I won't. I will be fine. Do what you need to do at work and then come back, okay? It will be good for you to get out of here for a little bit anyway. Don't you think so? I'm sure you are going a bit stir crazy."

"Sure," I agree with her even though I don't mean it. She has no clue I'm going to have to force myself to leave her side. I can't help but grit my teeth at the almost gut-wrenching nausea I feel rising in my throat at just the thought, but she will be fine. I know she will. I will keep telling myself that. Repeating it like a mantra.

I go to the bathroom, splash water on my face, grab the hand towel from the countertop, and then dry off. Bracing my hands on the outside of the sink, I stare at myself in the mirror. I've got some darkness under my eyes, and my hair has tracks in it from my fingers. Looking deep into my own eyes, I swear a little bit of madness shows through if I look hard enough. It's in the tenseness around my eyes and mouth and the little red lines outside of my irises. I am completely consumed with worry. I need to get a grip. She will be fine, she is fine.

I realize I'm stalling. Sighing, I walk out of the bathroom to the side of the bed and give her a kiss on the forehead when she looks up at me in question. "I'll be back later. Love you."

"I love you too."

Words that still make my heart swell in my chest. I hope I never tire of hearing them. When I close her door behind me I look for Pyper and am glad to see she's in the living room with a bowl of popcorn in her lap, staring at...

"What are you watching?"

Her reaction to hearing my voice is almost comical. The popcorn almost flies out of the bowl and she grabs at the remote, shutting the TV off. "What the hell, Luke?! Don't just sneak up on people like that."

"Sorry. I wasn't thinking. But seriously, what are you watching?"

"Nothing special."

I walk to the TV because I see the empty DVD box sitting on the TV stand and pick it up. "Supernatural?"

"Yeah, what of it?"

"I just had no idea you like this kind of thing."

"What's not to like? Two hot guys, occasionally shirtless, equals a win in my book."

I laugh, "I will take your word for it," and then, "Wait, does Olivia like this show too?"

She smiles, "Maybe." The look on my face thinking about my girl liking the shirtless hot guys makes Pyper laugh, "So, what's up? Olivia okay?"

I run my hand over my face, "Yeah, she's fine. At least, that's what she wants everyone to believe."

She sighs, and sets the popcorn next to her on the couch as if she's lost her appetite, "Yeah I noticed that."

"I honestly don't know what to do. I keep trying to get her to talk to me and she won't. I'm going to keep trying, but I think she needs some space. She's insisting that she's fine and that she wants to go back to things being normal and that I need to continue on as I usually would. She wants the old routine back, I guess."

"Maybe that's the best thing to do right now. I really don't know."

"I don't know either, but what I do know is that I am not okay with her being here alone."

"You and me both. If Deacon were to show up again, it's not like I would be able to take him on, but I might be able to slow him down enough to call nine-one-one."

"I don't even want to think about that. Hopefully, he's not so stupid that he would try coming back here again. Anyway, I'd feel a lot better if one of us tried to always be with her. Are you okay with that?"

"Of course. I agree with you, and she doesn't need to know what we're up to. It would probably only set her off."

"I agree. Alright, I'll be back later tonight then."

"Okay, sounds good."

"Oh, and Pyper? Do you need me to bring you back anything? Wine? More popcorn? More seasons of Supernatural? Or maybe they have action figures or trading cards you don't have yet?"

"Ha. Ha. Mock me all you want, Easton. You don't know what you're missing."

I laugh as she throws popcorn at me on my way out.

I THOUGHT I was starting to look haggard, but I look young, robust and trouble-free in comparison to my dad. Sitting in the living room in my childhood home, I take him in. I'm pretty sure he's lost weight. He has deep circles under his eyes and his cheeks seem more hollow that usual. His hair looks whiter too – it's a very distinguished salt and pepper, but he has much more white at his temples than he did before. He appears to have aged significantly in the little time it's been since I last saw him.

"Dad, are you eating? Sleeping?"

"I'm doing the best I can, son. Some days I take better care of myself than others. I miss your mother."

I feel the sting of unshed tears behind my eyes, but I refuse to be a baby and shed a tear in front of my dad. That's the last thing he needs. He won't talk to me if he feels like it upsets me too much.

"I'm sorry that I had to leave-"

He holds a hand up a hand, halting my words, "You know better than to apologize for that. I understand. Now, tell me how she's been doing since we spoke on the phone."

"I don't know, dad. She won't talk about what happened, but I know she's not okay."

"Well of course she's not okay. She was kidnapped and hurt. That would do a number on anyone. Lord only knows what really happened to her. I know you suggested something awful had happened to her when we spoke."

I debate whether or not to repeat what I heard and believe to be true but know my dad would never say anything. Moreover, his advice and understanding would once again be much appreciated. "Dad, when she was at the hospital, I told you I overheard something."

"Yes, I remember. And I told you that whatever it was to get your ass back to that hospital and to deal with what happened together."

I give him a small smile, but it quickly drops, "Dad, I know she was abused not only physically, but possibly sexually too. It's not anything one wouldn't have expected, I guess. But hearing it stated... well, it's one thing to wonder, it's another to know. "

My dad moves to sit on the couch next to me. He places his hand on my shoulder, lending his support. I don't even need to tell him how much this news is affecting me. He knows. He knows as a man that is dedicated to protecting the woman he loves. He also knows what it's like to be powerless in preventing harm and pain to the one you love. While the details may be different - Olivia was ravaged by a madman and my mom by cancer, I expect the feeling of helplessness is still the same. He can understand the loss I might feel – having had someone violate someone and something that was so precious. And my anger and rage – at Deacon, the situation, myself - yep, I think he gets it too.

"Tell me what you heard," he says. And so I do. I tell him where I was, what I overheard and how I freaked out so bad, I took off.

"Don't be angry at yourself for that, son. You had a very human reaction. When your mom told me she had cancer, I had a very similar reaction."

I look at him with surprise, "You did?"

"Yes. The fear and doubt was more than I knew what to do with. One night, when your mother was sleeping, I got in my car and drove away. Not with the intention of never returning, but because I needed to ask myself if I was strong enough to travel down what was likely to be a long and painful road. I needed to do some soul searching and prepare myself for what was to come."

"Did you feel like you were being weak? I did. I realized what I was doing and got my ass back there."

"No, son. Weakness would be if you had never confronted the fact and the ramifications that what happened to Olivia, will affect her and you. Just as I would hope that one day Olivia would be open to speaking with someone to get her through this difficult time in her life – to make sure she is dealing with it in a healthy manner, you should too. I suggest you also think about speaking to someone professionally. You gave yourself a little time, thought about what you needed to do, and realized your love for each other can get through anything. I believe it will son, but a little help, a little guidance from an unbiased third party, would be very good for you."

I nod, acknowledging his recommendation, "I feel like she is drowning and I can't save her. No matter what she says, I know that talking about it is what she needs to do. She needs to confront what happened to her in order to deal with it."

"Are you sure that is what she needs, or is it what you need?"

"What do you mean?"

"I mean, that this is about Olivia. Luke, she is damn well aware of what happened to her. She knows better than anyone. This isn't about her not talking about it. Right now, it's about self-preservation. She is doing what she needs to do for herself right now, just to get through one day at a time. It's no different than mourning, really. She's mourning the carefree way she was able to live her life before it was ripped away from her. The difference is, she can get that back. It isn't dead."

"But dad, I just don't think it's good that she refuses to talk about this. She needs to talk about it to someone. Even, as much as I hate to say it, if it isn't me, she needs someone. I know I keep saying this, but she needs to deal with this."

"And she will, but in her own time, Luke, not yours. Olivia finally stood up to Deacon and divorced him after living in pain for quite some time. She was ready to finally move on and start fresh. Then, because Deacon doesn't like her decision, he decides to take her choices away from her. Something as basic as being confident in your own decisions was taken away from her. How do you think that makes her feel? It's more than just, as you say, 'dealing with it'."

"You're right. I know you're right. I need to stop assuming I know what she should be doing right now. It's just really hard. It's like breathing, this need to make her happy."

"Oh son, that's called love. That will never go away, if you're lucky. And you know what the best part is? You'll be better for it. There's nothing better than taking care of the woman you love and knowing she loves you and wants to do the same for you in return."

"Like what you had with mom?"

"Yes, we got there eventually. Relationships aren't always easy. They take dedication and hard work. But, hopefully you will get years of love, joy, and contentment in return. And that my son, is worth all of the tough times in between."

"Thanks, dad. I really needed to hear this. I feel like I'm just screwing everything up."

"That's not the case. You are trying to figure out how to love and protect the woman you love, the best way you can. You will never go wrong when love is leading the way."

"Yes, that's what I'm trying to do, you're right." I take a deep breath, look at my dad and once again take in his appearance, "What do you say I make us something to eat?"

He smiles and pats me on the shoulder, "I'd like that."

13.

BLING!

Olivia

I'M CURLED UP on the couch with Pyper watching *Supernatural*. It's one of our favorite guilty pleasures. After Luke left she came to my bedroom asking me to join her and told me she had a surprise for me as well.

"I can't say no to Sam and Dean, I love that show!" What she doesn't know though is that one of the reasons I love to watch it is because of her commentary. She always says really naughty things about the brothers, and what she'd like to do to them. And on them.

"I knew you'd say yes!" Pyper jumps up and down clapping. Seriously, that girl goes overboard on the enthusiasm, sometimes. And I love it.

As I hobble my way into the living room, I see that Supernatural is already on the television. "Umm, what is this? You started without me?"

"Well, you were holed up in your room with Luke and I felt like watching it. I did not, however, feel like checking for a sock on the door. I figure you two have some catching up to do."

I smile, "A sock on the door? What are you, in college still?" She shrugs her shoulders, "Okay, fine, I guess I will forgive you this one time."

"Damn straight you will." Pyper hands me a glass of wine and I settle onto the couch, throwing a blanket over my lap. She puts a bowl of fresh popcorn in between the two of us, and it dawns on me she knew I would say yes because she has everything ready to go.

She starts a new episode and sure enough, it is one of her favorites. It's the episode where Sam and Dean try to figure out how to save Dean from an anxiety driven virus. Pyper's favorite part is when they open a locker looking for any clues and a cat is inside. Sam blows it off but the normal tough guy Dean screams like a girl and runs out. She's seen it several times, but she still laughs like it is the first time every time she sees it. And then she rewinds it over and over to watch again. I always laugh right along with her.

"Mmm, I really wouldn't mind being in a Dean and Sam sandwich," Pyper says smacking her lips together as if picturing it.

I raise my eyebrows at her, "Isn't that kind of gross? I mean they're brothers. If you had both of them in bed, wouldn't that kind of be like the brothers are having sex with each other too? Eww, talk about incestuous."

"Oh yeah, right. I'm sure if a woman had both of them in bed they'd be thinking, eww. I'm sure their hard pecs and well defined abs would drive those thoughts right out of their brain. Instead they would be thinking, 'OH MY GOD, I'm having sex with Sam and Dean from Supernatural!'

"Okay, good point," I laugh.

"I mean really, what kind of question was that anyway, Olivia? I expect more from you."

"I don't know, just something that came to mind."

"You're twisted."

"Ha! It takes one to know one."

She salutes me with her wine glass, "Guilty."

I laugh. I love this banter between the two of us. It's exactly what I need, and the wine tastes great and definitely doesn't hurt either. "I know you love Dean, but personally I'm a Sam kind of girl." Of course this is a conversation we've had many times, but it amuses me to get her going.

"Shocking, Livvie. You like the good looking, emotional, tortured and broody kind of guy."

"What is that supposed to mean?" I raise my brows at her, "Luke isn't broody, so your suggestion is way off."

"Whatever." She waves her hand as if it is a moot point. She leaves the room and comes back carrying a bag in her hand. "So, I thought we could do a craft."

"Um, what? Who are you and what have you done with my best friend, Pyper?"

"Ha. Ha. This isn't for me, it's for you and I thought I would put my good sense aside and think of you."

"Okay, well now I'm just plain scared."

"Very funny." She starts pulling things out of the bag one by one and sets them on the coffee table. There's a huge bag full of pink and white gemstones, all kinds of glitter, two new glue guns and glue sticks.

I just stare at her for a few beats, "I'm really trying to guess here, but I have no idea."

"I thought we could bedazzle your cast!"

"Bedazzle my cast? Where did you get that idea?"

"Oh, just something I saw on *Pinterest.*"

"Wait, you're on *Pinterest?* Seriously, are you possessed or something? Maybe a demon from *Supernatural* flew out of the TV and into you? Can you get possessed from watching television? Crap." I get close and look at her eyes, "No, they aren't all black."

"Ha. Ha. You are a riot. Come on; don't even think about telling me you don't want to do this. It's right up your alley."

"Actually, I kind of love the idea."

"Knew it. Do I know you, or what?"

"Okay fine, you got me here. I'm so impressed you actually one up'd me on this one. But I gotta say, this sounds like fun."

Pyper gives me a no duh look as she plugs in the glue guns, "This will be fun, and then your cast will be stylin."

"That it will," I smile and feel my eyes well up a little at her thoughtfulness. I blink rapidly to push them back. The last thing I want to do is cry like a baby and ruin our time together. It's just, when I think about how close I came to losing her. No. I'm not going there.

"So, tell me. After speaking about the hotness of Sam and Dean, what kind of guy do you picture yourself with? A serious, no-nonsense, tortured, book smart kind of guy like Sam? Or, the live-life-to-its-fullest, don't hold back, sarcastic, shameless flirt like Dean?"

"Honestly? The few times that I've seriously given that some thought, I would have to say neither."

"Neither? Really?" I give it additional thought as I watch Pyper check one of the guns. When she sees they are both warm she hands one to me and together we start gluing pink plastic gemstones to my leg cast. "I thought for sure you would say a guy like Dean. Remember the time we made a pros and cons list about the attributes of each of them?" We both giggle at the memory, "Your Dean list was like a mile long."

After gluing a huge silver gemstone, Pyper looks at me with humor shining in her eyes, "Yeah, I remember, I am definitely attracted to the idea of a badass like Dean, but I picture myself with a serious business man."

"A business man? Really? You want an uber professional kind of guy?"

"Well... yeah. Can you imagine me with any other kind? I mean, I know I'm pretty laid back, but I want a guy that is financially independent in his own right. One who wants to take care of me, even if I don't need that kind of care-taking, and doesn't just want to be with me because of my dad's money and the connections he would hope to acquire by association."

"You're really worried about that? You've never mentioned it before."

"Sure, wouldn't you be? Ouch! Son of a bitch!"

"Glue get you?"

"Yep, damn that hurts. Anyway, my dad isn't a celebrity like George Clooney by any means, but he's still well known. I worry about people using me to get to him."

"That makes sense; I never considered that, I guess. But you can't let fear of something that may or may not ever happen keep you from dating. You could find someone that will make you really happy. I'm not saying you need a man to be happy, but I know you. You are like most people, you'd like someone to share your life with; companionship. We all want to be loved like that, and no matter what you say sometimes, or how much you joke, you're no exception."

Pyper fills our wine glasses for the third time, maybe - I don't know, I've lost track. "Yes, you're right, I would like to find someone, but I'm sure as hell not going to settle for just anyone."

I nod my head, "No, you shouldn't ever settle," I agree. "Hey, remember that guy you told me you dated once? The artist?"

Immediately Pyper groans and pauses from gluing rhinestones. She looks up at the ceiling like she's recalling exactly whom I'm speaking of, "Oh God yes, anywhere we would go he would be all 'Oh wow, look at the naked beauty in the way this trash can sits there taking up space and holding garbage within. Can't you just see how the earth holds its balance of good and bad in its simplicity,' he was so weird. And made no sense."

I snort mid-drink and am surprised wine doesn't come out of my nose, "Didn't he ask you to pose nude for him?"

Pyper gives a loud laugh, "Yeah, that was the last thing he ever asked me. I dumped him after that. Freak!"

"That seems a little harsh. I mean, what's a little nakedness in the name of art?"

"Very funny, Livvie. You know very well you never would have done it if our roles had been reversed. Besides, he wanted me to pose nude on solar panels – he was really into the green planet as well."

"Solar panels?" I quickly recover when I see the claws coming out. "Oh come on now, I don't know. If I recall correctly, I seem to remember someone once telling me that I needed to take chances in life. That I wouldn't know what greatness is out there if I didn't jump in with both feet and put myself out there and blah, blah, blah. Seems you could have accomplished that... being out there." I can't help but goad her a bit.

Pyper's eyes widen and she gives me a mischievous grin, "Oh my god, that person sounds like a total bitch." She's waving the glue gun around as she uses her hands to emphasize her statement. She's at the top of my cast and precariously close to my lap as she's waving it around, making me a tad fearful. "I mean, please, like you aren't capable of making your own decisions, or something."

"Yeah, she's a total bitch. And it seems to me, she should take her own advice." I respond quickly, "Hey! Watch it with that glue gun, would ya?"

"What?" She looks down at herself and realizes she was waving it around, "Oh sorry."

I can't help but laugh, "After everything I've been through, that's all I need. I can see the headline now, 'Woman Dead After Suffering Third Degree Burns to Vagina."

I see Pyper's expression fall for a moment at my statement and I want to kick myself. I didn't mean to sound all serious or make her sad. I was trying to be funny. She quickly recovers, "Oh please, a few third degree burns never killed anyone."

I roll my eyes and change the subject, "Do you still have your dating profile up on Date Me?"

"No. I took it down while you were missing."

I wasn't expecting that answer, "What? Why?"

"That's a pretty dumb question, Livvie. I wasn't in the mood for that kind of thing while you were gone. My email would get overloaded with messages from the site, and I wanted to keep it clear in case any news came through. I finally just deleted my profile."

"Oh." I don't meet her eyes, even though I can feel her staring at me. I pretend to be very involved in opening the pink glitter, "Well, we should start a new one for you. Get you out there meeting people again."

Pyper gives me a sad smile, "Maybe some time, I'm not really in the mood for that right now."

"Why? Now is as good a time as any."

"Just because, Livvie," there's something in the tone of her voice that makes me meet her eyes. I don't expect the fear I see lingering in her eyes or in the way her whole body has tensed up.

"What's wrong?" I ask her confused.

She sighs, "I know you won't leave it alone, so truthfully, the whole thing with Deacon really scared me. It made me realize that you don't always know people, ya know? You just can't be too careful and it kind of put a sour taste in my mouth on the whole dating thing for right now."

My stomach clenches and I flinch when I hear Deacon's "*Hello Princess*" in my mind at her words. She couldn't be more correct. Nothing is scarier than thinking you know someone and finding out that you didn't really. Nothing at all. "I get it, and I'm really sorry."

"Don't you dare apologize," she points a finger at me, well more like points a glue gun at me. "This is not at all your fault. This is just me being smart. You're my best friend and I've had a front row to everything you've been through. Well mostly. Anyway, I don't think anyone with half a brain, could be close to what I've witnessed from Deacon, and not have a little justified fear in them."

I'm proud of myself for managing to keep myself from flinching at his name. That has to be progress. "You're right. I just hate to think that I've contributed to you not carrying on and living your life the way you should. Or that...he has stripped you of that."

She secures another gemstone to my cast and I see we've just about got the whole thing filled up. "Well you know better than that, and I'm sure my feelings are only temporary. I will get my mojo back eventually, I'm sure." She hesitates, and I can tell she wants to say something but when she presses her lips together, I can tell she's decided not to.

"What is it?"

Her eyes meet mine. "What?"

"I can tell you want to say something to me, but you hesitated."

"You're right. And can I just say for the record that I love the fact that you know me that well?"

I smile, "Well, of course I do."

She returns my smile, but it falls quickly, "Look, Livvie, I need to say something and it isn't easy because I know you don't want to talk about what happened."

My smile falls at her words and I feel my body stiffen. "But?"

"But I wouldn't be your best friend if I didn't tell you that while I understand that you can't talk to me right now, you still need to talk to someone. And I don't mean Luke, although you should talk to him too. I mean a professional." She stops and takes a big breath, it's almost as if she's trying to get it out as fast as possible before she loses her nerve, "Livvie, I can't even begin to imagine what you are going through. I know that my encounter with Deacon, while terrifying, was not anywhere close to what you experienced, and even I have decided talk to a therapist about it. Please, please, please talk to someone too, Livvie. Please."

Tears fill my eyes at her words but I'm too choked up to speak.

"You are one of the strongest women I know, but even you can't get through this alone. Just think about it, okay?"

I manage a nod, and swipe at the tears falling down my cheeks. "Thanks for loving and caring about me, Pyper. I'm lucky to have you."

"Yes you are!"

"It's true." We both sniff and I decide a change of conversation is in order again. So, I say what I know both of us are thinking, "So, it looks like Martha Stewart threw up on my leg."

She looks at me and I stand up, albeit awkwardly, and flash my newly bedazzled leg cast in the light. We look at it, then at each other, and laugh uncontrollably. The laughter makes me feel good; normal. This is what I need.

14

LAUGHTER AND LUST

Luke

WHEN I RETURN to Olivia's condo, I'm immediately met with the sound of laughter. I stop in my tracks for a moment and listen to the beautiful sound. The sound of Olivia's laughter is one of the best things I've heard in a long time. God, it feels like forever since I've heard her laugh like that. I feel a small twinge of jealousy that I can't claim it as my doing. And maybe a bit of guilt that perhaps she had been right about what she needed.

I follow the sound and find Olivia seated on the couch with a blanket thrown over her lap. Pyper sits at her feet with her back against the coffee table, facing her. The TV is on and there are two dudes on the screen arguing over something, but Olivia and Pyper aren't even paying attention to anything around them. Two wine bottles are on the coffee table, and they each have a glass of wine in their hands.

I stand quietly, unnoticed around the corner. My girl looks so beautiful. She's got her hair piled high in a bun, and a few strands have fallen around her cheeks and I swear they are glistening a little in the light, making me want to touch them. She's got a huge smile on her face while she listens to whatever Pyper is going on about, her cheeks are flushed from the alcohol, and her eyes are sparkling. Her body appears relaxed for the first time in days, her shoulders aren't tense and she's hunched a bit in comfort instead of ramrod straight. The haunted look that's been a constant in her eyes has disappeared – at least for the time being. She looks carefree and happy, and while sure, it may be that the alcohol is influencing her reaction; hell, I'll still take it.

I walk around and approach slowly because I've noticed that lately, any sudden motion makes her jump. She may try to cover it up when it happens, but I notice. I notice everything about her. When she sees me, her face lights up, I feel my heart skip a beat and my breath hitch in response, "Well hello there, handsome."

I try and smooth my features so I don't look like a love sick, pussy-whipped, sixteen-year-old, but I'm not sure I succeed when I see her smile widen, "Hi angel, looks like you are having a nice time this evening."

"We are. Why don't you join us?"

"Don't mind if I do, but first I'm going to grab one of those," I point at her glass. I go into the kitchen to grab a glass and then pour the last of the wine from one of their bottles for myself.

While I'm pouring, Pyper who didn't bother saying hello, other than giving me a smirk, asks Olivia, "Hey, remember the time we went a whole week without talking to each other?"

Olivia snorts, "Of course. How could I forget? I was so pissed at you, you bitch. You totally stole my crush, Adam." She points her finger at Pyper in emphasis and Pyper laughs.

I choke on my wine, "Adam?" I ask Olivia as I sit beside her on the couch. She places her hand on my thigh and it makes me twitch below the belt. My skin immediately feels hot under her palm and I can't help but wish she would move her hand higher. Stupid, traitor body can't control itself around her at all. I look from her hand to her eyes and see she's already looking at me. I raise my eyebrow at her and give her a smirk, admittedly because she finds both actions sexy, and the flush on her face deepens. Because I am sure that I am the cause, I can't help but lean in and give her an all too brief kiss on the lips. I taste the wine on her lips and she smells damn near edible. Her lips press against mine in return, and if Pyper wasn't here, I would push her down on the couch and take more right fucking now.

"So ANYWAY," Pyper interrupts rudely and I roll my eyes – it's a good thing I really like her. I growl a little under my breath making Olivia giggle, "Yes, you were mad at me because I talked to Adam." Pyper giggles.

Olivia chokes on the wine she was sipping and coughs a couple times, "Talk? Oh please." She turns to me, "I was looking for Pyper after school. I walked past the staircase, by the library, and happened to see red out of the corner of my eye. I turn towards the stairs and see that red-headed slut," She points at Pyper accusingly, "Lip locked with Adam in the alcove!"

"Who's Adam?" I ask again after getting ignored the first time.

"Adam Caruso," Olivia answers.

"Adam Caruso? The douchenozzle track star that walked around high school like he was God's gift?"

"That's the one," Pyper replies.

"She did you a favor if you ask me." I reply, not at all because I'm jealous. Not even a little.

"I had a crazy crush on him." Olivia swoons.

"Oh really?" I ask at the same time feeling the green eyed monster rear its ugly head and claw at my chest. I don't like thinking about my girl crushing on anyone else. At all. Even if it was years ago.

"Oh don't worry, lover boy, she was much crazier over you."

I can't help it. That makes me grin; huge. Damn straight she liked me more. I feel like I should do a victory dance or pound my chest or something. Oh man, I'm so whipped. Olivia laughs and I can't help but smile automatically in response at the sound. It's a sound that until tonight, I didn't realize I missed so desperately. Sure, she's laughed since she's been back, but the forced sound is absent this time.

"So, why would you be in the alcove with Olivia's crush? Not that I mind the fact that it was you instead of Olivia, but that doesn't seem like you to hurt Olivia like that."

"We were just talking, it wasn't a big deal-"

"Talking with her TONGUE," Olivia scoffs.

"You didn't let me finish! I was going to say 'at first'. Look, I don't really know how it escalated to kissing, one minute he wanted to ask me a question about our home economics class, and-"

"A question about home ec?" I laugh totally interrupting her and not caring when she sighs in annoyance. This is too good. "What the hell kind of question could someone have about home ec?"

"Yes, very good point, Luke. She never did tell me what happened. We eventually just gave in and started laughing after we bonded over a horrible outfit our nemesis, Kim Anderson, wore to school one day. I just let it go and moved on to my crush on you," Olivia says squeezing my thigh, making me twitch yet again. She needs to stop doing that or I won't care that Pyper is in the room.

"So now is as good a time as any to fess up then, huh Pyper?" I tease, "I bet I have a good idea what he said to you. Was it something along the lines of, "Hey babe, can I double stuff your oreo?' Olivia bursts into laughter which of course is gasoline to my fire. "Or was it more like, 'Can I slap my meat on your grill?'"

Olivia starts giggling out of control, "Oh my gosh... Luke.... I can't... I can't... breathe," I smile at her and laugh too. She's bent over at the waist and when she catches sight of Pyper, she places her hand over her mouth to try and stifle her giggles, to no avail. Her actions prompt me to look over at Pyper and I'm met with a death glare. Her arms are crossed over her chest and she's fighting a losing battle trying to keep a straight face. Her lips keep twitching at the corners, but then she straightens them again into a hard line.

Not one to be outdone, Olivia chimes in, "Was that what it was, Pyper? You just couldn't help yourself after that and the next thing you know you were sucking face?"

Pyper loses her battle and they both explode into a fit of giggles, most of it likely spurned on from the alcohol running through their veins.

"Good one, angel."

"Thanks, babe." I stare at her and then look at her mouth. I love her lips, her smile. Suddenly the air starts to feel thicker and all I can think about is how I want to take that mouth of hers. My clothes feel itchy and too tight, especially between my legs. I look back at her face and see her eyes are staring at my mouth now, and her laughter fades away. I smirk and it makes her look back at my face, and into my eyes. Her eyes reveal how much she wants me, and I know she sees my need reverberating back at her because her cheeks flush in knowledge. I want to rip her clothes off and have my way with her - on this couch, against the wall, on the floor, on the damn coffee table - I don't care. I just want her. I start to move my mouth towards hers like there's a magnet pulling us together.

That is... until we're rudely interrupted. Again.

"Ahem, excuse me. The third wheel redhead is still sitting in the room you two."

I curse under my breath and Olivia laughs. "Well then, I think it's time we leave the room. What do you say, angel? Ready for bed?"

She nods before she even realizes she's doing it, once again looking at my face, knowing going to bed doesn't mean sleep. Her gaze travels down and I swear each spot her eyes touch on their journey, makes my body tingle in reaction. When she reaches my lap, her eyes widen a little and she says, "I could go to bed now. Suddenly I'm really.... tired."

"Yeah, I'll just bet you are." Pyper teases.

Olivia glances at Pyper in embarrassment and starts edging to the front of the couch cushion so it will make standing up easier. I jump up and grab her crutches from against the wall, and turn back to her, stopping dead in my tracks.

"Babe...what the hell is that?"

"What?"

"That," I say pointing. Pyper is already laughing and I think even rolling around from it on the floor a bit, but I ignore her.

Olivia looks down to where I'm pointing and when she realizes it's her leg I'm talking about, she stares at it for a minute too as if she's seeing it for the first time as well. "Pyper had a surprise for me. It's called 'cast bedazzling.' Do you like it?"

"Umm," she starts twisting her leg back and forth and light prisms dance off the walls. How do I tell her it looks like a whole craft store is glued to her leg?

"Oh you know you love it! You think it's sexy!" Then she pushes her leg to the front showing it off a little more, "Do you want some of this?" She asks, turning it one way, "How about a little of that?" She twists her leg the other way. She's laughing and I start to return her laughter until she overcompensates on her twist and loses her balance. I drop the crutches, swoop in and pick her up, holding her close to my chest, while she cracks up at herself. "My hero!" She's drunk off her ass.

I start walking towards the room, "Night, Luke and Olivia," Pyper calls out behind me. "Night," I call and Olivia singsongs, "Nighty night, Pyper Wiper."

Once we're in her bedroom, I kick the door closed behind us and deposit her on the bed gently so I don't bump her cast. She sits there looking up at me, and I realize she's swaying back and forth a little, even as she's seated. "Let me get your pajamas for you."

"No."

I raise my brows in question, "No?"

"No, I want to sleep naked," she semi-whispers as if she's doing something naughty. I inwardly grumble. This is going to require self-control that I'm not sure I possess tonight.

"I don't know how well I will be able to control myself if you do that."

"Who says I want you to control yourself?"

"You're in no condition to fool around."

"Actually, once I'm naked, I will be in just the right condition."

I step towards her, "I will help you get undressed, okay? But that's it."

This time, she smirks at me. "We'll see."

She raises her arms inviting me to slide her shirt over her head. When I do, my breath hitches at the sight before me. Under her plain 'Fashion is my Passion' t-shirt, she is wearing a white lace bra that takes my breath away. Her flesh looks pearly white and so soft. I want to touch it. She locks me in a stare and seductively runs her fingers over the tops of her breasts that are overflowing over the cups of her bra. Fuck. Me.

She licks her lips and I nearly lose it, like an adolescent virgin seeing tits for the first time. "Olivia," I say warningly not moving my eyes from her breasts. She, of course, doesn't listen and keeps trailing her fingers back and forth. I bet I look like a man possessed. Possessed by boobs. Excellent. I'm such a weak bastard.

I swallow hard and take a deep breath, "Okay let me help you get your sweats off." I take a small step toward her as if I'm afraid her boobs will reach out and bite me. I inwardly call myself a pussy and close the distance, pulling her up to standing. I help support her so she doesn't topple over and she doesn't help matters by pressing her breasts against my chest, causing me to suck in and hold my breath.   I slide down her body, latching fingers of one hand into one side of the waistband of her sweats and pull down. It's rather awkward getting the pant leg down her cast. One arm is trying to hold her up and the other is trying to pull her pants down, one side at a time. The odd position has my face right in her breasts, and I swear she pushes them even closer to me, into me I'm going to deserve a fucking medal of honor after this.

Once I get her sweats pulled down far enough, I sit her back down. Letting out the breath I was holding, I squat down and slide them the rest of the way down her legs, and pull them off her feet. Her white lace panties are just as gorgeous as the rest of her and I just want to touch her. Of course my dick responds and begs, standing at attention. My jeans feel tight and in the way, my whole body hot. While I'm bending at my knees, the little devil opens her legs. I hurriedly stand up, after taking more than a momentary peek, and she laughs.

"Can you get the clasp of my bra? It's hard to get with this stupid gimp arm of mine. I'll be happy when it's healed. I hate needing help to get dressed and undressed."

I want to offer her encouragement, but the thought of pulling off her bra causes my throat to feel dry. I remind myself that we have had sex since she's been back, and that a gentleman should not take advantage of the fact she's been drinking. Even though the devil on my shoulder wants me to fuck being a gentleman, I'm really trying to ignore it. I reach behind her back, unhook her bra and slowly pull the straps off her shoulders, trailing my fingers down her arms as I slide it completely off. Her skin feels amazing. She bites her lip in response, and that's all it takes. I can't help but lean forward and take her mouth. God help me, but I am no saint.

I put my hands on both sides of her face and tease the seam of her lips with my tongue. When she opens for me and her tongue meets mine, I shudder in response. Her lips are soft, yet insistent against mine as she picks up the pace and kisses me like she can't get enough. She pulls on my shirt and pulls me closer and the sexiest sounds start coming from her mouth. Kissing this girl is something I could do for hours. I am unbelievably addicted to her – she's a drug I can't get enough of and I would do anything to feel the high her kisses bring me again and again.

Before I realize it, one of my hands is in her hair, and the other is touching her bare breasts. She's moaning into my mouth and I feel goose bumps break out on her skin. I tease her nipples, gently, but firmly, squeezing them as I sweep my tongue into her mouth over and over, holding her as tight as she's holding me.

I reluctantly pull away from her and place my forehead against hers, trying to catch my breath. She's breathing just as hard but whispers, "I love you, Luke."

"I love you too, angel. So much." Pulling away from her, I untangle my hand from her hair. "Here, let me get you settled into bed."

"Wait. I'm not completely naked yet."

I try, really try, not to look down. "I really think we should keep those on."

She makes a pouty face, "Party pooper."

"No, not a party pooper, I'm trying to be a good guy here."

"Who says I want Luke the good guy? Maybe I want Luke the bad boy."

I groan, she's killing me. "Don't tempt me."

"Oh, I'm tempting you alright."

"Well, let me at least get you a glass of water and some Motrin first, so maybe we can get a head start on that headache you're likely to feel in the morning."

"Oh, alright." She sighs and it makes me smile. She's cute when she pouts.

I ease her back on her pillows and pull a blanket over the top of her, covering her up, but not before placing some pillows under her leg, elevating it.

"I'll be back," I head to her bathroom and as I go I adjust my raging hard-on that is begging for attention.

"When you come back, I'm going to make it my mission to get you to remove that last annoying piece of clothing." Olivia calls out to me.

I laugh shakily. In the bathroom, I splash water on my face and sit on the toilet for a few moments to try to catch my breath. I put my head in my hands and run my fingers through my hair. I need to try and have some self-control here, but she's not making it easy.

My pajama pants are hanging on the back door, so I grab them and change into them, throwing my clothes into the hamper. Part of me wants to walk out there bare ass naked, but that really wouldn't help matters.

I take a deep breath and walk back into the bedroom. I stop dead in my tracks as I look at the bed and laugh. In the short time I stepped away, she has fallen asleep. Her head is lying back on the pillow, her mouth is wide open and she's snoring. She looks so cute, even if she does sound like a lawn mower.

After turning the light off, I climb into bed and lay as close as I can to my girl without bumping her leg. I wrap my arm around her and she sighs sweetly in her sleep. I fall asleep with a smile on my face and the memory of her laugh tonight resonating in my ears.

15.

WHAT CAN WASH AWAY THIS SHAME?

Olivia

WAKE UP from a dead sleep without opening my eyes, when I feel his fingers making their way up my leg. The tips of his fingers are soft, and they tickle me just a little, while at the same time instilling heat throughout my body as they move up inch by inch. Those fingers tease me over the front of my panties, making my breath catch in my throat and my stomach clench. His fingers become a flat palm as it moves to my tummy, and rubs in a circle.

Those sinful fingers then swirl around my belly button, and I wait in anticipation for them to tease my breasts next. They slide up the center of them and then instead of landing where I anticipated they would go – and silently want them, they proceed down my arms on one side and then up the other. I shiver at his touch, it feels remarkable, but I want them back at my breasts.

As if he hears my internal thoughts, his fingers trail back up my arm and finally touch one breast. Fingers circle around my nipple, and then I feel a slight pinch, before he moves to the other breast, repeating his actions. My breath picks up as his hand makes its way

137

back down to the front of my panties. I feel wetness between my legs in response to his teasing, and I lie still and quiet, eyes closed, excited for the moment when they touch me right where I want them to.

His fingers brush over and circle my clit through my panties for a moment, before sliding down the line of my entrance. I want him to move my panties aside and plunge his fingers into me, bringing me to a hard orgasm. Instead, he keeps up the teasing.

I can't keep still any longer and turn to my side, reaching out so I can touch him too. I begin mimicking his movements, and run my fingers over his chest, down his abs, brush over the front of his boxers and then his thigh as far as I can reach. I can tease just as well as he can.

I lift my head towards his, seeking his lips with my own. I kiss him; pushing my tongue into his mouth, I move my lips against his in earnest, trying to communicate my needs and wants.

I pull away, prepared to tell him with words now how much I want him. I slowly ease open my eyes and look right into Deacon's face.

A slow smile slides across his mouth, his eyes are hard and unforgiving, and his grip on me tightens, "You feel so good, princess."

My eyes fly open, then I sit straight up and scream. I don't think I'll ever be able to stop. I can still feel his hands on my body. Still feel his lips on mine.

"Olivia?" Luke wakes up and the tone of his voice reveals his fear, "Olivia? What's wrong?"

I hear Luke, but I can't stop screaming long enough to respond. Was that just a nightmare? Or was it a memory? Oh God, I don't know. I don't fucking know, please, oh please, let it just be a nightmare. But, how do I know for sure?

I finally stop screaming, and throw the blankets off my lap, inadvertently slapping Luke away in the process. I need to get out of this bed for a minute, I need to move around. In my frantic attempt to fly out of bed, I forget about my stupid leg, and quickly realize my error when I fall over and onto the floor. "Ouch, fuck!"

"Shit!" I hear Luke say and his feet pound on the floor as he runs around to my side of the bed, gathering me into his arms. I hurt my wrist trying to catch my fall, and rubbed my chin on the floor. It burns a little. All I can do is hold onto Luke and cry.

Suddenly, my bedroom door flies open and smashes into the wall. "Olivia? What's going on? Are you okay? Luke? What happened?"

I look over at Pyper through my tears and wonder what she has in her hands. Before I can give it much thought, Luke is trying to lift me off the floor.

"Nightmare." Luke responds to Pyper. He pulls me tighter to him as he stands, sits on the edge of the bed and rocks me back and forth in his arms. "It's okay. You're safe. I'm here. You're okay. I'm here." He repeats over and over again. I clutch at him the best I can, bury my head into his chest and sob uncontrollably. I just can't stop.

"Is she okay?"

I feel Luke's chin lift off the top of my head. He doesn't answer that question probably because clearly, I am not okay. Instead he asks, "A bat, Pyper? Really?"

"Yep, she sleeps right beside me."

Luke keeps rocking me, "She?"

"Damn straight."

"Remind me never to mess with you."

"That would be smart."

I'm sure later, I'll find their words funny, but right now, I wouldn't be able to find the humor in anything.

I feel unclean.

I feel violated.

Polluted.

I interrupt them, "Shower. Luke, I need a shower."

He doesn't even hesitate. He picks me up and starts to carry me to the bathroom, Pyper momentarily stopping him, "Do you need anything? Can I do something?"

"Thank you, but I've got her. Go back to bed and try to get some sleep, if anything changes, I will come and get you. I promise."

"Okay," she says to him and before she leaves, she places her hand in mine and gives it a squeeze.

I am shaking. I keep trying to calm myself, but fear and shame have absorbed into my very bones, and it will take more than wishing it would leave to remove it.

Luke takes me to the bathroom, sits me down on the toilet seat, then walks into the shower to start the water. I am shaking so hard my teeth keep chattering. He grabs a towel off the shelf and wraps it around me while I wait. I look at him out of the corner of my eye, too ashamed to meet his head on. He's concentrating on the circles he's rubbing into my back, brow furrowed, with tension lines around his mouth. I put them there. He's stressed and worried and it's all my fault.

Leaving me for a moment, Luke grabs the trash bags from under the sink and wraps my cast up so they don't get wet. He's gentle, but thorough. I don't think even a drop of water will try to penetrate the barrier he created. After he's finished, he removes my panties without a word.

"Come on, the water should be warm enough now." He eases me off the toilet seat and I limp over to the shower, thankful for the shower seat we purchased.

"You don't have to come in with me, I can manage," I toss over my shoulder.

"Not a chance. I'm not leaving you. Unless... unless you don't want me here."

I stop. I take a deep breath and turn around to face him. I look into his eyes and as I do my own fill with tears. I hate it, but I'm powerless to stop them. His own look is pained, and seeing it makes my chest ache in literal pain as though my heart hurts at the sight.

"I always want you here, Luke. Always. That is never ever a question. Okay?"

He nods his head and reaches out his hand. I take it and tug him toward the shower with me. I can't stand for long though, so I take my seat on the bench. I tilt my head back and let the warm water run over my body. Luke uses the shower head on the opposite side of the shower, letting me sit until I desire to do otherwise, not saying a word; silent, but his presence clearly known.

Images from my nightmare keep surfacing. I think of how he touched me. Where he touched me and worse, how I liked it. How I wanted more. The rational part of me knows that in my mind I thought it was Luke, but doesn't that make it worse? Worse because I didn't know. Why didn't I know that it wasn't him? I must stop these thoughts – this is dumb. I can't control what I dream. Yet, that sneaky, awful feeling that it wasn't just a dream recurs, and the awareness that I am remembering an event from that horrific situation makes me shiver once again in fear, rage, and shame. I reach back to make the water even hotter. As I feel the temperature change, I urge the heat to burn the images from my mind.

I jump as I feel Luke's fingers graze my cheek. "I'm sorry," he whispers, "I didn't mean to startle you."

I take his hand in my own and press my cheek into his palm, anxious to take the comfort he's offering. Without another word, he grabs my shampoo and starts washing my hair with one of my favorites. It smells like coconut and delivers a fresh, unspoiled scent. This is becoming a habit with us, and as his fingers massage my scalp, I find that strangely, I am able to relax and enjoy this moment. Perhaps this should be a nightly ritual. I will return the favor when I can stand without fear of losing my balance, I promise myself.

Luke tips my chin back with his fingers and runs his hands through my hair as the water rinses away the shampoo. When he's finished, I open my eyes and see my loofah hanging from its hook. "Can you hand me my loofah?"

Luke looks at me perplexed, "What the hell is a loofah?"

I can't help but smile at his question, even given the circumstances. "That brown scrub thing hanging on the hook behind you," I point.

When he turns to grab it, I let my eyes run over his beautiful body. Out of nowhere, I feel choked up. I love him. I love him so much. Sometimes, the fact that we're together again hits me right between the eyes. I still can't get used to it in some ways because I thought I might never see him again. I need to push this shit aside for him. For us.

But first, I need to finish showering. The need to ensure that I am clean lingers.

Luke hands me the loofah and I grab some body wash off the shelf and squeeze it onto the scrub, then methodically start scrubbing every inch of my skin.

Deacon's fingers trailing up my leg....

I scrub my leg up the same path his fingers touched in my dream. I go over it again and again, making sure I hit every spot.

"Olivia..."

His palm on my stomach; fingers swirling around my belly button...

I scrub that too. Hard.

Every. Single. Inch.

"Olivia... stop..."

I don't care now if he touched it or not, I want it clean, I need to be clean. I want the thoughts in my mind gone. I need to scrub them out.

He touched and squeezed my breasts... I liked it.

I press the loofah so hard into my skin that I feel pain from rubbing the skin raw. I don't care. My actions are frenzied now. I rub the same spot over and over again. On some level, I know I'm acting insane, but on the other, I don't care. I must do this. It hurts, but I don't care. I deserve it.

"Olivia... please..." I pause momentarily, hearing his voice in the background – and the pain. But another thought slams into my mind, making me forget my hesitation. I liked it when he touched me - it felt good. This should hurt, this should be painful; I deserve it. I want to be clean, I need to be clean.

"Olivia, no."

Suddenly, I'm crying and I can't stop. I'm crying and scrubbing as hard as I can, my fingers digging into the loofah so hard that they too feel raw with my efforts.

Luke's hands are suddenly on my own firmly holding, interrupting, and inevitably stopping my frantic motions. "Stop. Stop, Olivia. OLIVIA STOP IT!"

The sound of his voice startles me enough to look at his face. My thoughts are still trapped inside the dream in my mind and it takes a few moments for Luke to come into focus. I blink my tears away and stare at him. His eyes, oh his eyes are so sad and glassy like he wants to cry. His lips are pursed and he's breathing heavily, and I realize it's from his efforts to get me to stop.

"Olivia, you are here with me," he strokes the side of my face, "You are safe," he catches a tear trailing down my cheek with his thumb, "I love you. Please stop. Please stop this. You are hurting yourself."

I look down at my body; there are a couple of places where I scratched my skin and I'm bleeding a little. Not dripping or anything, but it's bad enough.

"I... I didn't realize," I look at his beautiful face again. It's calming. "I'm sorry. I'm so sorry. I didn't mean... I mean, oh God, I'm sorry." Embarrassment floods through me. What is he thinking? I wouldn't blame him if he wanted out. "I'm a train wreck."

"Please don't apologize to me, you don't have anything to be sorry for," I look from him to the wall at his words, but he grabs my chin and makes me meet his eyes once more, "Olivia, I love you. Nothing, absolutely *nothing* can change that. Do you understand? I'm here and I'm not going anywhere. You are not a train wreck, you are the woman I love, and we will get through this. Together. Do you understand?"

"Yes," I whisper as tears leave tracks down my face at his words. I'm starting to worry that eventually, grooves will appear in my face from all the crying I do on an almost daily basis.

He turns off the water and gets towels for both of us. Two for me, one for my hair and one for my body. He dries off his chest and puts the towel around his waist and then helps me dry off.

I watch his movements in fascination. There is tenderness in his eyes and love in his actions. With Luke, he doesn't just tell me he loves me, he proves it with the things he does. With a flinch I remember how Deacon would tell me he loves me too, but his actions proved the opposite. Affairs, verbal and physical abuse do not mean love. Not in any way, shape, or form.

The way Luke makes sure to put a towel around my shoulders so I don't get chilled, is love. He takes the plastic off my cast without me even asking him to help, that's love. When he's completed that task, he grabs my brush and runs it through my hair – love. I recall his whispered words to me when I woke up screaming and he held me, what he just said to me in the shower, the roses he brings me, the smiles he gives me, the way he touches me, all with love.

"Luke," I whisper.

He pauses in his efforts to untangle my conditioner-less hair, "Hmm?"

"Make love to me."

He places the brush back on the counter and bends at the knees until he's eye level with me, "Angel, I don't think that's a good – "

"Luke, I need to feel your hands on me. I need to feel how much you love me and know that you want me. I need it. Please."

Without a word, he puts an arm at my back and one under my legs, lifts me and brings me to my bed.

16.

SEX NOW, TALK LATER

Luke

I LOOK DOWN at the woman I love as I carry her to bed and see in her eyes the sincerity of her request. I also see love, and need, but behind that - trying but failing to hide-is fear. Remnants of fear left over from her nightmare are still reflected in her eyes. Perhaps I should insist on merely holding her or encouraging her to talk about her nightmare and what happened, but I can't. I can't turn down her request, even though part of me wonders if I should and perhaps, even wants to. I certainly don't know what she dreamed, but it's obvious, given her response, what it entailed. Will this set her back even more? Is making love to her wise after she had a dream like that? On the other hand, I would be crazy to turn her down, she needs me. And hell, I always need her. I'm like a walking hard-on with her, but it's more than that. I truly want to be here for her, to meet her needs, more than just physically- I want to fulfill her emotional, intellectual, and mental needs as well. In truth, I would pretty much give her anything she asks of me, any time, any day. But especially right now.

I place her on the bed like a fine china doll and standing beside her, unwrap her body from the towel that was hiding her from me. When it is revealed to me in all its glory, I run my eyes greedily from the top of her head, to her toes, taking it all in. She's astonishing, and all mine. I want to pinch myself. Instead, I reach out with my fingers and trace the lines of her face. I've thought it all before so many times, but I run through it again, like rediscovering something you thought was lost. I love the crinkles at the corner of her eyes when she smiles. I love the way her nose scrunches when she's thinking or when something grosses her out. Her full lips are a provocative invitation all on their own. I love how her mouth curves at the corners when she's amused at others or herself, and when she smiles. I lean down to place a soft kiss on her forehead and then follow with kisses to her nose, cheeks and then her lips.

I lower myself onto the bed, balancing myself on either side of her with my elbows and start to kiss her, wanting to take my time and be gentle with her. I want her to feel my love in every look, every touch, and every kiss. She clutches me to her and kisses me hard, as tears leak from the corners of her eyes. The way she's holding on to me, the firmness of her mouth, the noises of need she's making, I can sense her desperation, as well as see it. She's feeling wild and out of control.

I pull away from her and shush her, pushing the hair off her face and wiping her tears with my thumbs. "I'm here, angel. I'm here, you're safe. It's okay. Let me love you."

Her grip on me releases just a bit and she takes a deep breath. She doesn't respond to my reassurances, but her actions convey that she heard me. I lean back in, take her lips once more and kiss her. I move my mouth slowly, savoring the taste of her, keeping my passion at bay. I give her just enough in the way my kisses are soft, but purposeful, making sure my actions convey that my desire and lust and need for her rivals her thoughts for me. It's true. I need her as much as she needs me, If not more.

I regretfully leave her lips, but move on to other parts of her that I love. I leave trails of kisses down her neck, loving the moans she releases in response. She leans her head to the side, giving me better access, and I smile against her neck. I move up to her ear and nibble on her lobe, knowing how much she loves it. I kiss across her collar bone and bite down just enough for her to feel it and suck in air, but not enough to hurt her. She groans her pleasure, and I start kissing my way down her chest, keeping my hands at her side for now – just using my mouth.

I kiss my way up the side of her breast and then suck her nipple into my mouth. I release it from my mouth and then swirl my tongue around it, which makes her clutch my hair in her hand and press my head into her, silently asking for more. I bite gently and hear her hiss out a breath in response, and then move to the next, repeating the action. She's squirming under me already and it's going to take everything I have not to plunge into her and ride my raging hormones to completion.

I release her other nipple after one more swirl of my tongue, then kiss down her stomach, "Oh, Luke, that feels so good." I smirk to myself, then lick, bite and suck my way downward, at the same time I reach up with one hand to fondle her breasts. She's not a big talker during sex, so what she does say, I know she means. Plus, she speaks more with actions, not words. Her one good hand is still clutched in my hair, and the other one is alternating between gripping and clawing at the sheet.

I know she wants me to go right to her sweet spot but instead, I take my time kissing down one of her legs. I bend her knee and lick under it and work my way down her calf, then kiss her ankle, the sole of her foot, and each one of her toes. She smiles at me, and I return it, while placing her leg back on the bed and moving to the next one, but this time I start at her toes and make my way to the juncture of her thighs. I gently move her casted and very pink sparkling leg to the side, opening her legs further. I still can't resist telling her to, "Open up for me, angel," and then smiling in anticipation when she does.

I wrap one of my arms around her lower back, using my forearm to tip up her pelvis just a bit. I stare at the wetness before me and lick my lips with anticipation, and then with my other hand, I open her folds and don't waste any more time. I plunge my tongue inside of her, and when she says, "Oh god, yes," it makes me feel like I'm fucking king of the world.

I slide my tongue up and down and twirl it around her clit over and over. She's writhing uncontrollably underneath me, making me tighten my arm at her back. The unintelligible noises she's making, gets me even harder, which should be impossible. I'm so hard I can feel my heart pounding in my dick. I insert two fingers into her, curving them inside, searching for her sweet spot; wanting her to lose control. I can tell she's getting close, so I quit with teasing her clit with my tongue and instead, take it into my mouth and suck on it.

"OH FUCK!" She yells, and it spurns me on, making me suck harder. I fucking love it.

It takes her all of point ten seconds to fall over the cliff she was balancing on and I continue to suck on her, helping her ride it out.

She's gasping for air and her whole body is shaking with her release. She breaks out into goose bumps with her orgasm, and I smile knowing that means it was a good one for her. Hell yes, I'm good, I want to fist pump or do a victory dance.

I look up at her and she meets my eyes as a smile curves her mouth. Her eyes are heavy with relaxation and I know she's feeling spent. "We aren't done yet, angel."

I prove it by kissing back up her body, tongue swirling around her belly button, kissing up the center of her breasts and then I reach her face, and smile down at her. "That was amazing," she whispers while trailing her fingers up and down my back.

"I'm glad. I will try to refrain from bragging," I smirk at her, knowing full well I have a cocky look on my face. She laughs, the sound husky and sexy, making my chest flutter in a feeling I can't quite identify.

"I want to get on top," she tells me.

Hell yes. But wait, I push aside the horny teenager and try to be a caring boyfriend, "Are you sure? Would that be comfortable with your cast?"

She smiles sexily at me, "We can make it work."

I'm sure as hell not going to argue, I asked, she answered. Done. I flip over and lay on my back, then reach over and help her straddle my hips. Her knees are bent on either side of my hips, and her cast is running down the side of my leg. It can't be super comfortable, but she isn't complaining.

"God you're beautiful," and she really is. Her hair is all messy and it looks sexy all tousled about her shoulders. Her eyes are bright with lust and her lips are swollen from my kisses. She rises up on her knees, reaches down and grabs my cock. She rubs it over her clit and throws her head back at the feeling. "It's so sensitive," she murmurs. It takes everything I have not to lose it just at the sight of her, but I control it because the best is yet to come.

She leans back over me, tips of her breasts touching my chest, and kisses me. She plunges her tongue into my mouth and kisses me hard. When she pulls away, we're both gasping for air. She takes a minute and out of nowhere, caresses the tattoo on my upper arm with love in her eyes, and a smile on her lips. Then, in one move, she lifts up and slams herself down on my cock. I come up off the bed with the feeling.

"Shit!" I wasn't expecting that.

"Feel good?" She smiles evilly and then lifts up and slams herself down again.

I can't even form a word, but it isn't needed. She balances herself with one hand against my chest and moves against me over and over. Her wetness is pouring out of her and onto me and she's sliding in and out, in and out with no effort at all. Her head is thrown back again, my hands are clenched at her hips and her full breasts are bouncing up and down with her movements. I can't resist and sit up to take one into my mouth, sucking it hard.

"Yes, yes, yes, yes," she pants with each slam into me.

I'm not going to be able to hold it much longer. I'd like to think I have good self-control, but hell, this is just too much. "Angel, I'm going to come."

I lie back on my back and look up at her. I want my eyes on her when I let go, but first, I want to help her reach climax once more. She's bouncing and working me over so fucking good. I reach my hand between her legs and rub her clit. "Oh god, yes. Just like that. Don't stop." So I don't. I keep rubbing her until I feel her shatter over the top of me and then finally with a grunt, I let go and release all I have into her. I come and come and it feels like I'm never going to get out every last drop.

She collapses onto my sweat covered chest and we try to catch our breath. I run my hands up and down her back over and over again, my fingers leaving trails in her sweaty skin.

She whispers so softly I almost don't hear her, "I love you, Luke. So much."

"I love you too."

Words I promise myself I will never take for granted. I still remember when I never thought I would hear them from her mouth again. I still remember the pain when she left and the absolute defeat I felt when I couldn't find her, and thought I would never see her again. I choose to never forget that time because the memories of pain, even if they are just distant echoes now, help me to appreciate the new memories we are making, that much more. Every minute, every second, with her, matters.

"Thank you," she says.

"Why are you thanking me?"

"For taking care of me tonight," she lifts up her face and gives me a brief kiss on my lips.

"I will take care of you forever," I promise, and she smiles at me and gives me another kiss. She has no idea how much those aren't just words, they're a promise.

"I'm going to go into the bathroom to clean up."

"Okay." Then without another word, I lift her up and carry her inside the bathroom.

"Luke! I can do it!"

I smile at her, "I know you can."

I get her a washcloth and we remove the traces of our lovemaking. We wash our faces and grin at each other as we brush our teeth too. She starts to run a brush through her hair, but I take it from her fingers and finish the job while she closes her eyes, enjoying my help. This... this right here is my happy place. I want this forever.

I bring her back to bed and get her settled, then climb in beside her, pulling her to my chest. I revel in the silence, reliving the last hour, while I run my fingers through her hair. I will never get enough of this woman in my arms. She completes me in a way I never thought possible. She makes me want things I didn't think were in my future and she touches a place inside of me I kept off limits for so long. Now that she's been there, it's like she's left her stamp on my heart, my life, and I never want to let her go. The feeling is my high, she's my drug.

Remembering her nightmare tonight breaks my heart. I would give anything to find Deacon and rip his heart out for what he did. Being able to do so would bring both of us peace of mind. While he's out there, she isn't completely safe. The thought of losing her again... of anything happening to her again... I can't even... I can't even allow myself to go there. It's too horrifying.

I know her answer before I ask, but push ahead anyway. "Do you want to talk about it?"

"Well, okay, you were absolutely amazing, it was just what I needed-"

"No, that's not what I- wait- I was amazing?"

Yeah, I can feel my ego inflating at her words. Hell yes I'm amazing.

She laughs at me, "Definitely amazing."

I grin, then shake my head in order to get myself back on track.

"I'm glad it was amazing, it was for me too, but I meant, do you want to talk about your nightmare from earlier?"

"Oh." She's quiet for a few beats, "No, it was just... it was from-" she sighs. "Honestly, no, I don't really want to talk about it."

"But-"

"Babe, I'm fine. I'm better than fine, thanks to you. I don't want to talk about it right now."

The last thing I want to do is upset her. So I let it go, for now. But I can't help feeling like she's just a time bomb waiting to explode.

"Okay."

She snuggles closer to me and kisses my chest, "I love you."

"I love you too, angel. Go to sleep."

And she does.

17.

SCARS RUN DEEP

Olivia

"EW, IT LOOKS kind of gross," Pyper has a disgusted look on her face, which makes me feel self-conscious.

"It isn't that bad. Plus, it adds mystery."

"That's true."

"I'm just happy to have the dressings all removed. And converting the old cast to a walking one will be much better, though we may need to accessorize it a bit too. I was kind of getting used to the bling. That long leg thing, though, was really starting to itch."

"I bet. I wouldn't be able to stand having it that long either."

I smirk to myself because I think I'm pretty funny, "That's because you can't stand a long term relationship with anything other than your spa and your vibrator."

"Ha. Very funny. And okay, fine, kind of true," she admits.

"Well, I thought it was a good one." I notice her looking at my arm.

"Whatever. We could come up with some great stories about what happened to you."

"Oh! I think a knife fight. Sounds like I'm bad ass."

"You? A knife fight? I don't think so."

I sigh loudly, "You are great for a person's self-esteem, Pyper. I think I'll just keep it covered up for now anyway. That's better than the truth."

"No, that's not true, Livvie. You're survivor. There's no shame in that. You know I'm just teasing you."

"Yes, I know. I just hate having one more memory of my kidnapping."

Pyper rubs my back, "You are the strongest person I know. What's a little scar?"

"Yeah, I guess."

The doctor comes back into the room, "Okay, Olivia, you should be all set. Take it easy with that arm. Just because your stitches and bandage have been removed, doesn't mean the area isn't still sensitive. It can take up to two years for it to fully regain its near former strength and elasticity. And it may never be more than eighty percent of what it was before. You had a nasty injury there."

"Okay, I understand."

"I also prescribed a cream," he hands me a piece of paper, "It's a cream that will help the appearance of your scar disappear a little. Rub it on twice a day as it continues to heal."

"Thanks again."

"You're welcome. I will see you back in a few weeks for a checkup. Before you know it we will be taking your walking leg cast off. As you know, since the bone penetrated the skin, healing is going to take a bit longer on your leg."

"Yes, I can't wait to get it off. It's starting to bother me a lot. It's been itching like crazy at times. Sometimes I fantasized about busting it off myself. Will this one itch too?"

Dr. Osenhoff laughs. "Likely it will. It itches as it heals. Itching is a good sign, even if irritating. And, by the way, you're not the first person who has had some innovative ideas for cast removal. Try your best to leave it be. I know it's hard."

"I'll try. Thank you very much."

"You're welcome, Olivia. It was nice to meet you, Pyper."

"You too, Doc," Pyper quips.

As we make our way out of the doctor's office, hobbling a bit with my updated cast, and happy to be free of my crutches – well mostly anyway - I turn to Pyper, "Thanks again so much for coming with me."

"How many times do I have to tell you to stop thanking me? That's what friends are for."

"Well still, I appreciate it. I don't take it for granted."

"I know you don't. So Luke is still going to be at the club for a while, right?"

"Yeah I think so. Why do you ask?"

"Because your best friend booked you a manicure appointment. I thought maybe you'd like to get your nails done after your final appointment for your arm, so I took the liberty of booking us appointments."

"Aww, you really are the bestest friend ever."

"Don't I know it."

A little while later we pull up to the spa. I'm excited to get my nails done, it has been a long time since I've taken care of myself as far as beauty splurges go. I'm wearing my cute navy blue and white chevron skirt with a white, long sleeved tee, a jean jacket, and silver flats. My outfit is complimented with lots of silver chains and my silver tote. My skirt allows my now walking-casted leg plenty of room, and even though I'm hobbling along, I look cute doing it. I'm so tired of the constant sweats, t-shirts, or pajamas I've been sporting lately. Needing to make accommodations for my leg cast, didn't give me lots of options. I will be happy when I can slip my favorite pair of jeans back on. I confess though; my inner fashion diva has been dying a slow death and she was more than thrilled when I actually got dressed and did my hair and makeup today. I even had Pyper take my picture for an outfit of the day post for my blog. And it feels good. It feels normal.

Pyper walks slowly so I can keep up with her and when we arrive, holds the door open for me. She looks really nice today too. Dressed in a pair of jeans, she's paired it with a gray wrap sweater that ties on the side, gray heeled booties and a large Kate Spade tote bag. She looks amazing, red hair in tousled waves down her back. Once I'm through, she stalks ahead of me to the front desk, "Hi Penelope, how is business today?"

"Oh hello, Ms. Lexington. Everything is going well, we've had a full schedule this morning. Lexi, our massage therapist called in sick, but Kelly was able to come in and pick up her appointments that didn't want to reschedule, so it's all worked out.

"That's great. Good job holding down the fort." Penelope gives Pyper a brilliant smile as if Pyper gave her the best compliment she's ever received. "Penelope, I would love for you to meet my best friend, Olivia. Olivia, this is Penelope, my assistant manager."

I smile at Penelope, "Hi Penelope, it is very nice to meet you. I hope Pyper isn't too much of a slave driver."

"Oh no! Never! Ms. Lexington is a wonderful boss, I'm so lucky to work here. It's very nice to meet you, Olivia." Wow, she's not even smirking like she's joking. This girl is crazy serious.

I give Pyper a look and her lips twitch in response, "Penelope, will you please let Ginger and Sally know that Olivia and I are here for our appointments? Thank you."

"Right away, Ms. Lexington," and then she scurries, yes scurries, off to do Pyper's bidding.

"Holy hell, Pyper. What have you done to that poor girl? Did you go psycho boss on her ass or something?"

"No, not at all. Believe it or not, Olivia, some people are just really serious about their jobs and like working for me." I don't know how she manages to say that with a straight face, because I bust out laughing.

Fortunately, she isn't able to keep a straight face for long either and laughs too, because if she didn't, I'm pretty sure it would have been a sign of the apocalypse. "I have no idea what her deal is. Can you believe she's like that ALL the time? I mean, I'm glad she takes her job seriously, and she really is great, but I've made it a goal of mine to try to get the girl out to have some fun."

"I think some fun and some good sex would do her a world of good," I volunteer my opinion making both of us giggle.

SLAM

"You will fucking do what I say!" Deacon screams at me, shaking a gun in my face and then shooting it at the ceiling.

I gasp, slap my hands over my ears and let out a small scream. Fear grips my stomach and it feels like it just landed in a heap on the floor. I bend at the waist and get myself as small as possible, which isn't easy given my cast, but I don't want him to hurt me. Maybe if I make myself as small and quiet as possible, he'll just go away.

I'm shaking uncontrollably and tears are already streaming down my face in waves. My heart is pounding so hard I'm sure if I were shirtless you'd be able to see it through my skin. I start counting in my head, the repetition soothing me. I hear a high pitch ringing sound in my ears that makes me feel like everything is moving in slow motion.

I'm terrified.

Suddenly, like a car going eighty miles an hour, awareness slams into me.

"Olivia! Olivia!"

I'm aware that there are hands on my upper arms and I'm being shaken. Clarity comes to my mind and I realize Pyper is the one saying my name over and over. Very slowly - because part of me is afraid it isn't her face I'll see - I lift my tear-stained eyes up. Relief so potent it makes my body feel boneless, runs through me. Pyper's eyes are big, round, and full of fear and sadness.

"Pyper?" I whisper.

"It's okay, Olivia. It's okay," she whispers over and over like a prayer.

"What was that sound?" I choke out, my body still pulsing with remnants of fear, even though I know I'm safe. I'm fine. Deacon is not here.

"It was just Penelope. When she was coming around the corner she accidentally slammed into the chair, knocking it over. That's what she gets for being an over achiever and rearranging the lobby furniture." She laughs, but it sounds forced and hesitant.

"A chair?" I shake my head in confusion. I look around and see Penelope standing across the room, staring at me. When my eyes meet hers, she hurriedly looks away and begins to fuss with the furniture, trying to look like she's arranging it and not staring at me out of the corner of her eyes. Fortunately, no one else seems to be here witnessing my meltdown, but that doesn't stop my face from burning red in embarrassment anyway.

Seeing me staring, Pyper turns to see what has my attention and when she sees Penelope, her face hardens, "Penelope!" she snaps, "Get Olivia a bottle of water!"

Without a word, Penelope scurries off to do just that. Pyper somehow has a tissue in her hand like magic and is wiping my tears.

"Are you okay? We can leave. Do you want to go home? I understand if you'd rather go home. I'm so sorr-"

Whenever Pyper doesn't know what to do or say, she starts to talk too much. I love it because I would just sit there in awkward silence not having a clue and looking like an ass. Not Pyper.

"No, I'm okay. Oh god, I'm so sorry... when the chair fell, I thought...." I stop and swallow, not wanting to continue that sentence. But as is the case most times with best friends, Pyper knows that without me even having to say a word.

"I know, you thought mother earth was being invaded. It's okay. I think your theatrics scared them away."

I smile, "That was my plan all along."

"I knew it. It's rule number one in the alien invasion handbook. Create a diversion by screaming and curling up into a ball or by flashing them your boobs while running in zigzags. I see you went with option one."

I chuckle and then she asks, "But seriously, are you okay?"

"I'm fine, just really embarrassed. Can we carry on with our nail appointments?"

"Yes of course, as long as you're sure..."

"I'm sure. It's just what I need. To pretend this never happened."

A look of unease crosses Pyper's face but she wipes it away quickly, "Okay then. Penelope!!"

A LITTLE WHILE later I'm admiring my red manicure painted with *OPI's I'm Not Really a Waitress*, the most perfect red nail polish on the planet. Pyper went with a soft white color called Halo I'm Beautiful that looks perfect on her, but always makes my hands look washed out.

"So, I really want to do something nice for Luke. He's been taking constant care of me and we've pretty much been home bodies. I was thinking maybe I should take him out to dinner or something."

"That's a good idea. I'm sure he would like that. Are you sure he would want to go out?"

"Well, I don't know why he wouldn't?"

"Well because of the crowds and..." she trails off when she sees the look on my face.

"The crowds? What are you talking about?"

She sighs and her lips become a straight line. Just as I'm about to push her into telling me, she gives in to whatever internal battle she's fighting. "He prefers being at home with you because right now, crowded places make him nervous."

It doesn't take a rocket scientist to figure out why that would be, and it irritates me. "Are you kidding me?"

"No, I'm not kidding. He's got a point, Olivia."

"What? How can you say that?"

"Easy. He's right. He can't keep track of everyone in a crowded restaurant. It's easier for someone to hide in, create a diversion, trick you to going to the bathroom or something and taking you..."

"Are you serious? This isn't a Jason Bourne movie, it's my life."

"I damn well know it's your life! And you've already been kidnapped once, for God's sake, what's to stop it from happening again? If Deacon thinks he can get away with it, he's capable of anything and you know it. Why the hell would you want to put yourself in a position like that?"

"Because I will be damned if I let him control my life!"

"Well too bad! There is a difference between letting him control your life and just being plain stupid!" We are yelling now and I'm thankful it's just the two of us sitting here, although the irony isn't lost on me that we are sitting in the Zen garden being anything but... well, Zen.

I take a deep breath and count to ten because rationally, I know she isn't calling me stupid, I know she just cares and is concerned. "I'm not being stupid, Pyper. I'm taking back control."

We stare at each other for a few minutes and don't say a word. Both of us lost in our own opinions. Finally, she breaks first, "Look, if you want the truth, the truth is this. If you want to do something nice for Luke, cooking him a meal at home would go over better with him than going out somewhere." I start to interrupt and she holds up a hand stopping me, "I'm not saying he never wants you to go out. I'm just saying if thanking him and making it a night FOR him is what you're after, then staying in would be the way to go. Otherwise, he will be a nervous wreck, and both of you will be more annoyed with one another at the end of the night instead of enjoying each other's company."

I sigh, "You're right. I know you're right. I want the evening to be about him, not me. But, a home cooked meal? Um, hello? Have you met me? I suck at cooking. Must I remind you of the boiled egg incident?"

"Oh please, that wasn't that big of a deal."

"Really? Let me refresh your memory. I couldn't follow simple instructions to let the water boil, take it off the heat and then put in the eggs and cover the pan. Instead, I put them down in the pan while the water was boiling hot on the stove. Eggs cracked everywhere, leaving trails of white goo, and I splashed burning hot water all over my arms when I dropped them in! Burns, Pyper. Actual burns. On my arms. I can't possibly cook him a meal from scratch at home!"

"Actually, you're better than you thought. You just recited the proper way to boil eggs all on your own. Apparently, following instructions is just where you screw up."

"Ha. Very funny. Knowing and doing are two very different things." I have to admit though, my mind has already wandered to the thought of me slaving away cooking a meal for Luke and him coming home to a meal I prepared for him. I would be all cute in an apron and he would come up and kiss me on the cheek and ask, "What's for dinner?" I would be like a domestic goddess!

"Hmmm, then again, maybe cooking him dinner at home would be a good idea."

18.

RAGE REIGNITED

Luke

"I DON'T GIVE a shit, Chuck. You've told me you understand, but you keep screwing up. And it's happening on my dime, so I'm going to keep repeating myself until it's stamped into your brain, because nothing else seems to be doing the trick." I sigh to myself while I listen to him give me yet another excuse. I interrupt him before he gets far, "I'm tired of excuses. So either do what I say, or tell me you can't step up to the plate. Because, if you can't, then I'll send someone else to do YOUR job - that's all there is to it." I hang up the phone. I don't have time for his incompetence.

I have worked hard to not become known as being a prick for a boss. I have always found the balance between being easy going and rewarding staff that performs, but at the same time, not settling for less than my expectations of them. But, as I'm sure the case is in every company, there are people that even after giving them chance, after chance, still just don't get it. I run my business like a well-oiled machine. I'm certainly not a novice, so I don't do well with people questioning my directives. Feedback is fine. Improvement great. But some things are not up for discussion.

I'm sure the fact that I don't want to be here doesn't help my tolerance level of stupidity in the slightest. All I can think about is that I've left Olivia alone. Sure, she said she will be fine and she has articles to write and stuff to do for her blog, but I hate being away from her. It's become an irrational fear that is at times, uncontrollable. I often times feel physically sick being away from her. My body gets warm, my stomach in knots, and I feel a deep ache in my bones at the distance between us. It's so strange. I'm sure it's all in my head, but dammit, she's still in danger.

Pushing out another sigh, I tell myself that I'm going to push all these thoughts from my mind and work hard to concentrate on nothing but Zero Gravity for the next few hours. I'm thrilled that our intake continues to exceed plan. This longstanding trend – one we've seen since first opening our doors – makes me quite happy. Liquor sales are through the roof, the door charge is still competitive with other clubs in the area, and it has allowed us to pay good money for great entertainment. Which reminds me; I have a few new bands that are interested in playing here. I need to set up times to interview them, and if they pass the screening, try them out on open mic night; to see how they handle themselves and if they would be a good fit. I pick up the phone and start making some calls, filling the calendar quickly.

Aside from that, I have alcohol to order and a few resumes to review. Zero Gravity has four bars, one upstairs, three downstairs. We employ waitresses that also walk around taking orders. Since opening, we've only utilized two of the three bars on the lower level, but now that we are consistently exceeding our sales goals, the extra cost of an additional bar and the staff needed to run it will be paid for easily. Plus, an additional bar will keep traffic through the club decongested, since it will minimize the likelihood of crowding at any one bar. Picking up the resumes, I scan them, searching for one in particular. I promised an old friend that if a bartender position became available, I would give him a call. One of my best friends from college has had a rough time of it lately, and could use a change of pace. I pick up the phone, ready to call him about the position, but before I can start dialing, my cell phone rings.

Smiling to myself, I hastily look through the scattered papers on my desk trying to find where it is hiding. When I find it under a few files, I look at it expectantly, hoping to see the cute picture of Olivia making a kiss face on my screen, but instead it says "Blocked".

I slide my finger across the bottom and answer, "Hello, this is Luke."

"I'm going to fucking kill you."

I freeze and the breath leaves my body; my heart one second so normal, starts pounding in my chest like I've run ten miles – at a sprint. I may have only talked to him on the phone one time, when he was yelling at Olivia and I took the phone from her, but I would recognize his voice anywhere.

"Deacon? How did you get this number?"

He laughs, "You should really think about telling people not to share your personal information. With a little charm and alcohol, some people really are willing to divulge anything."

My mind races trying to guess who would have done such a thing, but really, it could be anyone. All of my employees have my number. It wouldn't really be that hard.

"What the fuck do you want, Deacon?"

"You know what I want. It's only a matter of time before I have her back with me again."

"Listen to me clearly, you son of a bitch. You will never get near her again. I won't allow it. You stay the fuck away from her. Do you understand me?"

"*You* listen to *me*. I'm watching. I'm *always* watching. And I will take what I want, when I want. I just haven't pushed her yet. I'm giving her time to recover from her fall. Did she tell you about that?"

"About how you made her fall over a railing, you bastard?"

"Did she tell you what she was doing before that? How she was kissing me? Had her hands on me? Where she touched me?" I hear him chuckle to himself, "Mmmm, she tasted so good. I can't wait to taste her again."

My heart feels like it trips over itself at the thought. Blood races to my face and saliva and bile fill my mouth as if I'm going to be sick. I swallow it back and take a deep breath. Through gritted teeth, I spit out each word, "You. Aren't. Going. To. Fucking. Touch. Her."

He laughs again, the sound making me want to punch something, "Oh I've already touched her. And I'm going to do it again."

"Over my dead body."

"That could be arranged. If you know what's best for you, you will back off. The right moment will come, and when it does, I will take care of you and get my princess back once again. She wants me, I know it. I still remember the way she kissed me that last day. I know she's forgiven my mistakes and if she hasn't, I'll make her."

I'm breathing heavy and I want to yell into the phone and tell him what a complete lunatic he is, but somehow a rational part of my brain knows that you can't talk sense to a mad man. "You will never lay another fucking finger on her again."

"Oh, I laid more than a finger on her, and she loved every second of it. She fucking begged for it. For me. And I can't wait to hear her scream again."

I see red. Nothing but red. I know this asshole likely forced himself on my girl, and here he is, acting like she wanted it. I can feel the edges of my sanity wavering - my vision is blurry and spotted with rage, and I would give anything to be able to wrap my hands around his neck. Anything. "There are so many people searching for you. It's only a matter of time before you're found. When you are, I will make sure that you pay for what you did to MY girl. Do you hear me ASSHOLE? I said MY GIRL!"

"SHE'S NOT YOUR FUCKING GIRL AND SHE NEVER WILL BE! SHE IS MY WIFE!" His yell is so loud the ear piece of my cellphone literally vibrates from the sound. I can't help but smirk - I can hear he's breathing heavy on the other end of the phone and I know my words have affected him. Luke-one, dickhead-zero.

I can't help but rub it in a little more, "You couldn't be more wrong. I had her first douchebag, and I will sure as hell have her last."

Somehow he's managed to calm himself, because his next words are spoken in a tone so calm and steady; I never would have known he had just screamed at me seconds before. "We'll see about that. I'm watching, and I'm waiting. You remember that."

I hear a click, indicating he's hung up the phone. I put my phone down on my desk, and put my head in my hands. This is a nightmare I just want to end already. The adrenaline high from talking to him makes my body shake, and it's a few minutes before I'm able to pick up the phone. When I do, it's to speak one sentence, "Max, this is Luke, get over to the club now."

I hang up without giving him a chance to respond. If he's smart, he won't waste any time getting his ass over here.

While I wait for him to arrive, I am thankful, not for the first time, that I have a mini bar in my office. I pour myself a glass of scotch and knock it back, reveling in the smooth taste. I pour a second glass immediately and take it back to my desk, intending to drink this one slower.

Looking at the papers on my desk, everything fades in front of me and my mind flashes to the way Olivia looked in the hospital when we were reunited. She was so bruised and hurt - desperate to shield the people she loves from the ramifications of her kidnapping. The worst moments still are when she looks off and becomes trapped in the memories that hold her hostage. She tries to hide it, but I can tell. She loses focus on everything around her, and her eyes become glassy while she gets a far-off look on her face. After the second time it happened, I started having dreams at night occasionally about murdering the son of a bitch responsible for making her look that way.

A knock at the office door startles me out of my unpleasant thoughts, "Come in."

"I'm sorry to bother you, sir," Brian, one of my newer staff members, stands at the door with an apologetic look on his face. Brian is a nice guy that has done a good job taking Kevin's place when I sent Kevin to help get a new club off the ground. "There is a Max Helms here to see you?"

"That's fine, I'm expecting him. Send him in, thanks."

Max hurries in with a flustered look before Brian can even say a word. "I got here as fast as I could, what is going on?"

Brian sighs and loiters near the door, unsure of what to do, "It's fine, Brian, thank you." He nods and leaves the room, closing the door behind him.

Before speaking, I take another sip of my scotch while staring at Max. He's an average looking guy with brown hair and glasses. He's got freckles on his nose, dimples in his cheeks and he's skinny as a rail. If you passed him on the street, you likely wouldn't give him a second look, and in his profession, I think he counts on that.

He looks nervous and I'm glad. He's a smart guy and he knows I'm unhappy. I pay him well, and he should be worried about not meeting my expectations. Because he's not. Although, I'm not so absurd that I don't realize it isn't entirely his fault.

"I just received a phone call from Deacon." I pause, letting that sink in before continuing. "He basically threatened my life and told me he is waiting for the right time to take Olivia again."

Max's eyes widen, "Well, of course you need to call the police about this."

"Yes, I know, and I wanted you to be here when I do that, since I want full disclosure. I want them to know you and your agency are working on finding him too."

"They may not see too kindly to that."

"I really don't give a shit. Olivia is my priority, so you all can compare dicks another time."

"I didn't mean..."

"I know what you meant, Max. Look, I hired you because I know you're good. If you weren't, we wouldn't be having this conversation right now." I take another sip of my scotch, "Now then, before I call them, I want a status report right now. Please," I throw in as an afterthought.

He starts shuffling through his files before grabbing a piece of paper and sitting back in his chair, meeting my eyes steadily. "The agency performed a complete background check on Deacon Brooks and we have a complete list of all his previous employers, friends, relatives, schools he's attended, even ones he applied to and didn't get into. I know he donated blood when he was sixteen, and that he had tubes put into his ears at the age of three. I know he received a ticket at twenty-two for speeding and that he appeared in court a year after that for expired license plate tags. I know everyone he dated and pretty much anyone he ever even looked at funny."

"So it sounds like you have a ton of useless information that isn't going to do shit for us."

"That's not necessarily true, sir," I can't help but smirk at the title. "I've spoken to pretty much everyone he's ever met in his life. Family that would talk with me, old neighbors, even old college roommates and pals."

"And?" I'm impatient. I don't have time for him to sit here and try to amaze me with his presentation and supposed thoroughness. "What has any of this information gotten you?"

"Apparently, Deacon was in therapy from the age of twelve to eighteen, at which time he could no longer be forced to attend sessions any longer and he quit going.

"Therapy for what?"

"Well as is the law, his psychiatrist wouldn't reveal information due to patient confidentiality, but from the police reports we were able to obtain, combined with talking to neighbors and friends, it appears it started with vandalism. He even did a stint in juvie for shoplifting."

"How do you go from shoplifting to kidnapping and sexual assault?"

"Well that's just the thing. Everyone we talked to said the same thing about the guy. He was egotistical and bullied fellow classmates. He was unemotional, to the point of being callous at times. His temper is legendary. Several accounts of him flying off the handle, whether it had been at his parents with neighbors hearing arguing and him storming out of the house, to stories his buddies told about bar fights and how he would antagonize people to the point of purposefully making them angry just to start something."

"But I just don't see how Olivia would fall for someone like that. It doesn't make any sense."

"Well it does if we are dealing with what I think we are."

"And what's that?"

"A psychopath."

I stare at Max trying to digest what he's just said. "Well we all know he's psycho. I mean, why else would he kidnap a woman?"

"No, I mean more than just the term you use to call someone crazy. I'm no psychiatrist, but I would bet money he's been diagnosed as someone to have psychopathic tendencies."

"Well, what exactly is a psychopath?"

"A psychopath is callous, impersonal, shows a lack of guilt, and is promiscuous, yes. But they're also impulsive, extremely charming, irresponsible, possessive, deny responsibility and have the special ability to manipulate others. He has all the classic symptoms."

"What does that mean for Olivia?"

"Honestly... it doesn't mean anything good."

I stare into Max's eyes for a minute, seeing his sincerity and with a nod of my head, pick up the phone to call the police.

19

WINE SAMPLES ARE THE DEVIL

Olivia

*L*EAVING THE BOUTIQUE with a special purchase wrapped in tissue, one that I know Luke will love makes me excited for the dinner I'm preparing this evening. I found the perfect black, sheer babydoll nightie that should make his jaw drop. I can't believe I'm going to attempt to cook dinner while wearing it. I stopped at another store and got a really cute apron to put over the top of it, in case I happen to splash or spill anything while cooking. He definitely won't be expecting me in that getup, that's for sure. Just thinking about it makes me smile.

Poor Pyper. I hope things are okay at the spa. She looked really concerned when she received the call that there had been an accident with a client. She made me promise to stay home and wait for her before running errands. And I did... for all of a half hour... but when she called and said it was still going to be a while yet, I got irritated, thought 'screw this' and left. With Luke working too, it gives me the perfect opportunity to escape – if only briefly - and be freed from their endless watching and waiting over me. I know Pyper and Luke are just trying to take care of me, but sometimes it feels like I can't breathe. Besides, I don't plan to be gone long. Just need to pick up a few things.

Finishing my self-talk, and reassuring myself that I deserve to be out on my own, I finally limp my way over to my car and get in. It feels good to drive again, even if it is a little awkward with my leg. Fortunately, the walking cast is not on my driving leg, so I can get around okay, and I even brought my crutches and threw them in the trunk in case I need a bit of extra support, but so far I am managing just fine without them. I adapted quickly to this new cast - I may not be a pro, but I am quite good. Pulling forward out of my parking space, a man in a dark SUV comes flying up the aisle, making me slam on my brakes. Fortunately, he slams his at the same time and I'm looking into his window, ready to scream at him through my windshield when his wave of apology makes me bite my tongue. He smiles and continues on his way and then so do I. Near disaster avoided.

I take a deep breath. I am not going to let anything ruin my good mood. This is going to be a great night! I may not have a clue about cooking, but I pored over recipes with Pyper that I printed off of the internet today, and I think I have it down. It can't be that hard and besides, what's the worst that can happen? If it sucks, we will order pizza, no big deal.

Next on my short list of errands is the specialty grocery store. I'm whistling a happy tune when I pull in and find a parking spot right in the front, like it was waiting for me. As I walk to the store entrance, I see the same SUV that almost ran into me drive down the front of the store. I stand there, waiting for him to drive by so I can cross the road and head into the store, but he stops and waves me across. My stomach drops and I can't help but feel uneasy, but I'm sure I am overreacting.

I brush it off and head into the gourmet grocery store in order to get a few items we don't have at home. Since we rarely cook, I find it fascinating that we manage to maintain a fairly well-stocked pantry and spice rack, though I sure as hell don't know how. I should ask Pyper about that. I can't help but stand by the carts for a minute and take in the rows upon rows of shelves. The food volume and selection could be overwhelming for a novice like me. Okay, I got this. Since I've moved here, this hasn't been a place I've exactly frequented, but I have been to plenty of grocery stores. Just because I don't have this memorized front to back like I did the old one in Boston, doesn't mean I should be intimidated. I am a grown ass woman, I can put a meal on the table. I'm going to all out roar at my womanly awesomeness when this is over. It's true, Pyper and I always order take out, or we heat up food from her mom, who has a tendency to keep us well-fed, now that I think about it. Anyway, there is always something around. Nevertheless, I can do this.

My list is simple, and hopefully cooking all of this will be too. I'm choosing to keep a positive attitude about it. This is going to work out and it will taste amazing. I nod my head, emphasizing my silent declaration and, having completed my pep talk, begin pushing my cart up and down the aisle.

I'm comparing two tomatoes for a salad when I notice a woman is managing a display consisting of samples of mini cheeses, crackers, and various types of wine for tasting at the end of the aisle. Hmm, what great timing! I don't mind if I do. The wine may be a nice complement to the dinner I'm preparing. Her back is turned and she's talking to a woman asking questions, so I grab a little plate and look around before taking three cups of wine. I should be ashamed, but I'm not – I mean how can I know which I may prefer? And besides, I didn't eat lunch, so I'm starving.

I also sample some of the cheese and crackers without even really tasting them. I'm like a whale with a fish, just swallow, no lingering over it. I down all three glasses of wine. It leaves a pleasant aftertaste on my tongue, but, I'm not really sure which was which. Did I like one better? It's as though I really didn't taste it, those damn glasses are so small. I look back toward the wine table and see that while I was swallowing my bounty, the sweet lady has replaced the glasses I took. I look left and right and make sure no one is looking, and I do another smooth walk by with my cart, acting like I'm very serious about getting to the lettuce across the way. I swipe a couple more glasses from her table while she is bent over throwing something away. My timing rocks.

I taste the wine, slower this time and realize I really do like it, both of them - and what a coincidence, I really do need some lettuce too! I grab a head of lettuce after looking it over, pretending that I can tell the difference and can choose the best one, place it in a plastic bag and drop it into my cart.

This time, I walk straight towards the woman with the tasty wine.

"Hello. Would you like to try a sample of Angel Kiss, a new white wine that just came on the market?"

"Sure, that would be great. I've never EVER tried this wine before. Especially not in a grocery store like this one." I snort. Oops! Shut up Olivia! What am I doing? I'm such a damn light weight. I already feel the effects of the few samples I've had. How pathetic.

The woman gives me a strange look, but it quickly disappears and she's back in selling mode, "Great! This is a great wine. It really complements chicken, turkey or fish very well."

"Oh," I pout, "But that isn't what I'm making for dinner."

"Oh, well that's okay. You don't have to eat those items with it, they just give you suggestions if you'd like."

"Oh okay," the best grocery store lady ever is now filling up my cup and I may have accidentally bumped her arm a bit, so she pours a little bit more than she meant to. "Oops, I am so sorry. I'm clumsy."

"That's okay," she smiles tightly and hands me the glass. I gulp it down in four big gulps and then smack my lips in enjoyment. Wow, that tastes better each time. When I look back at the wine giving goddess to tell her I will take two bottles, she's looking at me with a disgusted look on her face. "What's your damn problem?" I think to myself.

"Umm, nothing. I just see that you enjoyed that sample."

Oh shit, I must have said that out loud! I dab at the corner of my mouth with my finger trying to look like I'm daintily wiping wetness from the corner. Of course this would work better if I had a napkin. Whatever. "I would like two bottles of Angel Kiss, please."

"Okay, sure." She smiles tightly and turns to grab two bottles off the shelf behind her. While she does that, I swipe another glass full.

She stops and stares at me sipping when she turns around, but I just give her a big grin and place the bottles in my cart. "Thank you so much kind, wine tasting woman. May you have a wonderful afternoon and sell many more bottles of your kisses from angels." I think I even bow a little too. Then turn my cart around and head down an aisle to get away from her.

I find a few items on my list and throw them into my basket, but all I can think about is how good that wine tastes. I'm contemplating opening the bottle when I turn down the next aisle in search of bread crumbs and I almost smash my cart into another.

I look up with a startled, "Oh! I'm so sorr-"

The man I ran into is the man I saw in the parking lot at the boutique, who is the same man from the parking lot outside. Fear paralyzes me, and I can't speak or move my cart out of the way. I just stare at him. He's wearing a trench coat and has a suit on underneath, his tie loosened at the neck. His hair is dark, he's wearing glasses and he has freckles on his face. "I'm so sorry, I didn't mean to run into you."

My mouth feels dry and my body feels like it is shaking on the inside. I manage to give him a brief nod, then I disengage my cart from his and turn down a different aisle, walking as quickly as my walking cast will enable me to go. I keep looking over my shoulder, but I don't see him. I am in an aisle that has other people and it makes me feel a little bit better.

I take deep breaths and as I get to the end of the aisle, I see the man walk by again, but this time he's smiling at something and I turn my head to see where he's looking. There is a woman, blonde, dressed in a teal business suit headed his way. She's smiling back at him and her arms are full of items she's plucked off the shelf. She dumps them into his cart and gives him a kiss on the cheek.

I blindly reach for one of the bottles of wine in my cart and twist the damn cap off – thank goodness it's the twistable kind – and take some chugs as tears fill my eyes.

I'm so angry at myself. I can't even go to the damn grocery store without projecting my fears from kidnapping onto everything. I take a gulp and wipe my mouth with the back of my hand. I'm fine. I'm safe. Yes, Deacon's out there. No, I have no idea where he is. Fact is, he could walk up to me right now and take me. No doubt I would pee my pants right here, but I still adamantly refuse to live my life like a hermit because of something that might happen. If anything, I learned that I should live each day because you never know when it could seriously take a turn you aren't expecting.

Does that mean I'm over what happened? I laugh, literally laugh right out loud in the middle of the damn store just thinking that. No, I'm seriously fucked up. I can't sleep without having nightmares, I can't even function when something startles me, but whatever. I bury it and keep moving because this will not define me. I refuse to let it.

I take another chug of wine and limp my way to the checkout line after making sure all the items that were on my list are now within my cart. With any luck, they won't notice that there is some wine missing. But hey, I'm legal. I giggle to myself as I twist the cap back on.

Sure enough, I'm not so lucky. When the cashier gets to my bottle of Angel Kiss, he looks at the bottle, then at me, then back again. I just give him a huge grin and subtly push my boobs together, hoping my cleavage distracts him from calling the police or something.

Once outside, I'm beginning to wonder if driving home is a good idea. If it weren't for the cart I'm pushing, helping me keep my balance, I'm not sure I would be standing upright. I stand at my trunk for a minute and laugh when I almost fall over because I'm leaning against my cart and it starts rolling. I put the groceries in my trunk and then grab my phone out of my pocket. I hesitate before starting to dial Pyper because she's going to be furious with me. I look to the side, contemplating how I'm going to tell her I took off, when another store in the same strip mall catches my eye.

An Army Surplus store. The wheels start turning. Sure, that guy ended up not being a threat, but what if he had been? What if Deacon had been here and had approached me in the store? Before I can give it another thought, I'm making my way across the parking lot and into the surplus store. I look at the signs hanging from the ceiling and walk toward the area I'm looking for.

On my way to the desired department, I stop and look at a wall of hats and masks. They are the kind of masks that completely cover your face except for your eyes. I try on a few just for good measure and check myself out in the mirror. My eyes look huge and my head looks skinny. I never noticed its odd shape before. My mom must have always laid me on my back or something, because my head looks flat back there. I need to ask her about that someday.

I snort in amusement and accidentally knock down a hook holding a whole bunch of hats. They fall to the floor and I try to bend over the pick them up, but I start to lose my balance and almost, nearly fall to the floor. Awesome.

I upright myself, square my shoulders, look around, see that no one even noticed and decide to casually walk away. I head to the back of the store and get in line. There are several other people waiting, so it's a few minutes before my turn. A man behind the counter dressed completely in camouflage gear who has a pot belly so large the buttons of his shirt are ready to pop stares at me as I approach, "Hi little darlin'. What can I help you with?"

"Hi," I glance at the name patch on his shirt, "Pete. I am interested in seeing your canisters of pepper spray and I'd also like to look at and find out more about your taser guns."

"Sure thing, sugar. You expectin' some trouble or somethin'?"

"Not exactly. I just want to protect myself in case the need should ever arise."

He stares at me a moment and then pulls out a pink canister of pepper spray. "Pink?"

"Yeah well, yer a girl, ain't ya?"

I decide to let that slide, and retaliate instead with a sarcastic comment, "Good observation Obi Wan Kenobi."

He smirks and hands me the canister. "You been drinkin' at all?"

I snort, "Nope," I tell him, popping the 'p'.

He looks like he's not sure if he believes me. "Mmkay... it's just somethin' we're supposed to ask. Now, this here is really easy to use. You see where the top of this twists to the side, aligning the pump up along the arrows? If you need to use it or are walking in a parking lot that's dark you can twist it to have it ready. A lot of ladies like this here wrist strap because you can wrap it around your wrist like this," he demonstrates on me, "and if you let go of it, you don't have to search fer it on the ground."

I turn the nozzle like he showed me and press down on the pump to see if it's hard or easy to push. Just as Pete reaches his hand out and says, "No don't-" he spray is flying. I never would have thought Pete could move so fast. He ducks like I'm holding an AK47 and was ready to use it. The spray flies inches from his head and slams into some poor dude standing behind him. The man turns toward me, and that's when it hits his eyes because somehow miraculously the spray is STILL coming out of the can. I guess my finger has become glued to it, and even though I want to let go of it, I can't.

"AAAHHHH! Put it down, woman!" Pete screams at me.

I'm too transfixed on the horror playing out before my eyes. Dude is screaming from the spray hitting his eyes which sure, that's expected. What isn't expected is that everyone else in the vicinity starts coughing. I had no idea that pepper spray was so intense, it can take out people in the surrounding area too. This shit is awesome.

Pete finally pops his head up and peeks over the counter at me. I'm sure later when he looks back he will realize how hilarious this has been. He finally manages to pry the canister from my zombie like fingers and is breathing heavy while scowling at me.

"Oopsie. Sooo sorry about that." I think he wants to kill me. I'm completely unfazed, however. "Can I see a taser now?" Pete actually laughs at me. He laughs! I can't believe this shit. So of course, now I'm pissed off. "I want to see a taser now, please." Pete just stares at me and I ask, "Do you want to make a sale or not? I won't touch it this time. No worries."

"Lady, we already had to escort a customer out of here. I don't know about that."

"It was an accident! I'm really sorry! He'll be fine after he washes out his eyeballs." I try not to laugh at myself. I really do.

Sensing my seriousness – and perhaps aware that failure to fulfill my request could have significant bad results; he actually gets out the taser and shows me how it works. I notice that people are still wiping their eyes and I think there's a line at the bathroom. I've even gathered a bit of an audience as people gather to try and figure out the source of all the excitement. Perhaps they would like my autograph. But, I instead decide to ignore them. Someone comes up and asks Pete a question and he places the taser on the counter to grab something for them. I know I said I wouldn't touch it, but really, it's laying right there, begging me to see how it fits in my hand. And surely lightning doesn't strike twice in the same place, right?

So, I pick up the irresistible taser from the counter, and without any warning, the thing immediately releases. I guess I was gripping it too hard and my finger pressed the button, I don't know. I must have very good target capability, because some poor soul gets it in the ass and goes crashing to the floor, knocking over a display of some kind of canned bottle on his way. Oops. I can't help but laugh my ass off, because that fall was fucking hilarious.

The staff obviously doesn't think it's very funny though and before I know it, I'm on the phone with Pyper after all, "Umm, hi... so... you're going to be mad at me, but remember how I said I would wait for you? Yeah well, I didn't.... and there has been a little umm incident...."

20

NOT MY MOTHER'S MEATLOAF

Luke

I'M ANXIOUS TO get out of here and get home. I'm supposed to meet Olivia at the condo tonight. She said she has a surprise for me. The thought puts a smile on my face. I can't imagine what she has in store, but I have no doubt I will enjoy whatever it is.

I'm working on my own surprise for her. It's been hard to be secretive about it with all the time we've been spending together, so I've taken advantage of our time apart today.

I've decided not to tell Olivia about my phone call from Deacon. What would be the benefit? She has enough on her plate as it is. She's still dealing with a variety of emotions. She thinks I don't know it, but I can tell and I see the effect they have on her at times. I don't want to add this to her concerns as well. Additionally, she has no idea I've hired a private investigator and I want to keep it that way, if possible. Fact is, if Max finds Deacon before the police do, there's no telling how I will handle it. I've asked myself that question many times and my rage always gets in the way. I want him found soon, because as I continue to watch Olivia struggle, my worry over my reaction when the inevitable happens, concerns me.

I sigh as I count off the third and final reason. She's spent the day planning whatever this surprise is. I don't want to ruin her good mood. I may have selfish motives for that, but I'm not about to feel guilty for them. Wanting a fun night with my girl is not something I'm going to apologize for.

After making a few more phone calls and finishing a staff meeting with my employees, I'm ready to head out. Just as I grab my keys, the phone on my desk rings. I contemplate not answering for a moment, but then give in with a sigh and glance at my watch, seeing I still have a little time. "This is Luke."

"Luke, it's Pyper again."

As luck would have it, Pyper just happened to call earlier while Max was in my office, letting me know of her need to leave Olivia and that she was afraid Olivia may go out, despite the fact she asked her to wait. I asked him to keep an eye on the condo, and if Olivia decided to leave as we predicted she would, to please follow her and keep an eye on her to make sure she stayed safe.

"Hey, Pyper, what's up?"

I smile as Pyper quickly gets to the reason for her call. Apparently, Olivia, despite having promised not to, left the house by herself when Pyper had to tend to an emergency at the spa and got herself in a little bit of trouble today. Pyper says she should have known this could happen. Olivia's been acting like a caged, wild bird at times, so it doesn't fully surprise us that she would try something like this. Thank goodness for Pyper. I'm thankful she's so willing to keep me abreast of Olivia's actions. Pyper gets that while I understand Olivia's need for normalcy, it doesn't change the fact that it isn't safe – not until that asshole is dead or caught and behind bars.

No sooner do I hang up the phone with Pyper, it rings again and Max is on the other end to give me an earful as well. I understand that Max was spotted by Olivia and he could tell she got nervous with him. Fortunately, Max placed a call to his colleague, whom happened to be close by and she was able to show up and help him cover up his error, putting Olivia at ease. Of course, she somehow still managed to find trouble.

It makes me laugh. Only my girl would chug wine at a grocery store and wander into an Army surplus store and pepper spray and tase people. I bet her buzz from the wine wore off in no time after that. Envisioning the potential scene, I laugh out loud again. I can't wait to see her, and the thought makes me drive just a little bit faster to her place once I get in my car.

I don't know what I expect when I arrive at the condo, but it sure as hell isn't the sight I see before me. Upon arrival, I notice that Olivia has the table set for a candlelight dinner. It makes me glad I brought the pink roses I have in my hand. I start to walk in and make my presence known, but getting a look at what is transpiring in the kitchen, I find myself frozen in place. Fortunately, Olivia hasn't heard me yet, so I'm able to stand there and stare. And drool. I know my mouth has dropped open and for the life of me, I can't figure out how to close it.

She's wearing some kind of black, see-through, lace thing with the sexiest, and smallest, black thong I've ever seen underneath. Over the top of it, it appears she has an apron tied around her waist. I can see the white bow from where she's tied it at her back. She's bent over the oven and I can't seem to take my eyes off her gorgeous ass that is on full display. Wow. She looks like every man's wet dream.

I pull my eyes away from that glorious sight, which believe me isn't easy, and wipe my mouth, just in case. I collect myself, and take in the rest of the kitchen, hoping it will stop the rising that is occurring below my belt. I shake my head to help me concentrate and focus once again on the kitchen; it is in pure disarray. I have no idea what she's making, but she has ingredients all over the counter tops. The refrigerator is wide open and the drawers are open inside of it. It looks like she must have spilled something on the floor because she has a broom leaning against the counter, and the sink is overflowing with dishes needing to be placed in the dishwasher.

I smile. Huge. I can't believe she's doing this. I know her and usually a ready-made microwave meal or an easy pasta dish comprises her idea of cooking. My girl doesn't cook. But she's trying. For me. I feel that familiar ache in my chest and I absently rub at it. My throat closes up and my eyes burn. I love her. God, I love her so much. Without another thought, I walk into the kitchen. I need to take her in my arms right now. I'm so overcome with emotion that I clear my throat trying to push back some of my feelings. It makes her whirl around and face me at first in surprise, but then an automatic smile graces her lips. God, she's gorgeous. It takes my breath away. Her hair is pulled out of her face, but a few tendrils have escaped and are brushing her cheeks, making me jealous that they're touching her and I'm not.

Her cheeks are flushed from the heat of the oven and she has some flour on her nose and cheek. I decide right then not to tell her because it's too adorable. She's dolled herself up with makeup, even though she doesn't need it, and she looks absolutely mouthwatering.

"Babe! You're a little early," she says breathlessly.

I don't even reply, I just put my arms around her and kiss her. I needed my lips on her the moment I walked through that door. I hold her close to my body and kiss her hard and passionately. I place my hands on either side of her cheeks and tilt her head for me and claim her lips. She emits a small groan and returns my kiss just as greedily.

When I pull away, placing a small kiss on her nose, careful not to disturb the flour there, she smiles, "Well, hello to you too."

"Angel, what are you doing? Cooking? For me? You hate cooking."

I don't know how it's possible, but her cheeks redden a bit more and she shrugs, "I wanted to try."

"Well, I can't wait to eat whatever you've made. I'm starving!"

She smiles shyly and honestly, I don't care if it tastes like dog shit, I will pretend it is the best thing I've ever tasted.

"I hope you like it. I wanted a special evening for just you and me. Dinner is just going to be foreplay, the real fun will come later." She smirks and if her cheeks weren't already red, I know her words would darken them. This outright flirting isn't her norm, and I know she's trying to be sexy and it sure as hell is working. My dick twitches in response to her words, making me want to grab her and pull her close. I want to take that promised fun now, but she's worked too hard and for the love of all that's holy, I need to get my hormones under control.

"I'm sure I will love it. Here," I grab the flowers I threw towards the counter on my hurry to taste her, "these are for you."

Her smile lights up the room, "I love them, you know I do." She puts the pink buds to her nose and smells them. They pale in comparison to her. She turns and goes to get a vase out of a cupboard, giving me a perfect view of that ass again.

"I have to say," my voice sounds raspy from the sight before me, "I'm loving the outfit you chose for the evening. You are absolutely stunning, but I'm feeling a little overdressed."

She sets the vase and flowers down so she can turn to me. She looks me up and down, eyes moving slowly, "You'll do," she replies and then bites her lip, giving the impression I'm mouthwatering in response. Then, with a smile she does a twirl, faces me, and puts a hand on her hip. "With this apron on, all you see is the back."

"That's just fine with me."

She laughs, "I'm glad you like it. I got it just for you."

"Oh, I more than like it."

"You'll have to prove it later."

"It will be my pleasure," I promise. "So, what can I help you with?" I need a distraction from all that flesh.

"Nothing. I want to do this for you. You can sit if you want, or just hang out while I finish up a few things here."

"Okay. Am I allowed to ask what's on the menu for tonight?"

"Why yes, I'm so glad you asked." She walks past me with a shake of her hips and I follow her every move as she takes the vase with pink roses to the table and sets them down. "I thought I would choose a provocative menu for us this evening. We will start with a *tossed* salad and *clam* chowder. Then I made *meatloaf* with ground Italian *sausage*." She smirks like this is funny, but my eyes widen at the combination. I'm unsure of her choices until it dawns on me that she chose these items because they sound sexual. I almost let a laugh escape but then smother it with my hand, looking like I'm rubbing my mouth. I don't want to hurt her feelings. "And for dessert we will have *bananas* foster." Oh God, I almost lose my shit right there because she raises an eyebrow and her face shows how proud she is of the selection. Forget the fact that they don't go together AT ALL.

I struggle to maintain a straight face, "That all sounds really uhh... good. Really good."

"Great. Would you like a glass of wine to enjoy while I finish up a few things? I got it at the store today. It's quite good - it's called Angel Kiss. I found that fitting."

I smirk with knowledge, "Good? You tried it?"

She pauses for a moment as she reaches for a wine glass, "Um, yeah. They had some samples of it at the store for people to try, so I did." Her eyes are downcast and I know it is because she doesn't want me to see the truth in her eyes. I know damn well she more than tried it!

"Great." I will save my intel for the right time. This isn't it. "I think I will just hang out in here with you while you finish up," I tell her as she gives me a glass of wine.

"That's fine with me," she gives me a smile and walks passed me and to the stove. She's got something boiling on the stovetop. To my surprise, she reaches for a bottle of liqueur and pours it into the pot. She doesn't measure anything, just dumps that shit in like she ain't messing around. She turns to me, cocks her hip and gives me a wink. "So lover," she purrs, "tell me about your day."

I stare in fascination for a moment at this creature that has apparently inhabited her body. I open my mouth to respond but before I can utter a word, there's a loud WHOOSH and the pan on the stove catches fire. It's like a blazing inferno right behind her head! I burst out of my seat.

"Oh shit!" she yells and runs to the sink. I barely spare her a glance and run and grab the pot holder I see sitting on the counter and I remove the pot from the heat very carefully. Then I grab some flour from the canister she has open on the counter and spread it on the flame to put it out. Suddenly, I feel wetness. I blink and turn my head toward the sink. Olivia is standing there with the sprayer in her hand, pulled out as far as it will go and is trying to arc the spray in the air, trying to get it to reach towards the stove.

A strangled laugh escapes me before I can stop it. More of her hair has come loose and it is all around her face now. Her cheeks are heated and she has a panicked expression on her face. "It's okay babe, I got it. This flour put the flame out."

She just stares at me and blinks a few times while simultaneously spraying me and everything around her. She finally releases the trigger for the sprayer, stopping it. She turns to put it back and since there is water all over the floor from her firewoman attempt, she starts to slip and fall. I leap towards her to catch her before she hurts herself, almost falling myself. I managed to crash into her, but luckily, prevent us both from going down.

"Oh no, Luke. I'm so sorry. I hope the dessert isn't ruined."

"I'm sure it's fine." I pull her away from me and look her over, "Are you okay?"

"I'm fine, thanks to you. How about you?"

"I'm fine. Stay still, though. I want to get towels to clean up the floor."

"No, it's my fault, I can do it."

"Please angel, let me. I don't want you to slip and fall and break more bones, okay?"

She pushes the hair out of her face and smiles, "Okay. Thank you."

I clean up the water off the floor and when I'm finished, we finally sit down to enjoy our soup and salad. It's pretty good. Not that you can really mess up salad, but the soup is good too.

"How are things at the club?"

"Good. Nothing to report really. We are thinking about opening a new club in California, I tasted a new drink one of the bartenders made up, oh, and one of my old buddies from college is probably going to come and work for me."

"Oh really? That's cool! How did that happen?" She takes a sip of her soup and I can tell she's impressed with her own cooking, liking the taste.

"He had asked me a while back to let him know if something comes up. I need a new manager and bartender and he'd be good for the position."

"I'd really like to meet him."

"Oh yeah?" I ask her absently while taking a bite of salad.

"Of course. I bet he would have some great stories to tell me about your college days. I look up at her to smile and she winks at me. And then she winks again. And again. Oh, I think she's got something in her eye. "You okay?"

"Yeah, great. How's your salad?" She tries to act like nothing is happening, but her eye looks like it won't stop twitching. She's just ignoring it and takes another spoonful of her soup. She closes her eyes and one of her eyelashes falls off her face.

"Umm, Olivia?"

She opens her eyes and looks at me wide eyed, completely oblivious to the fact that her eyelash is now floating in her soup. "Yes, baby?"

She's looking at me so expectantly, with a smile on her lips and I can't tell her. I mean shit – how do I tell her? Oh, I know, "Um, I think I'm done with the salad and soup, can we have some meatloaf now?"

Just as I hoped, she gets up from her seat and takes her salad and soup plates with her into the kitchen while she grabs the meatloaf. Phew, crisis averted. I know it would have embarrassed her so much to know what happened. She doesn't need to do herself up like that anyway, not for me. But I know it's just part of her look for our romantic evening.

She returns with the meatloaf in her potholder-covered hands and sets it on the table to grab my salad and soup plates, taking them into the kitchen too. When she returns, she looks at me and I notice how her eyes look different now, one with longer lashes than the other. Damn, she's so cute.

She reaches for the meatloaf and cuts a piece, though some slips back in the baking pan, and places the remainder on my plate. "Oh, sorry it fell apart a little. That's likely a good sign, huh? I hope you like it. I've never made meatloaf before, but it was surprisingly easy."

"I'm sure it will be great."

She watches me as I grab a large forkful and put it into my mouth. I notice almost instantly that something tastes off. While the top has a nice brown, seared crust, the inside is noticeably chewy and mushy. I force a smile to my face and give her an, "Mmm," then look down at my plate. It looks cooked through just fine, but something is not right. Oh my god, suck it up Easton, you are NOT going to gag in front of your girl at this meal she prepared for you. You are going to chew and love it. I force a swallow and barely keep the grimace hidden from my face.

"You like it?"

"Mmm, good." I mumble and take another bite. Oh god it's awful, it tastes like ass. It's okay Easton. You will survive this. Besides, it's a small piece. It will be over soon. You've endured worse things...certainly you have. You will not disappoint her. You will love this. Or at least act like you do. You are a warrior. You got this. Chew. Chew. Chew. Swallow. Faster. Drink wine. Do not gulp.

I look up just as she's taken a bite. She chews for a moment and then spits the whole thing out on her plate. "OH MY GOD! That tastes awful! Luke!! That tastes awful! Why didn't you say anything?"

Oh thank god, I don't have to eat anymore. I could cry with relief. "I didn't want to hurt your feelings."

She pushes her plate away from her, gets up, walks to me and gestures for me to back my chair up from the table. When I do, she sits in my lap and throws her arms around me. "Luke Easton, I love you. I love you so much. I can't believe you were willing to eat that just to spare my feelings."

"You attempted to cook for me, angel. I would do anything for you."

"I know you would, I do. But you can't lie to me like that! That was awful. Next time, tell me the truth!"

"Okay. So then tell me, are you going to tell me the truth about what happened today?"

Her whole body and face stills. I can't help it, I laugh out loud. "How about this... you forgive me for not telling you the meatloaf is awful, and I let you off the hook about telling me about your antics today."

"Deal!" she hurriedly agrees, "Even though Pyper is a dead woman."

I laugh and nuzzle her neck. "How about we order a pizza later?" I suggest.

"I will do it right now!" She makes an attempt to get out of my lap, but I don't let her. She looks at me questioningly.

"I'm hungry, angel, but not for food."

She smiles and laughs as I grab my wine glass, down the entire glassful, then pick her up to carry her into the bedroom. I quickly take a glimpse out of the corner of my eye at the stove, ensuring a light or burner was not left on. After the dinner we had, I could just see the condo going up in flames.

Fortunately, the only fire will be between the two of us.

21.

SWEET CLARITY

Olivia

AS LUKE CARRIES me into the bedroom, all I can think about is how much I want his hands on me. All over me. I wonder if I will ever have enough of him. Of this. Of us. I hope not.

We reach my bedroom and he sets me down on my feet outside the closed door. I look at him in question, "You okay?"

"I'm perfect." He turns me to face him, my back to the door, then he surprises me by lifting me up again, "Wrap your legs around my waist. I need to feel you, to taste you."

I gesture towards my leg, "I'm not sure if I can."

"Just try, if it's uncomfortable, we will move."

I do as he asks and groan when I feel his hardness against me. I wrap my arms around his neck and lock my ankles the best I can around him given my stupid cast. I'm so over that thing – my leg doesn't even hurt, it's just a heavy hindrance. I want it off already. Pushing that thought aside, I concentrate on Luke and the fact he's placed my back against the bedroom door and is pulling the pins out of my hair. He throws them on the floor, then shoves his hands into my hair. I look up at him and he meets my eyes for all of two seconds before his lips come crashing down on mine.

I pull him closer to me and kiss him with everything I have. My lips move with his, our tongues twirling and stroking. I grip his hair at the base of his neck and grind my hips into his. I slowly pull away from him and bite his bottom lip, "I want you, Luke."

I swear a sound that sounds like a growl vibrates through his chest, making me smile. I need to feel him. Leaning back against the door, I start unbuttoning his shirt. He dressed up a bit for work today. Dress shirt and slacks. No tie, though. His shirt was open at his neck, hinting at his strong chest that I love so much. I begin to undo the buttons of his shirt, one down, two down, when I get to the third, a string from around the hole catches on the button, getting it stuck. I bite my lip and contemplate for all of a second if I should and then, with a smirk, I rip his shirt open with a sharp tug. The buttons go flying all over the place.

He laughs and winks at me, "In a hurry?"

I rake my nails down his chest and listen to his breath catch, "Yes. I want you now."

He doesn't waste any more time and opens the door at my back. I'm slightly disappointed until he just brings us inside, closes it and then puts my back against the door on the other side. Hot. My mouth forms a naughty grin, "Door sex. I like it."

He laughs and I reach for his belt buckle, hurrying to undo his pants. His hands are caressing my ass and with a sharp tug he rips the thong from my hips. I look at him and he grins, "I'm in a hurry too."

I laugh until I pull his erection from his pants with one hand. I slowly stroke him up and down and rub my thumb over the tip. Moving my other hand into his hair, I press my lips against his for a quick kiss, then I lick and suck his bottom lip. I love him so much, I can't wait another second to have him inside me. My legs have slid down, so he takes my casted leg behind the knee and places it over his hip, holding it there for me. I look at him as I place him at my opening. His eyes darken with passion and he pushes his hips towards me, entering me with just the tip of his cock.

I gasp at the sensation, craving more. "Oh god yes, I need more." I put my hands on his hips and dig my nails into his skin, trying to pull him closer. He pushes inside me more and I throw my head back against the door. He buries his face in my neck as he thrusts his hips forward and back.

Sweet sensations start building in my lower abdomen, and when he bites my nipples through my lace negligée, I swear I'm going to fall apart right then. "Harder," I instruct.

With a grunt, he heeds my demand and pounds his hips into me at the same time I put my fingers to my clit and start rubbing. "Olivia," he whispers. All I can think about is how much I don't want him to stop.

With a yell, I feel myself climbing even more, then falling over the edge when my orgasm hits me with a blast. At the same time, I'm aware of his thrusts increasing in speed. With a shout, Luke's body stiffens and he lets himself go. He's practically bent backwards with me just sitting astride his hips. His strength in that moment astounds me and I revel in the muscles moving in his chest. My man is sexy as hell.

He kisses my forehead and nuzzles my shoulder, then pulls away and looks at me with a sexy smirk, "Wow."

I giggle, "Yes, wow."

He turns around, me still in his arms, and places me on the bed. He removes the rest of his clothes, helps me with mine, and then we lie down. I place my head on his chest and he begins to stroke my hair. My eyes drift closed and I feel more at peace with him in this moment, than I have in a long time. I kiss his chest, "I love you."

His hand stills in my hair and I feel his fingers under my chin, nudging me to look up at him. When our eyes meet, he caresses my cheek with his thumb, "I love you too, Olivia. So much."

"I'm so sorry dinner sucked." I blurt.

His eyebrows furrow, "It didn't su-"

"Luke, it's okay. I'm a lousy cook, and I know it. I just wanted to try, for you. Thanks for going along with it."

He smiles, "Anything for you."

"Wow. You really mean that."

"Of course I do." I smile as he pushes some hair behind my ear, "Does this mean I have to try the dessert you made?"

I start to laugh because I can hear the desperate sound in his voice, hoping my answer is no. I can't stop giggling and eventually he joins in, his chest bouncing under my chin, "No, you don't have to try it."

"Thank God," he says, dropping all pretenses that I'm a good cook.

"Hey! You could have pretended a little longer." I push my bottom lip out into a pout, and he bends his neck down and bites it.

"You're sexy when you pout."

"Yeah well, lucky for you, I have ice cream in my freezer."

"You do?" He asks his eyes lighting up. "Is Pyper expected back any time soon?"

"No, she's staying the night at her parents' place."

"Okay, perfect," he jumps out of bed naked and makes a beeline for the kitchen. Returning a few moments later, he hops into the bed, showing me the ice cream and spoon he's brought back with him.

I sit up, "Hey, you forgot a spoon for me!"

He grins, "No, I didn't."

We both sit up, his legs crossed and mine on either side of his, facing each other while completely naked. I love it. He takes the top off the ice cream, scoops a spoonful and holds it out to me, waiting for me to open my lips. When I do, he pushes the spoon closer until I take the ice cream he offers. It's delicious. The vanilla and chocolate make my taste buds stand up at attention and crave more. He scoops more out, but puts that scoop into his own mouth.

He takes turns feeding me a bite, and then himself one. The fact we are sharing one spoon is very intimate and I've never felt closer to him. Something around my heart crumbles just a little and I feel compelled to tell him something.

He offers me another spoonful, which I accept. When he digs into the pint again to scoop another, I blurt, "I dreamed of you."

His eyes shoot to mine and his brow furrows, "What?"

I take a deep breath, "I dreamed of you," I repeat, "when I was taken." His eyes widen at my words and he doesn't move. I'm not even sure if he breathes. "When things were hard..." I look away and at my lap. My eyes well up and I sniff, trying to keep my tears from falling.

I jump a little when I feel his fingers at my chin, pushing it up until I move my eyes to meet his again. His hold mine steady and as one tear escapes down my cheek, he leans in and catches it with his lips. I close my eyes, reveling in the feel of his lips on my cheek. He pulls away and I open my eyes slowly to connect with his once again. He steadies me. He centers me. He makes me feel whole, even when I don't know if I've ever been more broken. In his eyes, I know I'm anything but, and that gives me the strength to continue.

"When things were hard and I was afraid I would never get out of there, I used to dream of you. I think it varied between day dreams and dreaming while sleeping, but they were always the same."

He swallows audibly and I watch his Adam's apple bob. "What did you dream?"

I smile then, because even in the middle of darkness and Deacon's madness, dreams of Luke brought peace, light, and hope. "I dreamed that you and I had a home."

"A home?"

"Yes. A big one, with a wraparound porch, and even a picket fence."

"What would we be doing?" he asks softly - like he's afraid I will stop talking if he talks too much, or too loud.

I look off to the side as if it will help me envision it once again, "We would always be sitting on the porch rocking in chairs."

"Rocking in chairs? Were we old and decrepit?"

I smile again and laugh softly, looking at the way his lips turn up at the corners, "No, we were just as we are now. It was always fall, and the leaves were amazing shades of orange and red. The sunset made the sky look like it was on fire, and we had blankets covering us. My feet sat in your lap, and you would be rubbing them, of course..."

"Of course," he agrees.

"And I would scratch our dog behind his ear."

"We have a dog?"

I nod, "Yes, a golden retriever, named Dakota," I state matter-of-factly, making him smile, "And sometimes..." I pause, uncertain of continuing.

"Sometimes?" he prompts.

"Sometimes," I whisper, as if talking loud will make the memory disintegrate, "while we were sitting there, I would look out into the yard, and under a tree would be two dark-haired little children.

They had their heads together and would be whispering thick as thieves as they sat in a pile of leaves telling secrets."

"Children? Our children?"

"Yes," I whisper looking at him. "You know, it was just a daydream."

"You want children with me? And a house? And a dog?"

I smile at him, reach out and touch his cheek. "More than anything."

He places the ice cream and spoon to the side and moves closer to me, capturing my lips with his. When he opens his mouth and I respond, he sweeps his tongue inside and I taste the sweetness still lingering on his lips. When he pulls away, he looks at me, "I want that with you too, Livvie. So much sometimes it hurts."

"You do?"

"Yes," he states emphatically, without hesitation. "Sometimes it still feels like a dream. I thought I had lost you forever. This second chance with you is everything to me. You're my everything. I don't let a day go by that I don't say a prayer in thanks that I get to hold you in my arms again."

"I feel the same way." I place a small kiss on his lips.

He pushes me onto my back and lays on his side next to me, the ice cream forgotten. "Thank you for telling me about your dream."

My brow furrows at his words, "What?" he asks reading me well.

"I know I haven't talked much about what happened..."

"Livvie - "

"No, let me say this. It isn't because I don't want to tell you or I don't trust you or anything like that. It's just because it's hard. Sometimes I feel like it is physically impossible to even get the words past my lips. My throat feels like it's closing and my chest feels tight. It's easier to push it away than to try and talk about it."

"That sounds like a panic attack, love," he states gently, as if afraid he will worry me. "That isn't something you should ignore."

"I know. You're right. And I realized something."

"What's that?"

"The dream that I had about us? That's my greatest wish, Luke. A life with you. If I can't get past this and start healing, I'll never truly be able to make my dream a reality. I will keep letting fear hold me back and it will come between us."

"That won't-"

"Yes, it will. I'm tired of having that man be a ghost in the room with us all the time. I know it is hard not knowing where he is and I do still think that the right thing has been to move forward and to continue on with our lives. But, I also think it might be a good idea to talk to a therapist about my kidnapping."

"You would do that?"

"Yes, on one condition."

"Anything."

"Will you come with me?" I ask shyly.

"Yes, of course. I will be happy to take you and wait outside the room for you - whatever you need – I'm here."

"No, Luke. Will you go to the therapy sessions *with* me? Inside. Like, let me lay my head in your lap on the therapists couch," I smile at the image I created.

"If that's what you want, then that's not even a question. Absolutely. I want to support you every step of the way. Even if you need nothing more than for me to hold your hand – I'm there."

"Luke, you are everything to me, I don't want to lose you. I've been so scared to talk to you about what happened because I don't know what I would do if you were unable to deal with some of the ugliness and move past it all. But suddenly, I realized that not talking to you and being honest, could do the exact same thing. And I realized I was not giving you the benefit of the doubt. You deserve more. You continually love me well and sharing this with you is of the most intimate ways I can love in return. I don't know if you will be able to deal with this. I don't know if-" I want to choke on my next words but I force them out anyway, "if you will want to be with me after you know everything, but lying... or always feeling like this is an elephant on my back, something to conceal, to keep from you, is not something I can continue doing. It is not loving you well. And I want that. "

Luke places his hands on either side of my face and looks deep into my eyes. They are glistening with his emotions from my words and his lips are tight. "Olivia, there is nothing, absolutely nothing you could tell me that would change the way I feel about you."

"Luke, don't be so sure."

"I am sure. I *know* it. What happened to you was *not* your fault." I choke again on my tears at his words, "Tell me something, did you want to go with Deacon?"

"Of course not."

"Did you try to get away?"

"Every minute," I whisper, my eyes locked on his.

"What happened was not your fault," Luke repeats again slowly this time emphasizing each word. "I can't even imagine how scared and desperate and sad you had to be. Anything, and I mean *anything* you had to do or were forced to do," he pauses and it makes me catch my breath. Does he know? But how could he? "I don't care about it. Not one bit. If I had the chance I would have told you to do whatever you had to do in order to come out of there alive, angel. THAT is all I care about. That you came out of there alive."

Tears start to fall freely down my cheeks now and he wipes each one of them away with his kisses. "I love you, Livvie. No matter what. NOTHING can change that. Do you understand me?"

I look in his eyes and I see. I SEE. Somehow beyond the pain that his eyes are reflecting from mine, beyond the concern and his need for me to hear his words, I see love. It's in the warmth of his eyes, it's in the way his hands hold my face. It's in the way his body is conformed to mine, and the way his lips kiss my tears away. It's in the way he eats my bad food and catches me when I fall. It's in the way he holds me, kisses me and loves me. It's there, shining in his eyes and I see it.

And I believe it.

22.

RUDE INTERRUPTION

Luke

I WAKE UP to a beautiful woman in my arms and immediately think that I always want to wake up just like this. Last night after we finished talking, Olivia and I made love again. This time, nice and slow. I wanted to again show her with actions, how much I meant my words. I love touching her, watching her move, listening to her sighs, hearing her words of love, seeing her need and satisfaction. She makes me whole, and I can't get enough of her. I don't think I ever will.

I look down at her face, she's so peaceful in sleep, I love watching her. She slept hard. I woke through the night checking on her like a new father, just wanting to make sure she was okay. Each time she was still in my arms, curled around my body, head on my chest, legs wrapped with mine. I'd pull her closer to me, even though there was already zero space between us, and listen to her sigh in contentment. She'd mumble something unintelligible sometimes, but never fully woke up or had a bad dream.

I can't help but run my fingers through her hair. It's so soft. I think back to our conversation last night, and my chest instantly warms. That spot in my chest aches again, but I know what that feeling is now. It's my love for her. I can literally feel my chest ache in response to my feelings. It's an ache I revel in, one I know I'm lucky to feel and one I know I will always feel with her. Only with her. Forever.

The dream she shared with me - I want to make that happen for her. For us. I can't look ahead into the future and not see her in it. The thought of losing her, or not having her in my life anymore creates a pain I quickly push away. I refuse to ever let that happen. I will spend my life making her happy; ensuring that she knows without any doubt, that she's loved, cherished, and safe. Sure, these are thoughts I've had before, but each time, I feel them stronger and with more conviction.

I want to ask her to move in with me. We are pretty much doing that now. We're never apart anymore. I only go back to my place to get clothes. I know she wants to stay close to Pyper, so I don't make her choose, I just come here. I wonder if I ask, and she says yes, if she will want to live here together, or if she will want to come to my place. Or maybe we will get out of the city and go to a suburb and find a place of our own. I'll do whatever she wants. None of the details matter to me. I just want her. Forever.

Snapping into my thoughts is the ringing of my phone. Olivia stirs, but doesn't wake completely at the sound. I sigh in relief, hugging her to me at the same time, and ignore the damn thing, just letting it ring. It finally quits and I let out the breath I didn't even realize I was holding, only to catch it again when my phone again starts ringing. I curse under my breath and glance at the clock on the bedside table and see it's seven o'clock in the morning. What the hell? Who would be calling me right now? A feeling of unease like a spider crawling down my spine occurs, and I wonder if it could be Deacon calling again.

"Luke? Is that your phone?"

I jump a little at her voice then sigh. So much for not waking her. "Yeah. I'm sorry it woke you. I'm not sure who would be calling. I tried to ignore it but I'm pretty sure whoever it is just called again."

She lifts her head and covers her mouth with her hand when she yawns. "It's okay. See who it is. I don't mind. It must be important."

She moves off me, leaving me frowning in displeasure at her absence, but I guess she's right. Just as she pulls away, my phone starts ringing once more. Apparently, it refuses to be ignored. I get out of bed and head for my pants that are lying in a heap on the floor. I smile a little to myself when I have a brief flashback of how they got there, then yank the phone out of my pocket. "This better be good."

"Sir, I'm so sorry to bother you."

"Your timing sucks, Brian," I snap, "what do you want?"

"I'm sorry again, sir. It's just, there's a situation at the club."

My brow furrows, "A situation? What does that mean exactly?"

"There's a fire."

"A fire? What do you mean, there's a fire? What happened?" I see Olivia sit up in bed and turn towards me at my words.

"I'm not sure, sir. The alarms went off and since I'm on call, the phone's forwarded to me. The police and fire department called letting me know about the alarms, and told me they are on their way to the club as we speak. I called you right away; I knew you would want to know. I'm headed to the club now and will fill you in once I get there."

"Shit."

"Sir?"

"Sorry. You did the right thing, thanks for letting me know. I'll be on my way over as soon as I can get there. I'm with Olivia, and don't want to leave her alone if I don't have to. I'll figure something out and be there soon." Brian knows full well about the situation with Deacon. During his shifts at the club, he saw firsthand how well I didn't handle it while she was taken. I want to go to Zero Gravity and find out what is going on, but that would mean leaving Olivia here alone, and I'm not willing to do that.

Olivia, having heard my conversation with Brian, pulled herself into a sitting position and has her hands on her hips. This action made the sheet fall to her hips, giving me a fantastic view. Smiling is not appropriate given the situation, but damn, I can't help it.

"Just a second, Brian." I move the phone to the side, "Any chance you can call Pyper to come here?"

"Why?"

"I should head to the club, but I don't want to leave you here alone," I admit.

She rolls her eyes at me, "Luke, that's ridiculous. You need to get to your club. I will be fine. Stop worrying about me."

Doesn't she realize that's not possible? It's okay, plan B. I will call Max and ask him to head over here, or text Pyper myself. As if reading my mind, she frowns. My eyes slowly travel from the frown on her lips, to her waist where the sheet sits. I would very much like to put my hands all over that amazingly soft flesh of hers again. Right now. My train of thought is interrupted by the clearing of a throat.

"Luke?"

My eyes shoot to Olivia's, "Hmm?"

"The club."

"What? Oh! Shit!"

"Sir, with all due respect..."

"What is it, Brian?"

"Well, I was just thinking, I will go and meet the police and firemen at the club. It may be nothing more than just a false alarm, for all we know. I will handle it and call you when I find out what is going on. You can trust me to handle this."

He makes complete sense, "Okay, Brian. Thanks. I owe you one."

"Okay, call you soon."

Brian hangs up and I turn to Olivia, once again devouring all the flesh that is on display. The fire is quickly removed from my mind. No sense worrying about something that may be nothing. Olivia's hands are on her hips once again, and she's giving me a stern look, "Luke, that was silly. You need to go to the club."

"I need to be with you more."

Olivia bites her lip and I lick mine in response, "You shouldn't have done that. What if it's serious and the club burns down?"

"It may be nothing. No sense worrying about something I can't control. I have insurance. I'm not going to worry until I know more."

"Okay, I guess you're right. He may call back and tell you that you are needed there, any time."

I give her my best mischievous smirk, "Then I guess we'd better hurry," and I dive into bed next to her pulling her on top of me as I land.

Olivia giggles and I laugh. I roll on top of her and hold her wrists to the side of her head on either side and kiss her with abandon. All thoughts of my previous conversation have fled my mind and as I take one of her nipples into my mouth and hear her whimper, all I care about is this.

I tease her nipple and release it and make my way back up to her neck, burying my face there. I take in her feminine smell that has a hint of lavender. I release one of her wrists, push her legs open with my knees then grab my cock and slip inside of her with a groan.

We both reach climax quickly and roll away from one another, catching our breath. My phone starts ringing almost immediately and I'm thinking Brian deserves a bonus for his good timing. I likely wouldn't have answered the phone had it been a few minutes before.

I reach for the phone off the bedside table where I placed it. Looking at the screen, I see sure enough, it's Brian, "Yes?"

"Boss, you are going to want to come here after all."

"Talk to me."

"I don't know. The police and fire department won't tell me anything since I'm not the owner, but something is going on. They're talking in hushed tones and won't let me into the kitchen where the fire originated."

"Okay, can you tell how bad the damage is?"

"I know it is inside the kitchen, and there isn't any damage other than smoke in the air inside the main part of the club, so it was at least contained to one room."

"Well that's at least something, I guess. Alright, I will leave here in five. See you soon."

"Alright, boss? Do you need me to stay with Olivia so you can get to the club? I would be more than happy to help."

"Thanks for offering, I may take you up on that. I'll get back to you if so." I tap end and turn to Olivia, "I'm sorry, angel, it looks like I need to go to the club after all."

"What did he say?"

"Not much, really. They won't tell him anything since he isn't the owner, but he said something is definitely going on."

"Okay, no problem, like I said, I will be fine. You go do what you need to do."

I pause in the middle of putting on my pants, "No way. You're coming with me."

"Luke..."

"It's either that, Brian can come here, or you can call Pyper to see if she can come here and be with you. I would prefer you stay here because I don't know what the situation is, and it sounds unsafe. You would be safer here where I don't have to worry about you being in the midst of the chaos and smoke."

With a sign, Olivia picks up her phone and starts dialing Pyper. I smile and give her a kiss on her nose. She rolls her eyes at me, making me laugh. "Hi Pyper? Hey... are you coming back to the condo any time soon? Oh you are? Just fifteen minutes? Okay, great! Luke has a situation at the club he needs to check out and doesn't want to leave me alone. Okay, thanks."

"Thanks, Pyper!" I yell out. Olivia chuckles, "She says 'no problem'."

Olivia hangs up, "There, are you happy?"

"Yes, very."

"Will you call me as soon as you know something?"

I go grab my shirt off the floor. "Of course." I shove my arms in my shirt and try to button it, forgetting that my buttons are scattered all over the carpet. A smile touches my lips at the memory of Olivia ripping my shirt off, "Crap, I forgot. I guess I can't wear this shirt."

Olivia gets out of bed and I admire her naked body as she disappears inside her closet. She reappears moments later with one of my shirts. "You still have these here from when you stayed in my room when I-"

"Yeah," I interrupt, not wanting the reminder, "I forgot about those. Thanks."

I take the shirt from her, pull it off the hanger, and put it on. Then, I walk into the bathroom and quickly straighten my hair and brush my teeth. When I come out, I see her standing there in comfy pajamas and a robe, I can't help but feel a little sad she's no longer naked. She comes to me and gives me a lingering kiss, nibbling on my lower lip as she pulls away.

"I'll be back as soon as I can. I love you." I give her another kiss.

"I love you too. See you soon."

I get a heavy feeling in my chest as I leave her apartment. I know I'm just being overprotective. She's safe and secure in her building.

I take the elevator down to the parking garage and run to my car, breaking all the speeding laws on my way to Zero Gravity. On the way I try to call Max and get his voicemail. I leave him a message and do the same with Pyper when I get hers too.

Mia, one of my employees, meets me at the door. "Sir," she nods at me, which I return, "Officer Phish and Officer Knight are in charge. They've asked to speak with you."

"Okay. Where's Brian?"

"It looked like he got an important call and then left sir. He said he would be back."

Two officers I'm assuming are Phish and Knight walk over to me, "Mr. Easton?"

"Yes, that's me."

"I'm officer Phish," a tall blonde holds out his hand to me for a shake and then gestures to the officer beside him, "this is Officer Knight. It appears that the fire was contained to only the kitchen area."

"That's good at least."

"Yes, it could have been much worse. But, we have a couple concerns."

"Concerns?"

"Yes. Do you have anyone that would have a reason for wanting to cause damage to your club?"

"Want to cause damage?" My head whirls at the thought, "I'm confused, what are you suggesting?"

They completely ignore my question, "Mr. Easton, we are going to need you to hang around until Detective Goldridge gets here to ask you a few questions."

23.

PRINCESS

Olivia

FTER LUKE LEAVES, I find myself standing in the kitchen with the refrigerator door open, trying to determine what I'd like to make myself for breakfast. I know I should feel guilty for lying to Luke about Pyper being on her way, but when I called her and got her voicemail, I reacted. His club is important, and he needed to be there. I locked the door behind him, I'll be fine. I need to go set the alarm though – but first breakfast.

I decide on eggs with ham and cheese, since it is one of the only things I know how to cook. I may not be able to boil an egg, but I can sure as hell stir them in a pan. It's likely they will only be a little burned. I pull the ingredients I need from the refrigerator, when I hear the front door open and close. I spin around with a smile on my face, wondering what would have brought Luke back so soon.

"Hey babe, what happened?"

The person I see walk into the kitchen makes my face fall instantly, and my blood run cold. Every hair on my body stands at attention and a feeling of foreboding enters my stomach, making me want to vomit. My body starts to shake as fear sets in.

"Hello, princess."

Everything I'm holding crashes to the floor, and I want to join them. Deacon stands before me looking as though he has all the right in the world to be standing in my kitchen. He leans his hip against the counter, crosses his arms across his chest and looks me up and down with a mocking smile upon his lips. His eyes almost bring me to my knees. Hard, unfeeling and full of lust, I can see the determination in them to get his way. Fear fills my whole body, paralyzing me.

"What's wrong, princess? Too surprised to greet me with a proper hello?" He starts walking towards me while speaking and for each little step he takes, I back up with one of my own.

"Wh-what are you doing here, Deacon?" My voice is shaking with each word.

He rolls his eyes with a careless gesture that puts me even more on edge. It's like he really doesn't think he's doing anything wrong. "Well, isn't it obvious? I'm here for you. Your time's up. It's time to come back to me now."

"Are you crazy? I'm not going anywhere with you! Get out of here before I call the police!"

The smile on his lips disappears and a hard look covers his face. I can see he's clenching his teeth by the way his jaw tightens on both sides. He's so close to me now, my nose is at his chest and his toes are touching mine. I raise my eyes one slow inch at a time until I reach his face. He moves his face inches from my own. His breath is warm on my face, and the stench of alcohol makes me wince.

"I've been biding my time, waiting for the right moment to see you again. I've missed you, princess."

He runs his hand along the side of my face and I turn my head away, trying to get as far from him as I can. "Don't fucking look away from me," he spits while at the same time yanking my chin so hard it makes me face him again. His fingers are digging into my chin and I know he's going to leave bruises.

"How many times do I have to tell you? You belong to me."

"No, Deacon," tears pool in my eyes, "I don't." It's hard to speak with him gripping my chin so hard, but I refuse to make this easy for him.

"Stop playing hard to get, it's starting to piss me off. You know as well as I do that I'm the one you want to be with. Now go get dressed, get your things, and let's go."

As he's talking, his hands have grasped my upper arms, his fingers digging into my flesh, causing me to grit my teeth. "I'm. Not. Going. Anywhere. With. You." Maybe enunciating each word will help my comments penetrate his crazy, fucked up mind.

He shakes me hard, making my back smack against the counter behind me. A burst of pain runs up my spine, making me cry out. "You do not want to fight me on this, Olivia. Now let's go; get your shit, so we can get out of here. You're lucky I'm even letting you do that much."

"Okay," I whisper, putting my hands up in an "I surrender" gesture. My eyes dart to either side of him, and I think if I can make it down the hall to my room, I can get to my phone and call for help. As soon as he steps away clearing my way to my room, I take off.

I run as fast as I can out of the kitchen and past the living room and just make it to my bedroom door when suddenly, I feel the air burst out of me in a whoosh. It takes me a second to realize I'm airborne and heading towards the ground quickly. Deacon has tackled me. When I land on the floor, we slide a few inches, and I feel fire on the palms of my hands and knees from my skin rubbing against the carpet. My already injured cheek hits the ground and I hear something crunch.

I would cry out in pain if I could, but I can't because Deacon's body is pressing mine into the floor and taking a complete breath is impossible. I'm trying to suck in air, but I can't, and it makes my chest hurt. Water leaks from my eyes when Deacon rolls me over. He pins my wrists to the ground next to my shoulders while adjusting his weight to straddle my hips.

I wish I had been able to run faster, but with this stupid cast on my leg, I'm already at a major disadvantage. I knew it would be hard, nearly impossible to outrun him, but I had to try.

Bringing his face so close to mine, our noses almost touch, Deacon says, "You are going to regret that, you bitch. I'm done playing nice."

A sound that I hope sounds like me trying to laugh, comes out of my mouth. I'm able to take short, shallow breaths now. I try to focus on breathing deeper.

"What were you hoping to accomplish, princess? Did you really think I was just going to let you run away to your room and call the police?"

I wriggle my arms in his hands, trying with all I have to get loose from him. But he's too big and too heavy.

"Baby, you are hurting me. How could you forget the times we shared together? The times we laughed, talked, and made love? Don't you remember? How much we love each other? I know I made mistakes, but I apologized for the other women already. I'm done apologizing to you."

I just shake my head back and forth slowly, not because I don't remember the good times but because I don't want to. The bad times more than outweigh the good, and what does it matter? I couldn't love him or forgive him again even if I wanted to. I am completely owned by a dark-haired, blue-eyed man who had my heart from the time we were teenagers. As Deacon starts trailing his fingers up my leg, I do my best to block it out. I close my eyes. I picture another above me. His smile, his hair ruffled from all the times he runs his hands through it. I see his eyes shining with love and happiness and my heart bursts at the image I created. I love him so much, and I know he loves me. The way I've been acting. It's so stupid. He loves all of me, no matter what. As I love him.

My thoughts are scattered when I feel Deacon has released my wrists in order to separate my robe. He curses under his breath when he reveals the hot pink chemise with lace panels that I'm wearing underneath. "Oh baby, I missed you. Maybe you just need to be reminded of our time together."

When he trails his fingers down the middle of my breasts and then over to one, squeezing my nipple hard, I panic. Dread fills me at the look of unbridled lust Deacon has in his eyes as he watches himself touch me in rapt fascination. I start to fight.

"NO! NO! NO! Stop, Deacon please. Stop touching me! I don't want your hands on me!" I smack him over and over and try to land punches. Even though he's sitting on my hips, I start kicking my legs as if I'm swimming, trying to knock him off of me in the process.

"Knock it off, you bitch!" He gets furious when a couple of my elbow jabs somehow make contact. He takes one hand and wraps it around my throat – tight - choking off my air supply and I tell myself not to panic, to conserve whatever oxygen I can. I do my best to pull them from my neck. I claw my fingernails into his skin, and jab at him with all my might. I know I break skin when I feel the warm, wet liquid under my fingers, but Deacon makes no indication that I'm hurting him in any way.

His other hand moves my robe to the side once again and he pulls my chemise up to my waist, exposing my black panties underneath. He loosens his grip just a little, which makes me gulp for air, but as he lowers his mouth to my throat again and alternates licking and biting me, his grip tightens once more. I'm running out of strength. I'm still trying to claw at his hands, but my attempts feel halfhearted at best now.

Deacon is completely unfazed and pulls the fabric away from my breasts. As I'm starting to see black around the edges of my vision, his mouth moves to one of my exposed breasts. I realize that his face is within reach. With all the strength and anger I have I give him a good whack across the face. He immediately lets go of me, grabs his cheek, shrieks out with pain and I take in huge desperate gasps of air.

Seething with anger, he spews words at me like venom. "Fine, I guess we are going to have to do this the hard way." I look at him and recognize that from somewhere he has produced a roll of duct tape. He sits down even harder on my hips, making me bear the full weight of his frame feeling like it will crush me. He pulls the tape away from the roll and grabs both of my hands, yanking my wrists together in an unnatural and uncomfortable way with one hand, while he wraps massive amounts of tape around them with the other. The tape is so tight that my hands immediately start tingling with loss of circulation and feeling begins to escape me.

When they are taped to his satisfaction, he stands up. I immediately start flailing my legs again only to hear him curse at me as he reaches for my ankles and wraps them up in tape as well.

"No!" My voice sounds raspy and comes out in a whisper, "No, please. Don't do this! I promise, I promise to behave. Please, please don't." I can hear my phone ringing and I wish more than anything I could answer it.

"Stop begging. You're out of chances. This is all your fault! If you would have listened the first time, this wouldn't be happening."

"I promise now. I promise now to listen."

He just ignores me, "I'm really tired of having to be intimate with you restrained in some way. First it was drugged all the time and now this. Where is the fun in that?"

Everything in me stills at his words. I can't move, I can't breathe.

"I tried several times to just not care and have sex with you anyway. I mean, it isn't like that would be a whole lot different than when we had sex when you were coherent, am I right?" He laughs at his own joke, "I mean, why do you think I had to find sex outside of the marriage too?"

He looks down at me and gives me an evil smirk, one that will haunt me for a very long time, if I get out of this. His eyes chill me to my core. They look empty. I don't even know who he is anymore. I don't know if I ever really knew him to begin with.

"So, we never had sex? All the times you kept me drugged and tied up, or locked in the room you never touched me?"

"Now I never said that. Touched you? Sure. But sex? No way. What do you think I am? Crazy? I tried, but I just couldn't bring myself to do it. Especially when Ronnie told me I should anyway. He was completely nuts!"

I can't help but feel relief at his words. All this time, not being sure if I was raped or not has been horrible. I know he still touched me and it's all still awful, but somehow, in some way, the horror of it all lessens just a little.

"It is too bad though that Ronnie isn't here to see this. He's an old juvie buddy, you know. I don't know if I ever introduced you properly. He inherited that property you were at from his aunt after he killed her." My eyes widen, making Deacon laugh, "Yeah 'ol Ronnie had his issues, but Aunt Louise was a real bitch. Anyway, he told me one too many times that going after you was crazy and I was wasting my time. We got drunk one night and he started in on me again, so I went a little too far when I beat the shit out of him. That bastard deserved it. He would have only been in the way, although it sure would be nice to rub his face in it now.

"You're insane."

"Aw baby, I'm just insane for you. You are the one who makes me do this. It's all your fault. If you had just stayed with me, none of this would have happened."

He sits down on my hips once again and takes my chemise in both of his hands. He pulls and rips it down the middle, making rage burn in my chest.

"I don't want to be with you, Deacon! Why don't you GET THAT?!"

He has totally turned me off and doesn't hear me at all anymore, "This isn't exactly what I had in mind, but you know, it's still better than being drugged. At least you're coherent. I'm good with that. I couldn't do it before because you were so out of it, it isn't like you could reciprocate. This dick can't suck itself, you know what I mean?"

He laughs at himself like it's the funniest thing he's ever said and the laughter has an insanity ring to it that makes goose bumps run down my legs and arms. I'm going to be sick.

He looks down at my body again and at my exposed breasts. He lowers his mouth to me and I start shaking my head back and forth. "No, no please," I keep begging him over and over again to stop. I don't want his hands or mouth on me. I want this to stop. "I don't belong to you! I belong to LUKE. I LOVE LUKE!" I scream, trying to hurt him, trying to get him to stop.

And he does. He lifts his head and looks at me. Then rears back his hand and strikes me in the face again. "NO! Don't you fucking TELL ME THAT. You belong to ME! You just need a good fuck to remind you of how good we are together. I can help teach you how to fuck the right way and we can make this work."

"No. I only want to be with Luke," I mumble through the blood in my mouth from his last strike. "He's the only one I care about." I look him dead in the eyes, "HE thinks I fuck just fine."

That, of course, earns me another blow, and instant pain floods my cheekbone again. It was worth seeing the anger in his eyes. "SHUT UP, YOU BITCH! I won't listen to this." He grabs the tape, removes a piece and puts it over my mouth. "There. Much better."

He returns to my breast and starts yanking my panties down my legs. "Ahhh yes, now this is what I'm talkin' about. I'm going to show you who you belong to."

He brings his hands to the front of his jeans and starts unbuckling his belt as tears leave my eyes, roll down my temples, and into my hair.

I close my eyes, and picture the face of the person I love.

24.

DEVIL'S DESTRUCTION

Luke

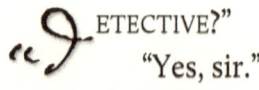ETECTIVE?"

"Yes, sir."

"I don't understand."

"You will. He will be here shortly," Officer Phish explains.

"Okay, well until then, can I see the damage to the kitchen?"

"Of course," Officer Knight answers, "Follow me."

I follow the officers into the kitchen and see the extent of the damage. One side of the kitchen where the oven and cupboards are located is completely destroyed. The other side, where the refrigerator and sink are looks completely untouched. There is, however, wall and ceiling damage from the smoke, though it is minimal. The worst part is the water damage caused by the firemen extinguishing the blaze. I'm standing in a half inch of water around the whole room and all the appliances and walls are just dripping. In some places, water is even falling from the ceiling, splashing onto people's heads.

Some of the small kitchen appliances on the counter by the stove, where the fire was obviously located are melted, but those are all easily replaceable. I look around the room and see one of the windows has a hole in it. I'm assuming the firemen must have busted it to get water into the kitchen. Or perhaps the fire caused it from the pressure, but that seems unrealistic as the oven is across the room from the window.

I run my hand through my hair and let out a sigh. I can't believe I have to deal with this right now. I would much rather be with my girl, but there's nothing I can do about it. I turn to the Officers, "I'm going to go to my office and call my insurance agent to get the ball rolling on the claim for this. Do you know how this happened yet?"

"When Detective Goldridge gets here, we will come to your office to discuss that."

"Okay, thanks."

I head out of the kitchen and up the stairs to my office. Already I'm counting off a list in my mind of all the things I need to do in order to handle this calamity. Once I'm at my desk, I pick up the phone and call Olivia so I can let her know that this could take a while. It goes straight to voicemail, so I leave her a message, "Hi, love, I'm calling like I promised. The fire was contained to the kitchen, fortunately. It is a mess, but honestly, it could have been a lot worse. It looks like I'm going to be tied up here for a bit. I need to call the insurance company and get the claim started and I will probably need to close the club for a few days, so I need to call the staff. Anyway, I love you. I will be back there as soon as I can."

"Sir?"

I look up and see Mia in the doorway, "Do you want me to get the insurance agency on the phone for you, or call the staff?"

"No, thanks, I can do those things, but what you can do for me is to make a sign and put it on the door explaining why we will be closed for a few days. Also, grab a paper and pen and make a list of the small appliances in the kitchen that will need to be replaced. Then, give Chuck a call and tell him I want him to replace them all."

"Okay, will do."

When Mia closes the door behind her, I pick up the phone and call my insurance agent to fill him in on the situation here and get the ball rolling for the claim submission. Then, I pull up the staff list on my computer and start making calls.

"Hi Jeffrey, this is Luke Easton from Zero Gravity calling to let you know that the club will be closed for a few days due to a fire. Your pay will be compensated as usual for the days you were scheduled to work during this time, and Brian or I will give you a call when we are once again open for business." I listen to Jeffrey on the other end, "No, thank you for asking, but there is nothing you can do right now. I will be in touch...thanks. Bye."

I make it through the list and am about to call my dad to give him a heads up about what's going on when there is a knock at my door.

"Sir?"

"Yes, Mia, it's fine, come on in."

"Actually sir, Detective Goldridge is here to see you."

"Okay sure, send him in."

Officers Phish and Knight enter first with a man who must be Detective Goldridge following behind them. He's dressed in a black suit and blue tie and must be in his early fifties. He's got salt and pepper hair with the salt primarily at his temples. His eyes are friendly, but his face is weathered and I can't help but wonder what kind of toll his job has taken on him.

Officer Phish gestures towards Detective Goldridge, "Detective, this is Luke Easton," he swings his hand back towards me, "Mr. Easton, this is Detective Goldridge."

I shake the Detective's hand and get a firm shake in response, "Hi, Detective Goldridge, I would like to say nice to meet you, but honestly..."

A small smile curls at the edges of his mouth, "No, I understand completely. I'm sorry about the fire in your club."

He gives me a nod, and instead of sitting in one of the chairs at my desk, chooses to stand behind me.

I nod my thanks, "So, Detective. The Officers told me you would explain what is going on once you arrived here."

"Yes, they are correct, but first I have a few questions for you."

"Okay." I furrow my brow in confusion. I really don't understand what is going on.

"Do you have any enemies, Mr. Easton?"

I know my brows have hit my hairline, "Enemies?"

"Yes. Do you know anyone that would want to cause harm to your place of business, Mr. Easton?" Detective Goldridge has a pad of paper in his hand and a pen that he pulls out of his suit jacket pocket.

"I'm sorry, I don't understand."

He actually has the nerve to sigh at me. It isn't my fault no one has filled me in on what's happening here. "The fire in your kitchen was not an accident."

"It wasn't?"

"No, in fact, Mr. Easton, we believe it was arson."

I stand in outrage, "What?! Why do you think that it was arson?"

"Please have a seat, Mr. Easton," I do as I'm told, but feel anger burn through my veins in outrage. He waits for a moment for me to collect myself, but I'm honestly just good at disguising my feelings, apparently, because I'm anything but fine, "did you see the hole in the window of your kitchen?"

"Yes, I thought it was caused by the firemen needing to get water into the room to put out the fire."

"No."

"No?" I'm starting to get irritated with Detective-- man of few words-- Goldridge.

"No. A bottle that contained a gasoline soaked rag that was lit on fire was thrown through the window. You are very lucky that the damage wasn't more extensive."

I vaguely realize Officer Knight is speaking into his radio, but my mind is too busy reeling by what Goldridge has told me that I don't have a clue what he's saying. A feeling of dread makes my stomach fall, but I feel almost disconnected with this news that I'm not able to pinpoint why I'm feeling this way.

As if he hasn't just dropped a bomb in my lap, Goldridge continues with his questioning, "So again, Mr. Easton, why would someone want to do this to your place of business?"

Before I can answer, an officer knocks and comes into the room and hands Officer Knight a bag. "This is the bottle," Knight shows me the bag, which contains pieces of what appear to be a green bottle. "It's been dusted for prints and they are running them right now."

"Okay."

Goldridge gets my attention again, "In the meantime, as I've asked, can you think of anyone that would want to do harm to your place of business."

And now, the feeling of dread drops on me again like a piano and I stand up with the feeling, "Oh God. Olivia." I grab the phone out of my pocket and start calling her cell phone again.

Ring....... Ring........

"Olivia? What do you mean?" Goldridge is staring at me intently.

"Olivia Brooks is my girlfriend. The only person that would have interest in doing me any harm is Deacon Brooks."

Ring.... Ring......

I stare at him, waiting for recognition to come over his face. Olivia's kidnapping was all over the news. He would have to have been on a deserted island somewhere to not have heard about it. I can tell the moment he makes the connection.

"Brooks," Goldridge looks at the ceiling as if it holds all the answers, "The girl who was kidnapped and her abductor hasn't been found."

Ring.... Ring....

"She's not answering, I have to go."

I start to make my way to my office door until Detective Goldridge makes the mistake of getting in my way. "Hold on there a second, Mr. Easton. What's the hurry?"

I look at him in pure disbelief, "The hurry is that if Deacon threw the bottle into my club, he did it to distract me, which means Olivia could be in danger right now."

I move around him and open the door, he places a hand on my shoulder trying to stop me again. I spin around. "Look, you can try to hold me here with your fucking questions, but I'm telling you right now, it isn't going to work. That's my girl that could be in danger and nothing and no one is going to keep me from getting to her right now to make sure she is okay."

"I understand. Just hear me out a second, have you spoken to Olivia since you've been here?"

"No, I tried calling earlier, but she didn't answer." The unease takes me over and I can't stand it any longer. "Look, we're done here. I need to go make sure she's okay."

"Alright, we are coming with you."

I don't even wait for them. I'm down the stairs, to my car and taking off as I hear someone, Goldridge maybe, yell to me to slow down because they need to follow.

I probably should have slowed down or let them give me a police escort, but I don't even think about it. My only thought is to get there and make sure she is okay. Of course, I break all kinds of speed laws on my way there, but I couldn't care less.

I don't bother with the underground garage, I just pull straight up to the front of the building. The concierge runs out to me as he sees me park crookedly, "Sir, you can't park there."

I throw the keys at him, "Then tow it."

I'm lucky and the elevator opens just as I get there. I debate for just a minute if I should take the elevator or the stairs but then I throw my body quickly into the elevator and stab at the button. It would be faster to take it up then to run up several flights of stairs. I need to save my energy for whatever may meet me when I walk into the door.

Each and every floor feels like an eternity. I find that I'm bouncing from foot to foot, clenching and unclenching my hands. My heart feels like it is going to explode out of my chest. I'm scared. So fucking scared. I can't lose her again. I would probably die. That's not being dramatic. If he got to her and she was taken, again, there is no one to blame but me. No one.

My breathing is out of control by the time the elevator opens onto her floor. I approach her door slowly and almost stop breathing all together when I see it is ajar. I push it open slowly, trying to be quiet not to startle him in case he is still in the condo.

I walk through the entryway and walk by the kitchen. On my way through I see a bunch of food that was dropped on the floor. The sight makes my heart stop. I run now and what I see, when I reach Olivia's bedroom, makes me stop cold.

25.

VENGEFUL RESCUE

Olivia

EACON PICKS ME up and carries me into my bedroom. It is obvious that his goal is to place me in bed to finish his act, but the thought of being with him in the nearly sacred place where I share my love with Luke is unbearable and makes me go crazy. I start wiggling like a possessed woman in his arms, screaming as much as I can with the tape over my mouth. Resigned and angry, he rolls me out of his arms and drops me on the floor. His apparent haste to have his way with me wins out over the need for a bed. He doesn't try putting me there again, and makes it obvious that any place will do.

Suddenly, everything feels like it is happening in slow motion. He rips my chemise the rest of the way down my body. The tear of the fabric sounds loud in my ears, resounding off the walls. My panties are long gone too. He rips them off when he realizes he can't slide them the rest of the way down my legs with the duct tape around my ankles. I try to bend my good leg's knee to get him in the balls, to no avail. The action only angers him and he pulls my hair and screams in my face for me to stop.

He takes his shirt off and I turn my head to the side while he undoes his buttons one by one. When he presses his skin to mine, I have to swallow the vomit I feel rise in my throat over and over, my throat burns with the effort. With my mouth taped, I need to force it back down. I do not want to drown in my own vomit. Not at all the way I want to die. But then again, perhaps it would be better than enduring this.

The sound of my breath whistles loudly out of my nose and comes in scared pants. I try to calm my mind and focus on something else. I beg my mind to disconnect from my body, finding another place to go, a happy place, but it's difficult. He keeps whispering in my ear how much he wants me, and how he knows I want him too. He keeps running his lips all over my body. Once he goes below my waist, I am finally able to check out completely. I am looking to the side, towards the door and I keep hoping and praying I see someone standing there. "Please help me. Please help me," a repeated mantra and prayer in my head.

He's at his pants again and when I feel his hardness touch the side of my hip, I instinctively squeeze my legs together as hard as I can. Tears run unabashed down my face and I've given up trying to beg and plead through the confines of the tape on my mouth. It doesn't matter anyway, so I keep up the silent plea in my mind instead.

He tries to push my knees apart, "Come on baby, this is going to feel so good."

How crazed he is. I have no idea how much time he's been in the condo now – time is standing still and it feels like hours; I really have no idea. Isn't he afraid of getting caught? Or is his need to power, to claim me, more important? Is he so cocky that the idea of capture doesn't even faze him because he thinks he's invincible? I don't know.

He gives up trying to pull my knees apart and I know he doesn't want to take the tape off from around my ankles, so he flips me over onto my stomach. My hands are trapped under my body, and it pushes my ass up and towards him. He takes the opportunity to slap it. Hard. Then he rubs his hands all over it as if trying to rub the pain away.

He pulls my hips up and I try to check out again, once again staring at the doorway. My heart bleeds for Luke. Not just because I would give anything for him to appear at the door, though I do not want him to see me or to be seen by him in this lunatic's crazed act. More than anything, I need and want my knight to rescue me, but I worry that should he return, and I am once again gone, it will break him. I know him. He will never forgive himself for leaving today, and I don't want that for him.

I wish for so many things. I wish for the life with him I always dreamed of - the one with the amazing house, dog, rocking chairs, and of course, the children. I want a picture perfect, picket fence life with him. A future and a purpose. I know we would be so happy together, and live out all of our pretty little dreams. We would make them a reality. His and mine, we would make them one. We would make them ours.

My wishes become so vivid it's like I see him standing in the doorway looking at me. I try to smile at my vision of him, but when his gorgeous face becomes twisted in disbelief and pain, I realize he isn't just my imagination. My dream Luke would never look so sad, so furious.

Oh God, it's him! Really him! For the first time since Deacon arrived, I feel hope bloom in my chest. I make a sound behind the tape. I feel relief, fear, embarrassment, and shame all at the same time. I hate that he is seeing me like this, and I don't want Luke to get hurt trying to take matters into his own hands. But again, I know him, and he wouldn't have it any other way.

I don't think Deacon has a clue he's here because he has not paused at all, completely focused on his task. That is until an almost inhumane roar catches his attention. I watch him pause, experience a moment of inquiry, and then surprise as Luke quickly lifts him off of me. Their bodies collide with a loud slap and they go crashing into my dresser, knocking it aside, tipping it nearly over and causing items to crash to the floor. The blow they take doesn't seem to faze either Deacon or Luke, as they go rolling across the floor.

As they roll out of my sight, next to my bed, with great exertion, I roll first onto my back and then on to my side. While the movement hurts like a bitch, I finally have Luke within my sight.

"YOUR ARE A SICK FUCK! I'M GOING TO FUCKING KILL YOU!" Luke screams and Deacon is unable to even mutter a word. Luke is enraged. Deacon is about to feel the full wrath of a man possessed; possessed with hatred for the person who dared to abuse and hurt the love of his life. And he deserves everything he's about to get.

Surprise works to Luke's advantage. He's bleeding from his temple, but as they stop rolling, Luke manages to take control. He seizes Deacon by the throat as he positions himself to sit astride him. He stops mid move and forcefully punches Deacon in the crotch. If not for this tape over my mouth, I would be cheering Luke on. I realize that sometime in the process of grabbing Deacon, Luke has thrown the comforter toward me and that it partially covers my exposed body.

Deacon turns to the side and vomits from the pain of the punches. This also brings me complete satisfaction. The vomiting doesn't even faze Luke. He uses Deacon's vomiting to his advantage, and takes the time to sit on top of Deacon's chest and punches him in the face. Over and over and over, again. Deacon is bleeding from his nose, from his eyes, from his mouth. His whole face is covered in it. But Luke doesn't stop, even when Deacon gets in a good hit of his own, it doesn't matter. Luke is a machine. I feel a deep sense of satisfaction as Luke lands each blow.

I'm startled when I hear additional voices and I try to roll back over to see what is going on. People holding guns enter the room. One in a policemen's uniform and another in a suit immediately run to Luke and Deacon and try to pull them apart. Luke isn't making it easy. His eyes are glassy looking and focused, and he keeps swinging, even when his target is moved out of range. The man in the suit is almost falling over in his attempt to get Luke to stop. At one point, Luke actually manages to break away and gives Deacon a hard kick in the side. I hear something crack when his foot connects and Deacon bellows in pain. Deacon is quickly placed on his stomach, regardless of the pain to his side, and the Officer gets his handcuffs out, "You have the right to remain silent..."

While all this is happening, another officer enters my bedroom, covers me completely with the comforter. His eyes are kind and I appreciate his thoughtfulness and attempt to provide me a bit of modesty in this unfathomable moment. He sits on the floor beside me and immediately removes the tape from my mouth, which is quite painful. It feels like I lost some skin in the process and my lips burn. "So sorry," he mutters and then starts working at freeing me from the tape around my wrists and ankles.

I hear the man in the suit talking to Luke, "Mr. Easton, calm down. Get yourself under control or I will slap cuffs on you too." I don't think Luke even hears him. He's still struggling against the man and his gaze hasn't left Deacon. I barely hear them. I look down at the officer working at freeing me and see that in his haste to help me, he set his gun on the ground instead of holstering it. I can't stop staring at it and thinking about everything I've experienced because of Deacon. I close my eyes and can feel his skin against mine, his mouth on my body, the blows to my face. Once free, before I even realize what I'm about to do, I grab the gun from the floor and stand.

I hold the gun out and hear a chorus of "Whoas," from the officers around me. But all I can feel at the moment is exposed. My ripped clothes gape around me, my hair is in disarray and hanging partly in my face, and I feel a twinge of humiliation and embarrassment. But, as I look at Deacon, and relive what he put me through, those feelings are nothing compared to the way the man before me has hurt me, and violated me. The Officer that untied me holds up his hands and backs away from me when he sees me with the gun. "It's okay," he says. But it's not. It will never be okay.

I have one purpose, one thing on my mind. I slowly raise the gun higher, pointing it straight at Deacon's head. The whole room goes quiet and I can feel every eye on me. One time for fun, Pyper and I went to the firing range and learned how to shoot, so I know damn well how to remove the safety and hold a gun. I take the safety off, and the sound is loud and my intent, very clear. Deacon, who was looking at the ground, slowly raises his head until his eyes are locked onto mine.

Like a horror movie, memories of him touching me, talking to me, hurting me, yelling at me, squeezing me, terrifying me, enter my mind once again. They come at me, one after another, until it's all I can see. I can't even see him or anyone else anymore, I just see the way he terrorized me for months. For years. The happy good times are long forgotten, buried by the horrors reality brings. Tears carrying pain and sorrow fall from my eyes and slide down my face. How the tears keep coming, I will never understand. Does one ever shed so many that they dry up? Do they ever stop? Will mine ever stop?

I blink repeatedly, trying to push those memories away, needing to focus on what I'm about to do. I stare at the man who is the cause of them all. "Princess?"

"DON'T CALL ME THAT! I HATE when you call me that!" My hand is shaking so hard and hate flows from every pore on my body. "How can you look at me like that? With such shock...such surprise?" I shake my head in disbelief, "Do you really have no idea what you've done to me?"

"I just wanted you. I just wanted us to be together." He starts crying. Tears pour down his face, and his eyes are laced with fear.

"Oh, please. Save it, you bastard. You don't deserve to shed tears."

"I'm crying for you."

"Fuck you. I don't want them."

"I want you. That's all, Olivia. Don't you understand? Everything I did was because I want to be with you."

"WELL I DON'T WANT TO BE WITH YOU!" I scream. I start shaking harder, head to toe, and the gun shakes even more in my hand. All I can think about is how much better I would feel if he would die.

26.

RIGHTEOUS RAGE

Luke

RAGE. PURE, UNADULTERATED rage is all I feel when I see Olivia tied up in her room with Deacon over her. Two seconds. Two seconds is all it takes for my heart to stop, my world to crumble and for my life to implode. Her nakedness bared, her eyes lost, my soul shattered. Two seconds.

Fear, anger, disbelief, and then revenge bleeds from my pores, screaming at me to make him pay. An inhumane sound twists its way out of my throat before I even realize I'm doing it. I'm on Deacon in no time, my one mission to make him pay for hurting my girl.

With every brutal pound, every slap, every jab, every kick, I feel like I'm vindicating Olivia. Problem is, it will never be enough. I could beat him until every orifice of his is leaking and gushing blood. I could make sure every inch of his body is black and blue with my stamp of hatred. I could pound him so far into this fucking floor that they would need a damn crowbar just to get him out of here, but it will never be enough.

How do you pay someone back for four weeks of terror? How do you pay someone back for years of verbal, mental and physical abuse? I don't speak at all while beating him. I'm completely focused on the task of making sure he never hurts Olivia again. What he was doing to her... I can't even... I can't even let my mind go there. I may have arrived just in time, but what if I hadn't? How would she ever come back from that? Is that what he did to her before? He would have taken her again.

I could have lost her.

Again.

The thought makes my fists fly faster, harder. Every grunt he makes in pain; every time I feel his flesh give against my fist gives me a deep feeling of satisfaction. I'm vaguely aware that I'm sitting on him and pummeling his face in, when suddenly strong arms are trying to pull me away.

I resist. I need to make him pay. It isn't enough. It will never be enough. I'm not done yet.

"Luke! Luke, enough. That's enough now."

I flail my arms and kick like hell, trying to get out of Detective Goldridge's grasp. Who the fuck does he think he is, taking me away from Deacon? Doesn't he understand? He's a man. How would he feel if he found a sick fuck trying to rape his girl? He'd be doing the same thing. I know that for damn sure.

"Luke. Enough. Stop. She needs you."

Those words are like ice water over my whole body, bringing me clarity. I immediately look over to my right and see her. And oh hell, my heart bleeds, every part of me screams in agony at the sight of her.

Olivia stands to the right of me, practically naked, her ripped clothing hanging off of her body. But it isn't her nakedness that captures my attention for once, it's the gun she's holding and pointing directly at Deacon. Her hands are shaking and the skin around her wrists is red and raw. Her gorgeous face is battered and already bruising. One of her eyes is almost completely swollen shut, and her mouth and the skin around it looks red and swollen. Some of the skin is even bleeding a little from where the tape was removed. Her nose is running blood and it's dripping down her mouth, chin, and to the floor. Deacon must have hit her hard a few times and the thought almost makes me charge after him again. Instead, I take a deep breath and die a little more inside at the look of pure determination in her eyes.

I hesitate for a moment. I admit, part of me wants to cheer her on. Tell her to do it, hell I would even put my finger over hers and help her pull the trigger, but the fact is, this isn't her. And he deserves far more than the easy way out.

"Livvie?"

She doesn't move, but I know she heard me by the little jerk her body makes at the sound of my voice. I want more than anything to gather her into my arms. It takes physical, as well as mental effort to stand still and do this the right way.

"Livvie?" I repeat, but this time, I'm standing right next to her, facing her. I don't want to get in front of the gun, just in case her trembling gets worse and it accidentally goes off.

She turns her head towards me and blinks as if she's trying to bring me into focus. Her head tilts to the side, making her look as if she's confused, "Luke?"

I give her a small smile. I can feel blood dripping down the side of my face and under my nose. I start to bring my hands up to wipe my face, but realize my hands are covered in blood. My knuckles are cracked and bleeding. I can't help but give a soft grunt in satisfaction, knowing that the majority of the blood is not mine. "Angel, you need to put the gun down."

Tears fall from her eyes, each one taking my heart with them. She's cried so much since her kidnapping - I don't want her to ever cry again. I vow right then to spend the rest of my life making sure my girl laughs more than cries for the rest of our days. "I can't," she whispers, "He tried to hurt me," I grit my teeth. "He did hurt me."

"I know. I know, angel, and I'm so sorry." I take another step toward her.

"Don't." I stop moving, but then quickly realize that's not what she means, "Don't you dare apologize. Not for him."

"I'm not. I'm apologizing for me. I left you alone. Again." The thought of what could have happened if I had not arrived in time, makes me feel physically ill.

"No," she whispers, "no, this is not your fault. Don't you dare take ownership of this. It belongs to him," her vehemence makes her shake the gun in the direction of Deacon. "This is *all* his fault, and I'm going to kill him. I'm going to make him go away, so we never have to worry about him again."

"Livvie, no. This is not you. This is your anger, fear, pain, and hurt talking. Look, I understand," I try to reason, "Believe me. No one wants him dead more than me. He hurt the one woman on earth that I love more than anything, and I want to see him dead as much as you do. This, however, is not the way. This is not you."

"Luke, I can't. I can't let him get away with this."

"Ma'am if you don't put down the gun, we will have no choice, but to make you." Detective Asshole decides to take this moment to declare. If I wouldn't get arrested, I would punch him in the face. That would likely be pushing my luck though.

I see Olivia briefly look over at him, then back at me. I turn my head towards Detective Dick and whisper, "Just wait," and then look back at Livvie. "You aren't letting him get away with anything by not shooting him. But Livvie, if you do this... if you pull that trigger...then he wins."

"I don't understand. I would win. He would PAY for what he's done." The gun shakes in her hands when she speaks, emphasizing her words. In response, Officer Knight and Detective Douche, pull guns from their holsters, and point them at her.

"Whoa! Put your fucking guns away! Just give me a minute to talk to her!"

"We can't take a chance that she won't pull the trigger."

"She won't shoot me, she doesn't have the guts," chimes in Deacon right then and it takes everything I have not to take the gun from her and shoot the bastard myself.

Olivia however, only gets emboldened by his words, "Oh, I won't?" I swear I see her finger twitch on the trigger making my heart stop for at least the tenth time.

"Livvie! No! I will NOT let you do this! This is not you!"

She looks at me and the look in her eyes makes me hold my breath. It's like after all this time, she's finally letting me get a real look inside her mind. Inside her heart. And I'm seeing everything she's been trying so desperately to keep hidden. She looks utterly and completely lost.

"Not me? Luke, I haven't been me for weeks. I've been trying like hell to keep it all in. To cover everything up with forced laughter and normalcy. I thought that moving forward and being normal would make things better. But it hasn't. I don't know if it ever will."

"That's not true, Livvie."

"Isn't it? When is the last time that I've been shopping or read a fashion magazine and lost myself in the world I love? I hardly blog anymore - just enough to keep it going. I haven't had a writing job in weeks, I've hardly left the house. I don't even know who I am anymore."

"I do. I know exactly who you are. You're *my* girl." I take a step toward her, "I've known you since we were sixteen. Then, and now, you are the same girl inside that you've always been. Funny, beautiful, passionate, and smart." I take a small step and touch the side of her face. "You have a crazy obsession with shoes and handbags. You know every color, trend and style that's been popular over the last several years. You make me laugh, like no one else can." I see a small smile on her lips and I keep going. "You also turn me on like no one else can." She flushes a little at my words, "Your cheeks flush when you're embarrassed or excited." I smirk at her while brushing my thumb across her cheek, "You have a best friend that adores you. You are a bit clumsy," I get a small laugh then, "and you are a horrible cook." I get a full laugh this time. "The sound of your laugh is the best sound I've ever heard, and you fit perfectly in my arms." I hold them open now.

"You are the other half of me. I thought I lost you once, Livvie, I won't lose you again. Not for him. He's not worth it." The gun she's holding lowers an inch, and out of the corner of my eye I can see Detective Idiot's shoulders relax just a bit.

"I get that you are confused and you've been through hell, but you see, angel... I know exactly who you are. Whenever you aren't sure... whenever you feel lost. Lean on me. I'll hold you, kiss you and love you, and whisper reminders whenever you need them, reminding you exactly who the girl is that stole my heart all those years ago."

Silent tears pour down her cheeks again and as she finally lowers the gun, I step the rest of the way towards her and finally take her in my arms, kissing her tears away.

"She's my wife! Don't you touch her!" Deacon screams, but we ignore him. Lost in one another's arms, he's on his way to becoming just a very bad memory.

Officer Knight steps behind Livvie, "Technically, I'm supposed to arrest you for taking my gun and threatening to shoot someone," he holds his hand out for his gun and Olivia gives it to him. "But I didn't see anything... did you, Officer Phish?"

I turn to Phish, to see him look at the Detective and Officer Knight. A small smile covers his mouth, "See what?"

"She threatened my life! You're just going to let her get away with it? I want an attorney! I want her arrested now!"

"Those punches must have screwed you up because you are out of your mind, that never happened and we were here the whole time," Detective Awesome says.

I breathe a sigh of relief and pull Olivia closer to me. "I love you," I whisper in her ear.

"I love you too," she breathes.

"What the hell?!"

We both pull apart to look towards the door at the fiery redhead that's standing there, looking around in pure confusion. The minute her eyes take in Deacon in cuffs and Olivia's state, she stifles a sob and runs to Olivia. "Oh my God, are you okay? What happened?"

"Pyper," I put my hand on her shoulder, "I promise to fill you in later, but for now, can you get a robe for Olivia?"

She looks from me to Olivia and her face flushes a little as if she just noticed Olivia's basically undressed. "Yes, of course. I'm sorry!"

As she starts walking to the bathroom, Officer Phish starts to take Deacon from the room. Pyper stops right in front of him, and once again everyone in the room stills as Pyper looks Deacon straight in the face.

"Pyper?" Olivia says, her voice shaking in nervousness.

Pyper looks at Olivia, then at Deacon. Before I can even comprehend it, she spits a giant wad of saliva in his face and kicks him in the balls. "That's for tying me up and kidnapping Olivia, you stupid, fucking piece of shit!"

It takes me a minute before I realize my mouth has hit the floor. I look at Olivia and see she is nervously looking at the officers, afraid of the repercussions for Pyper's actions.

Officer Knight smiles, "Man, something is seriously messed up with my eyes," he says rubbing them. "How about you, Detective?"

"Yeah, things are just really out of focus for some reason."

"I didn't see shit." Officer Phish says, while pulling on Deacon's arm to try and get him standing to pull him out of the room.

"Well, I certainly feel better," the spitfire throws us a smile over her shoulder before she heads to get a robe for Olivia.

I look at Olivia and see her watching Pyper with a smile on her face. She looks back at me and her face falls. "I need to talk to you."

Before I can respond, we're interrupted by Pyper returning, and Officer Goldridge, "I'm sorry to interrupt, but I have to take your official statement, Olivia."

"Is she allowed to get cleaned up first?"

"Yes... yes of course. We don't need to collect any evidence from your person. There's no question here what happened and who did it."

I nod and begin walking Olivia to the bathroom, "You know we sure are spending a lot of time in the bathroom lately."

She smiles a little and I ease her onto the counter and grab a washcloth, intending to help her. I hold the washcloth to her face, intending to wipe the blood from under her nose when she grabs my wrist, stopping me.

I look into her eyes and she whispers, "Thank you."

"I want to help you."

"No, that's not what I mean. Thank you for saving me in there. Thank you for loving me, thank you for knowing me. Thank you for finding me in the middle of my madness. You're my heart, Luke."

"I'll always find you if you get lost, Livvie. Always."

27.

HEALING TEARS

Olivia

*A*LL I WANT to do is talk to Luke. Instead, I have to give the police a statement regarding what happened before they arrived. Luke sits on one side of me during my question and answer session, and Pyper on the other. It feels like a cross-examination at times, instead of merely providing my recall of events. Each of them hold my hands the whole time – I'm not sure if they are offering comfort to me, or to themselves. I think both. When I get to the parts that are too upsetting for Luke – recounting Deacon tying me up, hitting me, and ripping off my clothes - Luke is off the couch. Pyper squeezes my hand so tightly, I'm afraid she will break it. She's gritting her teeth; I can hear them grinding and see her jaw flex on the side. I know she's trying to keep from crying, so I give her a reassuring squeeze in return.

Luke stands and paces, his hands fisted at his sides. He mumbles under his breath, but I can't make out what he's saying, other than a four-letter-word now and then. At one point, he walks to the window, grips the ledge and stares outside. It's obvious he's not really seeing the gorgeous view before him; he's lost in his own thoughts.

The entire time I'm speaking to the police, I'm hanging on by a thread. My face and body are in a lot of pain. The paramedics get called immediately and they check me out and treat what they can. I refuse to go to the hospital, so there is nothing else they can do for me. They said to put ice on my swollen face, take non-aspirin pain relievers, to call my doctor immediately if the pain persists or gets worse. I swallow some ibuprofen to hopefully lessen some of the pain.

Initially, the police thought that Deacon was hiding out in the hallway, waiting for Luke to leave. When he saw him go, he came into the condo. They had theories about how he would have gotten into the secure building or obtained the key to the condo. All were pretty much mysteries until they can interrogate him, but then Deacon's car provided all the answers.

It was parked in the garage below the building. Obtaining a search warrant must have been easy, because it sure happened fast. The officers found guns, rope, knives, more duct tape, wire, a small suitcase with personal effects for him, a few women's clothing articles, and fake passports he had made – one for him and one for me.

Luke and I looked at each other in confusion when the police asked us to follow them to the parking garage. They led us to a car that had crime tape surrounding it and a trunk propped open.

"Please brace yourselves; there is a dead body in the trunk of Deacon Brooks' car. We would like to know if you recognize him, Olivia, and we assumed you would want Luke to be with you."

"You assumed correctly." I blindly reach out for Luke's hand and grab it as I approached the car. I felt brave with Luke next to me and didn't hesitate, walking right to the back of the car. At the same time I said, "That's Ronnie," Luke gasps and said, "That's Brian!"

Officer Phish later explained, "Our assumption is that Deacon didn't want to leave any loose ends when he took you this time," he says looking at me. "Ronnie Holt, aka Brian West, was Deacon's buddy. When we ran a background check on Ronnie and Deacon, we found the connection. The two of them started getting in trouble when they were younger – and ended up in juvie at the same time, like he told you. They stayed in touch it appears, and Ronnie had a stream of arrests - drunk and disorderly, DUIs, petty theft." He hesitates, "He... he was even accused of assault and rape, but the charges were dropped - the girl disappeared with no evidence. The house you were kept in belonged to Ronnie's aunt, like Deacon told you, Olivia. She died, leaving the house to Ronnie. Events surrounding her death were suspicious - but there was never any evidence found - only rumors. We don't have proof that Ronnie murdered her, even though Deacon told you that. We will be looking into his aunt's death again."

"You found all of this out already?" Luke asked surprised

Officer Phish smiled, "It pays to have connections." Luke and I looked at each other, both shrugging our shoulders.

"Ronnie obviously got a job as Brian at your club, Luke, in order to keep a closer eye on what was happening with Olivia. This also explains how Deacon got in the house. We believe Ronnie lifted your keys at the club and made copies."

Now, as I contemplate all the information we've been told, I realize I obviously didn't know Deacon at all. He was truly psychotic. It's hard to believe that I ever could have loved him. Or thought he loved me. Even after experiencing his evil, it is difficult to accept the fact that he was so incredibly sick that he could actually murder someone – well, I have a hard time wrapping my mind around it all. It makes me aware of what he was truly capable of doing, even to me and to Luke or Pyper. Until now, it was all speculation, theory, wonder. But it's the truth. He was my worst nightmare. The thought makes me shudder with revulsion and horror.

By the time I finally get Luke alone, several hours have passed. We barely walk through my bedroom door and I turn to look at Luke. I can see conflict on his face, not knowing where to begin or what to say. I open my mouth to say... something...anything. He reaches a hand out and touches my cheek. His eyes are a mixture of love, compassion and sadness and I feel my whole face crumple, the breath leaves my lungs, and a sob rises in my throat. Out of nowhere, every suppressed and unexpressed feeling and emotion of the last several weeks comes hammering down on me and I can't breathe, can't bear the secrets and evasions any longer. My legs give out beneath me, and Luke grabs me and eases us to the floor as one.

I sob. Gut wrenching, soul moving, deep heaving, nearly hysterical weeping that starts in my soul and erupts up and out of my throat, infuriated at being denied for so long. Massive tears flow, forming a salty pool where they fall. I grab for and hold onto Luke, dig my fingernails into his shoulders. I pull him so close to me, there isn't a breath of space between us and his body shakes with every tremble of my own. Like flashes of a movie, my life plays out before my eyes, and with each scene, tears fall, but also cleanse and offer the purification I have been seeking.

I cry for the teenager I was that fell in love with a boy and made a hasty, life-changing decision upon hearing something not meant for her ears. I cry because instead of trusting and confronting Luke, I made an assumption and ran. I cry for the naïve lost girl I became, so desperate to fill an ache inside of her, that she allowed it to be filled with the vileness of a man like Deacon. I cry for my stubbornness and pride that prohibited me from accepting that the only one who would ever be able to fill that ache, was the man currently in my arms.

I cry for every angry and defiling word, every painful touch, grab, pull and tear of my flesh at Deacon's hands. I cry for the girl who made excuses each and every time, when she should have said enough. I cry for the battered, insecure girl who never stood up for herself, for the girl who never felt she deserved more. I cry for the woman who felt broken when she found her husband cheating. A part of her already knowing, yet not accepting the finality, and lacking the courage to end things, so staying and taking even more. I cry for the moment the reality of her marriage was thrust into her face in such a repulsive way.

I cry at the fear I felt when I found my best friend bound and gagged. I cry for each time I woke up naked next to a madman, not knowing what had occurred between us. I cry for each puncture I felt from the needle. I cry at the loss of hope I felt each time I looked for a way out but found none. I cry for my broken bones, the bruises, the injuries sustained. I cry for my family. Seeing their troubled faces and pain, but instead of allowing them to offer me love and comfort, I pushed them away.

I cry for today. I cry because I have lost a piece of myself – and I don't recognize this fearful, angry, revengeful self. Who is this woman that wants to kill a man - that has so much hatred that she wants him to feel the same pain he's inflicted upon me? That wants him to pay. I was violated. I was hurt. I was hit. I was touched. I was drugged. Scratched. Bruised. Assaulted. Practically raped. But worse of all, I cry for the times when I wanted to give up. To give into the pain and misery and just let go. I cry for the times I hoped he would go too far and put me out of my misery. For my broken spirit. For my ravished soul.

Finally, I cry for the man that loves me. Who wouldn't let me push him away, who was strong, consistent, and unfailing and who has loved me through it all, unconditionally, waiting patiently for me to work through my hurt, my bitterness, my despair and struggles.

My sobs turn into silent shuddering and slowly, the tears begin to subside and I realize that Luke is murmuring words of love to me, has been rocking me back and forth. "It's okay, Livvie. I'm here. Let it out. You are safe. I love you. I'm here. Let it out, angel. I love you."

As my sobs quiet, I'm left with little hiccups and I pull away and look at him. He immediately wipes the now slow falling, faint trail of tears from my cheeks and attempts a smile, "Feel better?"

"A little. I'm sorry for blubbering and getting this....on your shirt," I rasp, gesturing at the river on his chest.

"It's just a shirt, angel."

My body and face hurt from all of the abuse. I feel emotionally spent – exhausted– I could sleep for days. "Luke, I need to talk to you."

"There's no rush, love. Maybe now isn't the right time. You need to rest."

"No, I can't," I shake my head, emphasizing my words. "I've stayed quiet for too long, and I can't do it anymore."

"Okay," he whispers uncertainly. Luke looks at me, waiting patiently for me to begin.

"I don't even know where to start," I admit. "I need to tell you some things about when I was kidnapped." My heart starts to pound in my chest. I'm so afraid of his reaction. Part of me would like to tell him I changed my mind and that I do need rest after all, but I can't.

"Livvie, I really don't thi-"

"No. Please don't argue with me," I look down. "I need to tell you now, I need this for me too. I can't, no, I must not, keep quiet any longer." I take a deep breath and look up again to meet his eyes,

"I know that you know the basics. I was kept in a room, drugged most of the time. When I was alone, and coherent, I would try to find a way out. I never found one, but I would still look, try again, determined not to give up."

I swallow and take a deep breath, look up to the sky and then force myself to meet his eyes again as I continue. "But sometimes... sometimes, in my darkest moments, when I couldn't be comforted by dreams of you, I wanted to give up, Luke. I'm so sorry!" My words catch on a newly formed sob, and I do my best to fight it down. "There were moments, just a few, where I didn't want to fight anymore. It all felt so hopeless."

"Baby, that's understandable. All that matters is that you didn't give into it. You didn't give up. You're here, and you're going to be okay."

"Deacon. He... he would make me sleep with him... n-naked," I blurt.

Luke's only reaction is to curse low under his breath and to increase his hold on me.

"When I would sleep, almost always my dreams would be about you and I...I would dream we were together, happy. Sometimes we would just be talking about random things in my dream like the weather, or trips we wanted to take together. Other times, we would be intimate. I would feel you touching me."

I stop.

Tears gather in my eyes.

I try to stop them, but they start their silent descent down my cheeks, not caring for my wishes.

I take another deep breath.

"Your hands would run up my legs or over my breasts, and I would wake up, wanting you so much. I would turn to you, eyes closed, wanting to return your touches and words of love, only to open them and find it wasn't your face looking back at me. It wasn't your hands touching me. It wasn't you in bed with me."

Luke lets off a stream of curses this time, flashes of pain he tries his best to cover run over his face.

Now that the words have started, I couldn't begin to contain them even if I wanted to. He needs to know – and I need to tell.

"Luke...I...what I'm trying to say..." I hesitate, these next few words feeling stuck in my throat.

"Angel -"

I hold up a hand, stopping him once again. "No, Luke, please. Let me get through this." He nods his head, looking conflicted, but I continue, "What I'm trying to tell you is that I thought Deacon raped me. When I was awake and aware of my surroundings, it never happened. We never had sex. But, I was in and out of it most of the time, and until he told me today that he never went further, I wasn't one hundred percent sure if he tried to take advantage of that. He insinuated more than once that he had." I look down, momentarily have those recurrent feelings of being ashamed and unclean. I wonder if I will ever truly feel clean...pre-Deacon...again. It's as if a tainted film covers my whole body.

I still can't bring myself to look at Luke's face as I continue, "I want you to know that they did a rape kit at the hospital. They tested for STDs and did a... a pregnancy test," Looking up now at Luke, I see him running his hands through his hair in that all-too familiar nervous gesture. He has turned his face to the side, and a lone tear falls down his cheek. "They got the results rather quickly, and I was told they were all negative. I wouldn't have been with you sexually if it wasn't safe. I hope you know that."

Luke sighs, "Angel, can I talk now?"

I place my finger over his lips, silencing him once more. "Just a minute. I want you to know that I know you love me. It isn't a question of that. It's a question of whether or not you can live with this. I'm a bit messed up. I tried, oh how I tried, to get back to normal. I really thought the best thing for me was to keep marching forward, to go as far away from it all as I could and hopefully, eventually, my fears would calm and my anxiety would lessen. Sometimes that worked – like dinner for example." The memory makes me flash a smile, "But, honestly, that was so dumb of me. So short-sighted. Instead of lessening, everything just intensified. It's been building inside of me, so much so, that at times, it was hard to breathe and I thought I might explode. Or worse." I pause for a moment and take a deep breath. "I'm so sorry that I kept this from you. I should have told you what happened before I was ever even intimate with you. But I just couldn't bring myself to. I was so afraid to tell you because I don't want to lose you."

"Livvie, I really need to tell you something."

I keep going, determined to get the rest of this out, "As much as I love you, Luke, I know that it isn't healthy to keep doing this to myself. I can't keep living this way – I have to deal with this. Like it or not, this has affected me and it's going to take time for me to work through this." I take his hands in mine, "I love you and I don't want to lose you. You've been amazing these past few weeks, and I am so in love with you. I've never loved you more. I promise, that I will find myself again. I promise that I will work through this, given time, and I will be the girl you fell in love with again. If you just give me a chance…" I stop, breaking off with a sob, the pain of these words catching up with me, surprised that I have the capacity to even produce more tears.

Luke places his hands on both sides of my face, waiting for me to meet his eyes. Once I do, he gives me a small kiss on my lips. Another tear falls down his face, and the sight almost breaks me. I reach out and catch it with my fingertip, then bring it to my lips and kiss it. He kisses me again, this time, letting his lips linger on mine a little longer.

He removes his hands from my face, and takes my hands in his own, "Do you remember that day we were at the hospital and the police officers made us leave the room? They said they had to ask you some questions in private."

"Yes, I remember. After you left they asked me-"

"They asked you if Deacon physically or sexually assaulted you."

"Yes. How...how do you know that?" I look at him confused.

"I had just gotten you back. If I couldn't see you with my eyes, I was going to make damn sure I could hear you instead. I left the room, but being the protective ass I can be, I didn't close the door all the way and I heard what they said to you."

My mouth falls open, "Wait... so that means..."

"It means that all this time, I've known. I've known all along. Livvie, how could you think that I would possibly care about that? I love you. That means always and forever. It doesn't come with a disclaimer. All I cared about the whole time you were gone was getting you back, safe and sound. I thought I would never see you again. I thought you were gone from my life. That things would never be as we both dreamed. You have no idea what that did to me. If that meant you had to sleep with the devil himself to keep you safe, and give you more time until you were found or escaped, then I'm glad you did it. If it meant keeping you alive and saving your life, then I would have been the first person to tell you to do what you had to do to stay alive. Whatever the fuck it took to bring you back to me, that's all I care about, and that's what you did. You endured hell so you could come back to me."

"I can't imagine how you must have felt when you heard that."

"I'm not going to lie, it broke me. Not because you may have had sex with Deacon, and believe me I'm SO glad that didn't happen, but because you were forced into that situation to begin with. On some level, I still blame myself that you were ever kidnapped, and I have my own issues to work through with that. Being with you and loving you, even after this, was never a question. Don't you get it, Livvie? You're it for me. You're my *everything.* You say that you will get back to the girl I love, but baby, that's all you've ever been. I wanted you to let me love you *through* this – and you have. I knew you would tell me when the time was right for you. None of the other stuff matters, all I care about is that you are here, in my arms, and that nothing ever hurts you like that again. Everything else? We will figure that out."

"Luke, I love you so much. Thank you for loving me. I'm the luckiest girl ever."

"I love you too, angel. So much. And we are going to get through this. Together. One day at a time."

Epilogue

DREAMS DO COME TRUE

Olivia

NE DAY AT a time. Luke couldn't have been more right about that. Some days, it's minute by minute, and other days I don't think about it at all. I look at my therapist and know it is due in big part to her. Dr. Helen Roberts has been my confidant, life saver, and my own personal champion. When the anxiety and memories become too much, she has given me tools to help me calm myself. I was diagnosed with post-traumatic stress disorder and it hasn't been an easy walk – but it is a journey I'm determined to finish. With her help, and of course, with Luke's.

"It sounds like those breathing exercises are really helping you, Olivia, and that your episodes are happening less and less."

"Yes, I really am doing much better. The medicine really helps with my anxiety and of course Luke is sometimes all the medicine I need." I smile mischievously, making Dr. Roberts laugh.

"I have no doubt about that, but remember that while it is important to have your support from him and working through your couples issues is important, you need to continue to strengthen and get through this individually. That's how you will bring your best to your relationship with Luke. You are making tremendous progress, Olivia, you should be very proud of yourself."

"I am, thank you." These past several months have been a mixture of difficult, and wonderful. For a long time, nightmares would wake me almost nightly such that I feared falling asleep. Even though Deacon is in jail, without bond, awaiting trail, I continued to have an irrational fear at times that he would come back. Luke and Dr. Roberts have really encouraged me to take everything one day at a time and to stop being so hard on myself. Luke even comes to couples therapy with me, insisting that this journey be one we go through together, side by side.

Thinking about him brings a smile to my face. A knowing look crosses Dr. Robert's face, "Well, that is all the time we have today, I will see you and Luke next week."

"Okay, thank you very much." I stand, smoothing my black pencil skirt and balancing on my brand new Jimmy Choo heels. I've finally got my love for fashion back in full force. I'm blogging daily again, posting pictures of my outfits of the day, and have started writing for other magazines again as well.

"Oh, and tell Luke that I really enjoyed his column last week on your blog. That tip about romancing a woman was great."

I laugh, "I will tell him!" Thinking about Luke's new column makes me chuckle to myself. I love that he is so involved with what I do, so much so, that he wanted to contribute. 'Luke's Love Tip List' has become a hit among my readers.

I give Dr. Roberts one more goodbye and head to my car. The silk of my top sliding against my shoulders, the summer sun on my skin, the sound of birds in the sky, all make me smile and stop for just a moment and take in the beauty of the day. I continue to my car and feel my surprise quickly replaced with a moment of worry as I look up and see Pyper standing next to it. My steps pick up as I race to her, intent on making sure everything is okay. Pyper has no reason to be here. When Pyper finally sees me walking toward her, a smile lights up her face, which makes me instantly relax. She wouldn't be smiling if she had bad news or something was wrong.

"Pyper! What are you doing here? You're smiling, so I'm guessing that means everything is okay, right?"

"Oh! Of course everything is fine. I'm sorry I scared you. I'm just here to make a delivery."

My brows furrow in confusion. "A delivery?"

Pyper smiles wider and pulls a pink rose out from behind her back with a white note card and hands them to me. "Here you go," she says and then starts to walk away. I start to ask her what the hell this is all about but then she stops, turns around, and gives me a big hug. "I love you, Livvie."

"I love you too." My words are slow – confused. "Pyper? What's going on?"

"Just read the note. And call me later, okay?"

"Okay," I murmur absently as I look down at the note and see Luke's handwriting. I open the envelope addressed to me and begin to read.

"My life was forever changed the first time I saw you. I think I knew at that moment that I would never be the same. Did I ever tell you that health class wasn't the first time I saw you? No, it was at your locker. Locker number 1021. Already a fashion queen, you were standing there with Pyper, laughing at something she said. Your laughter drew me in like a bee to honey, and all I remember thinking was that I had to make you mine. Get in your car, and go to that locker. I love you."

I don't waste a moment, intrigued and excited by Luke's note, I can't wait to find out what he is up to. I make the trip quickly and practically fall out of my car in my haste to meet him at my old school locker. I can't believe he even remembered the number! I sure didn't; only its location.

I enter the school, somewhat surprised the door is unlocked, since all are away for summer break, and make my way to the hallway where my old locker resides. I notice a secretary sitting at a desk in an office off of the entry, she catches my eye and I see her smile slightly, seemingly acknowledging and expecting my presence. Curious. As I turn down the hall to where my locker was located, I'm disappointed that I don't see Luke standing there. Instead, as I approach my locker, I see another pink rose, with a note taped to the front.

"Imagine my excitement, at finding out you were in the same health class as I was. Teasing you, charming you, and asking you out daily became my mission. I never let the fact you said 'no' bring me down or deter me, because I could see the twinkle in your eye every time I asked. I knew it was only a matter of time until you gave in to my undeniable charm," I laugh. "The day you said 'yes' was a day I will always remember. Go to the place you finally spoke that word."

I put the rose to my nose for just a moment and take in its sweet scent and then walk down the echoing hallways towards the classroom that we shared for our health class. While some things have changed, the old high school is much the same. As I walk, my memories continue. I remember his cocky smirk and the way our hands touched accidentally when he helped me with a chair. Shivers of excitement ran through my whole body at that simple touch, and now, years later his touch still emits the same feeling. I remember the surprise I felt the day I came to class, already prepared for his daily question of 'will you go out with me' but he did not ask. The memory makes me laugh now. Then, I was a bit disappointed. Once I reach the classroom, there on the door, is another rose, with a note.

"Aside from staring at you the entire hour of class we shared together, I think one of the things I loved most about high school was watching you cheer for me when I played football. I would look over during the game, when I was supposed to be paying attention to the field, and see your hair glistening in the lights, and your cheeks flushed from the cold. You were so beautiful, it would take my breath away. If you caught me looking at you, you'd blow me a kiss and I could practically feel it meet my lips. Go there."

I walk to the back of the school, increasingly captivated by this whole scavenger hunt, out the doors, nearly skipping towards the football field, hoping to finally find the man of my dreams. This has to be the most romantic thing anyone has ever done. I feel so loved by him that it takes my breath away. When I reach the gate to the field, instead of finding him, I find yet another rose and note.

"While my childhood home is full of great childhood memories that I will cherish forever, there is one that will always haunt me. Go to my house."

I make my way back to my car and head to Luke's childhood home. A momentarily feeling of uneasiness and dread hits me. I haven't been back since the day I left it...that day so long ago. Deep breaths. When I pull into the driveway, memories of that day assault my mind and attack my heart. I hear the dreaded words from his mouth spoken to his mother and see myself run to my car, eyes full of tears and stubbornness in my heart. How I wish I had done things differently. I park my car, and slowly, even reluctantly. get out. My anxiety is quickly relieved as I look towards the door with tear-filled eyes and see Luke's father standing there, holding a rose, with a smile on his face.

"Olivia. Long time no see," his smile is warm and kind. And he reaches out to provide me an embrace.

"Mr. Easton, it's so nice to see you again. I'm so sorry for your loss. I apologize that I haven't had the chance to tell you sooner." I graciously accept his hug and return one of my own.

"It's okay dear, and thank you." He holds the pink rose and note card out to me and I take it from his hands. "He loves you so much, Olivia. The day he lost you... well I wasn't sure if he would ever be the same. I'm so glad that you both found one another again."

"Me too," I whisper.

"I will leave you to read your love note. Please come by again soon, okay?"

"I will, I promise."

He nods, gives me a smile and walks back into the house. I open the note card from Luke, "While the moment I lost you here is one of my saddest, it is also significant and part of our story. I wish it had never happened, and I had not missed out on so much time with you, but I know now that we are stronger for it. Losing one another has only made us appreciate one another more. Now that we've found one another again, I know we will never take one another for granted, or do anything that would purposefully hurt the other again. The night I finally found you again, I will never forget. Go to Zero Gravity."

I take one last look at Luke's home and get into my car. And smile. I drive across town, wondering if this will be my last stop, if he will finally be at the club. I want to kiss him. I want to tell him how much I love him. These reminders of our love, our story, soothe my soul. He excites me, he ignites me, and I want to show him.

When I finally get to the club, I practically run to its doors, eager to see the man I love. As I go through the doors, I'm surprised to see shoes in the middle of the dance floor, surrounded by pink rose petals and a rose with another note card.

Curiously, I pick up the card and read, "These shoes are the very ones you threw up on that night. I couldn't bring myself to throw them away. I had them cleaned and then kept them as sort of a memento. When I was in my office, looking down at the crowd, I remember my heart stopping when my eyes happened to fall on your face. At first, I thought I must be dreaming. Seven long years of imagining I would see you somewhere...and to see right here...in my place...to finally have it occur, well... I thought I might be seeing things. I slowly made my way down the stairs, never removing my eyes from the spot you appeared. When I saw those guys start manhandling you, I almost lost my mind. When I came close enough that I could reach out and touch you, I spoke your name. When you turned, and your eyes met mine for the first time in our seven long years of separation, the sight took my breath away. I imagined it so many times before – all the daydreams different, but of course, each one ending with us falling into one another's arms. Never did I imagine you would throw up on me instead. To say that wasn't quite the hello I was expecting is an understatement, but it truly was unforgettable. In that moment, I couldn't have loved you more, and I was more determined than ever, to once again, make you my girl. Come to our tree."

Tears are running down my cheeks and I clutch his note to my chest. He wants me to go to our tree. Excitement fills my chest with anticipation. I know without a doubt, he will be waiting there for me.

When I arrive, I'm not disappointed by the sight before me. Laying eyes on my love, I burst into tears. He has a blanket spread under our tree among the tall grass. There are pink rose petals everywhere. And Luke, he's in the center of them all, down on one knee, with dozens of pink roses in his hands.

My hands cover my mouth and I stifle a sob at seeing him and knowing what all this has been about. I can't contain my feelings, not a second longer. I run into his arms, making him drop all the roses. With a surprised expression, he briefly looks at me before I practically knock him over. I laugh and so does he, the perfect sounding harmony of our voices ringing as one.

"YES! YES LUKE! My answer is YES!"

Luke laughs so hard, "I haven't even asked yet."

My face becomes red as I pull away, "Well, your intentions were clear, I think and I reacted, I'm sorry!"

"I mean, I have a whole speech planned and everything."

"Luke, I don't even need to hear it. There is no convincing or speech needed. I was always meant to be with you, from the moment I met you. You have always been the only thing I've ever wanted. The only person that has ever made me feel the way that you do, the only man that I've loved with every single part of me. I don't need a speech, I don't need anything, Luke, but you. Always and forever, you."

"I love you, Livvie. So much. Will you marry me?"

"Yes! A thousand times yes, Luke."

He brushes the hair from my face and pulls a box from his pocket. He holds eye contact with me as he opens it and I look from his face to the ring and gasp. The diamond is very large and square cut. It's set in a platinum band that has small diamonds in a row on either side. "Oh Luke, it's gorgeous. And more than I need."

"No, it's perfect, for you. I love you, Livvie. You've made me so happy."

I look at him for a moment and then kiss him. We waste no time tangling our tongues together and trying to say with our lips, what we said in words. I feel so happy, so alive, so excited for the future and what it will bring.

For the first time in months, I see my daydreams of Luke, becoming my reality. As he slowly lowers me to the ground and starts to move his hands over me, I know that everything that has happened has led me right here.

"I can't wait to be your wife, Luke. I love you. I love you. I love you." I place kisses on his lips in between each declaration.

"I love you too. I'm the luckiest man alive. My life became complete again the minute I found you again, Livvie. I thank God he led you back to me. I can't wait to get you to that alter."

I smile, "I have an idea for what we can do until then."

He returns my smile, "Oh yeah? Why don't you show me?"

And so I do.

ACKNOWLEDGEMENTS

I never thought I would write one book, let alone two. I couldn't do it without the support of so many that were constants at my side throughout this journey.

First and foremost, to my husband Jake, and our daughters – I love you more than you know. Thank you for putting up with my craziness after many sleepless nights, for understanding when my mind is in the clouds with my make believe characters, and for loving me despite my madness.

Mom, my dedication speaks for itself. I would be lost without you. You are the best editor a girl could ask for. You know my heart and soul and when I'm not quite explaining or communicating how I should be, you don't hesitate to point it out and challenge me to go deeper and show more. I will say my favorite edit ever is your comment about if "pussy" is really the proper term for Luke to call himself. I don't think I've ever laughed so hard. Sorry to tell you mom, I kept it in the book.

Georgia, I find myself never knowing quite how to thank you properly. When I was so nervous about how this book was turning out to be so different from the first, your insistence that I follow my instincts was what spurred me forward many times I felt unsure. I hope I can prove to be as invaluable to you, as you always are to me. I look forward to the magic you are creating, and above all, I thank you for your friendship and love.

Angela Corbett, Mary Ting and Espe – thank you for always checking in with me, seeing how my writing is going and always offering your encouragement and support should I ever need anything. I'm lucky to have friends in you.

To all my beta girls, I love your faces. You helped me make this book what it is and your love of my characters rivals mine. I was so afraid that readers would be disappointed in the darker turn this novel takes, and you insisted all it did is show my range as a writer. Thank you for believing in me, and never losing faith in me, even when my faith wavered in myself.

Jen Joanisse, you are the best PA a girl could ask for. I love that I can bounce all my crazy ideas off of you and you go with it and encourage my creative process. Thanks for always looking out for me, and becoming one of my best friends.

Tara Brown – thank you so much for your help with a certain part of writing that I hate with a fiery passion. Your talent never ceases to amaze me!

To the InDivas – I love you all. What a wonderful group of women we have that reach out and lift each other up. That kind of support is invaluable in this industry and I know we were all brought together for a reason. Thank you from the bottom of my heart.

To all of you that have read this, thank you for helping my dreams come true. I have made friends with so many of you and I look forward to your emails and facebook posts. XO!

ABOUT THE AUTHOR

 Author Jennifer Miller was born and raised in Chicago, Illinois but now calls Arizona home. Her love of reading began when she was a small child, and only continued to grow as she entered adulthood. Ever since winning a writing contest at the young age of nine, when she wrote a book about a girl with a pet unicorn, she's dreamed of writing a book of her own. The important lesson she learned about dreams is that they don't just fall into your lap – you have to chase them yourself. Most importantly, she is a wife and mother, and is very lucky to have a family that loves and supports her in all things. She also has an unhealthy addiction to handbags and chocolate covered strawberries, neither of which she cares to work on.

UPCOMING RELEASES:

Whispering Wishes (Spring 2014)
Pretty Little Lies Book Three – Pyper's Story – (Summer 2014)

CHECK OUT THESE OTHER GREAT AUTHORS—THE INDIVAS

Angela Corbett

Alexandrea Weis

Melissa Keir

H.P. Landry

Brenda Pandos

Adam Kunz

Bethany Cross

Cameo Renae

Margaret Taylor

Mary Ting

Carlyle Labuschagne

Carol Kunz

M.r. Polish

LP Dover

L.b. Simmons

Rhonda Raymond Dennis

Dawn Pendleton

Marsha Casper Cook

Chrissy Peebles

Rose Garcia

Jennifer Domenico

A TEASER FROM MY CLARITY

by M. Clarke/Mary Ting
Coming May 12, 2014

TOLD FROM ALEXANDRIA'S & ELIJAH'S POV

When we got home, I thought Lexy would have left, but she stayed. I headed straight for the bathroom to take care of my wound. Lexy followed behind me and leaned against the door.

"Sorry, Alex. I shouldn't have brought you there. I thought it would help get your mind off your dad." Her tone was apologetic at first, and then it became filled with excitement. "But wasn't it fun?"

"I did have fun, Lexy," I confirmed. I didn't want her to feel bad for doing something thoughtful. "I'm glad you took me. I've never been to one of those before. It was exciting. But do the cops come every time?"

"No. Sometimes we get lucky. They change the location every time. The guys who were taking the money are the ones who arrange it all. Either someone ratted the location or the cops played a hunch this time. If you get caught, they'll throw you in jail and let you out the next day."

"How do you know?" I asked, pumping liquid soap in my hands, and then running them under the sink. Thankfully, I only had minor scratches.

Lexy gave me a sly smile and handed the towel to me. "Cause Jimmy got caught before."

"Really?" I said, laughing as I hung the towel back on the rack. Our laughter was cut short when we went to the living room and saw Seth and Elijah walk through the door. Elijah was still huffing mad. His jaw muscles were tight and his lips were pressed in a thin line.

"Out!" Elijah was short and to the point. He made everyone jolt.

Thinking he meant me as well, I started heading to my room. I didn't want to be around him either.

"Alex, where do you think you're going?" he said softly, confusing me.

I stopped when he called my name. Without answering, I went to the kitchen instead and waited for him. I heard harsh whispers, as if they were arguing and didn't want me to hear, but it didn't last long.

"Good night, Alex. See you tomorrow at work," Lexy said.

"Good night, Alex," Seth said next. "Go easy on her." I heard him say to Elijah. Why would he say that?

"Bye," I said loudly without a thought to walk them out the door.

Feeling restless, my heart hammered faster as I took out the milk carton and a bag of chocolate chip cookies. It was late at night, but I just felt like having something. After pouring milk into the cup, I took out a cookie, as I watched Elijah walk in.

Though his shoulders were relaxed compared to a minute ago, I could see the worried look in his eyes, but not for long. "What are you doing," he chuckled lightly, apparently finding humor in what I was doing.

"Dunking my cookie in my milk. Haven't you ever done that before?"

"No."

"Oh, then you're missing out. Want some?" As I wondered if he would maintain his calmness, I took a bite.

"No thanks. Not right now. I'm not a big fan of milk." He paused for a second, dragged his hair back with his fingers, and released a short, sharp sigh. "Look. I'm sorry I got angry earlier. It wasn't toward you. It was toward the situation and Lexy. She shouldn't have brought you there."

After I swallowed, I retorted. "Why not? You've seen the crowd. Why can't I be there?"

"I can't believe you're asking me that question?" His face tilted, angling his brows at me, as if I should have known better. "Have I seen the crowd? Have *you* seen the crowd?" He blinked rapidly, rattling off his words, but his piercing, beautiful brown eyes and long lashes were distracting me. "There are gang members, gamblers, drug addicts, not to mention the cops."

"I didn't know about the cops, and who put you in charge of me anyway?" I challenged.

"I did."

"I don't need you to take care of me just because I'm Jimmy's cousin. I wish everyone would stop doing that." My tone went up a notch.

"That's not the reason."

"Then what is? Oh, and I didn't see any gang members or drug addicts. Although I wouldn't know what they look like." I dunked the cookie again and took another bite.

"Exactly. And have you ever been in a jail before?"

"No." Biting my cookie helped me deal with how he continued to distract me. Something about the way he was being so protective and how he was staring at my mouth, oozed sex appeal.

"Exactly."

"Stop saying 'exactly'. Have you?"

He didn't answer. I'd guessed that was a yes, and before he could walk away from me, I pointed at him with the half eaten cookie in my hand as I asked another question. "How about the other students and your friends? They were all there too. Aren't I good enough to be there?" I don't know why, but anger boiled inside me.

"No...you're not!" he stammered, startling me. As he took a step toward me, I backed away and bumped into the cabinet.

His words were like a dagger to my heart. He did not say that to me, making me feel worthless. How DARE he?

With his hands planted on either side of the cabinet just inches away from my face, his body was way too close to mine. I couldn't help but stare at the tattoo that curved as his muscles flexed. His broad shoulders and his hard, defined chest were too much for me to handle, especially recalling how he looked without a shirt on.

Blistering, heated energy ignited in the space between us. I was drowning into his smell...into him...into that cage he created around us, and I wanted to dive into his arms. Lowering his head and brushing his lips against my ear, accentuating one word at a time, he murmured. "You. Are. Better." Then he paused. No movement...completely still.

I don't know how long we stood like that because a second seemed like an eternity, and I had no control over what I was feeling at this moment. After a soft intake of breath, he continued. "I don't know what I would have done if something were to happen to you."

His words quickly soothed me, making me melt in awe. I tried not to choke on the chewed up cookies still in my mouth. I swear I felt the warmth of his breathe against my neck and I wanted so badly for him to devour me right there. The heated feeling got worse when I saw his lips heading toward mine with a slow hesitation. My heart went into overdrive as the room spun around me. We were now face-to-face as he stared into my eyes with want and need.

Never taking his eyes off me, he rested his hand on my shoulder, and then gingerly slid down my arm, giving me pleasurable tingles...EVERYWHERE. Afraid to move the tiniest of my muscles, I felt locked in place. I was enjoying him way too much and I didn't want it to end. When he finally reached my hand, he pulled it up to his mouth and made the most pleasurable groan I've ever heard.

Looking exhausted and dazed, he shifted his eyes to the cookie in my hand, and mumbled slowly, "I think I'll have that cookie now."

Nothing registered until I saw his lips part, and my fingers disappeared in his mouth. OMG! My pulse skyrocketed, and I whimpered from the warmth of his tongue and the sensation that shot down my arm. My fingers were very wet sliding out of his mouth. I even felt the feather-light graze of his teeth; and I could swear every single muscle in my body became limp.

His jaw worked quickly, chewing. It was the sexiest thing I'd ever seen. He made eating a cookie SO hot. After he swallowed, he turned the other way, picked up my cup of milk, and chugged down whatever was left.

Looking like he just couldn't believe he drank milk, he placed the cup down. "Good night, Alex. Don't ever go racing without me," he ordered, and then he left.

What just happened? Milk and cookies will never be the same for me...EVER.

THE DEVIL DRINKS COFFEE
by Destiny Ford

"Why is it," Drake asked, coming closer to me, "that whenever I think I'm going to spend some time with you, another guy shows up?"

I backed up to move away from him. "Well, that's not really what happened, is it?" I pointed out. "Spence was already here when you arrived."

"Is there a reason you invited him?"

"Does the reason concern you?"

He put his hands out and looked at me like I was an idiot. "I'm here aren't I? So yeah, it concerns me. I thought I was coming over for a family dinner."

"So did I," I said. "But then you showed up."

"I was invited."

"Not by me."

He moved closer. I moved another step back. "You know," he said, pointing at me with an annoyed look on his face. "I saw a video of you today. I knew you wouldn't listen to me when I told you to stay away from Hawke, but practically having sex with him on the tabletop of a family restaurant with kids in the room is bad manners at best."

"That's quite an imagination you have."

"Have you seen the video?"

"I was there; I don't need to see the video to know what happened," I answered, and then took it a step further. "And I can promise you" —I paused, letting the corners of my mouth slide into a sly smile— "I would remember if I'd had sex on the table—especially if the sex was with Hawke."

Drake scowled and a vein near his temple was so enlarged it looked like it was about to burst. "You could see what Hawke wanted just from looking in his eyes, Katie. And I was watching a grainy cell phone video," he shook his head. "The Bradford story is dangerous for you to keep pursuing, and so is Hawke."

My eyes narrowed into slits. "Here's the thing about me, Drake," I said. "And it's probably something you should remember. Write it down if you need to because you might even have to do some research to understand it. I'm not the type of girl who does what she's told, or gives people what they want just because they want it."

"Is that so?" he asked.

I nodded.

"Well, here's something you should remember, so write it down if you need to," he said as he kept walking toward me. I backed up until I ran into the countertop and I was literally in the corner. "Hawke's not the type of man to stop until he gets what he wants." He moved in until our bodies were parallel and we were standing only an inch apart. The tension was running at an all-time high. I was dangerously close to giving in to my hormones. "And neither am I."

MEANT FOR ME

by bestselling author L.P. Dover

PROLOGUE
-MASON-

The silence in the car was deafening. The beat of my heart pounding in my ears was all I could focus on as Claire drove me to the airport with tears streaming down her cheeks.

Claire.

What the fuck had I done? I knew it was a mistake to let things go as far as they did, even though we both promised none of it would mean anything. It was a lie.

My flight back to North Carolina would be departing in three hours, and it would put thousands of miles between us. My life was back in North Carolina with my badge and my gun while hers was in California managing her family's vineyards. I didn't belong there. We were completely different people, but there was a spark in her eyes that drew me to her when I met her through my cousin, Melissa, years ago. It was the same spark that ignited every desire, every hope of being able to touch her just once. One time was all I wanted, or at least that was what I thought.

The spark that I loved so much about Claire wasn't in her blue gaze as I peered over at her from the passenger's seat. She was pissed at me and I couldn't blame her. Hell, if I was her I would've beaten the shit out of me for doing what I did.

My cousin was the reason I was in California in the first place, and if it wasn't for her wedding I wouldn't have stepped foot on this side of the United States. Melissa used to live in North Carolina, too, but she inherited part of the vineyards from Claire's family when Claire's mother died. Brett was her fiancé at the time, and once he had everything squared away with his job they both packed up and moved across the country. They had just gotten married a couple of days ago and were already on their honeymoon in St. Croix ... hence, the reason why I had no one else to take me to the airport other than Claire. I could've called a taxi, but Claire insisted on taking me.

I wanted to make things right, but there was nothing I could say that would make up for what I did. I screwed up and let my dick take the reins on my behavior. I couldn't deny the chemistry Claire and I had, especially the sexual tension, and every time she brushed up against me when we danced my cock immediately sprung to attention. It wasn't until later that night—when I found her laying across my bed with nothing but a pink, lacy babydoll that I could see straight through—that I finally gave in to my desire.

I wanted to taste her, to feel her ... to finally get her out of my system. What I got was an addiction, and what's worse was that I craved her even now.

We finally passed a sign for the airport indicating we only had one more mile to go, and I knew I was running out of time. The tension hung heavy in the air as I turned to the blonde haired knockout clenching the steering wheel so tight her knuckles were turning white. She wore a bright pink tank top with exceptionally short denim shorts that showed off her long, tanned legs. She was beautiful.

"What do you want me to say, Claire?" I asked softly, hoping to get something out of her instead of silence. "I told you I was sorry. What can I do to make you talk to me?"

What I did to her was something I would regret for the rest of my life. After a long, wild night of sex, love making, whatever you want to call it, it finally came time to wind down. The look in her eyes when she told me she was falling in love with me would forever stay ingrained in my mind. My reaction would haunt me forever as well.

Being the asshole that I was, I told her I wasn't good enough for her, grabbed my pants off the floor, and left the room. I realized my mistake as soon as I shut the door, but it was too late. The damage had been done. Claire cried for what felt like hours, or maybe it was my misery that made it seem longer. Meanwhile, all I did was sit there, leaning up against the door and listening. I wasn't prepared to hear those words come out of her mouth, and I sure as hell wasn't ready to face her this morning.

Holding her chin defiantly in the air, Claire kept her eyes on the road. However, I couldn't miss the undertone of hurt in her voice when she said, "Look, Mason, I get it. You don't do relationships. I was the one stupid enough to think that after the night we shared things would be different. I guess that's what I get for thinking."

I wanted things to be different between us, to be something real, except I knew it wouldn't work with the way we lived our lives. Sighing, I tried to reason with her even though I knew it was hopeless, "We would never see each other, Claire. I work long hours and the work that I do is dangerous. You deserve so much better than me. Someone you wouldn't have to worry about all the time."

She pulled up to the airport terminal and put her FJ Cruiser into park before crossing her arms over her chest. Her breasts peeked up over her tank top, and I could see on the mounds of her breasts where the stubble on my chin had rubbed her skin raw. I wanted to kiss her again and tell her everything would be all right, except the look in her eyes when she turned to me let me know I had missed my chance. All I saw was anger ... and pain.

Leaning over my seat, she reached for the handle on the door and pressed it down, opening it wide. Closing my eyes, I breathed in her scent—which always smelled like raspberries—as her body brushed up against mine.

"You're going to be late for your flight. It's time for you to go," she snapped.

I reached for her chin to get her to look at me, but she jerked away from my touch. Gritting my teeth, I released a heavy sigh. I slid out of her car and fetched my bags from the trunk. Before I went inside the airport, I leaned into the window of her car and let every ounce of regret I had pour into my words when I apologized, "I really am sorry, Claire. I need you to believe that."

Pursing her lips, she nodded her head and met my gaze head on, narrowing those gorgeous blue eyes in disdain. "Yeah, well ... I'm sorry, too. However, there is one thing you were right about in all of this."

Knowing the final blow was coming, I had to ask, "What exactly would that be?"

A tear escaped the corner of her eye and she hastily wiped it away, ashamed at letting me see her pain. "It would be the part where you said I deserved someone better than you. Before I would've said you were completely wrong, but now ... you were absolutely right. Good-bye, Mason."

With those final words, she turned her face away and sped off out of the terminal, never once slowing down or looking back. I had lost her, and after today there was no way she would ever come back to me.

I was a fucking idiot.